D0409600

Faithful

Faithful

ALICE HOFFMAN

SCRIBNER

LONDON NEW YORK TORONTO SYDNEY NEW DELHI

Faithful

First published in Great Britain by Scribner, an imprint of Simon & Schuster UK Ltd, 2017
A CBS COMPANY

1 3 5 7 9 10 8 6 4 2

Simon & Schuster UK Ltd
1st Floor
222 Gray's Inn Road
London WC1X 8HB

www.simonandschuster.co.uk

Simon & Schuster Australia, Sydney
Simon & Schuster India, New Delhi

A CIP catalogue record for this book
is available from the British Library

HB ISBN: 978-1-4711-5771-4
TPB ISBN: 978-1-4711-6293-0
EBOOK ISBN: 978-1-4711-5772-1

"Anthem" excerpted from *Stranger Music* by Leonard Cohen.
Copyright © 1993 Leonard Cohen. Reprinted by permission of McClelland & Stewart,
a division of Penguin Random House Canada Limited.

Selections from *Faithful* have appeared in *The Harvard Review, Prairie Schooner,
Five Points, Kenyon Review, Southwest Review, Story Quarterly,
Iron Horse Literary Review,* and *Ploughshares.*

Printed and bound by CPI Group (UK) Ltd, Croydon CR0 4YY

Simon & Schuster UK Ltd are committed to sourcing paper
that is made from wood grown in sustainable forests and support the Forest
Stewardship Council, the leading international forest certification organisation.
Our books displaying the FSC logo are printed on FSC certified paper.

Ring the bells that still can ring
Forget your perfect offering
There is a crack in everything
That's how the light gets in.

—"ANTHEM" BY LEONARD COHEN

Faithful

CHAPTER

1

In February, when the snow comes down hard, little globes of light are left along Route 110, on the side of the road that slopes off when a driver least expects it. The lights are candles set inside paper bags, surrounded by sand, and they burn past midnight. They shouldn't last for that amount of time, but that's part of the miracle. On the second anniversary of the accident, a gang of boys creep out their windows and gather at two in the morning to see if Helene's mother, Diana Boyd, drives along the road replacing each melting pool of wax with a fresh candle. They're hoping to reveal a con in process and dispel the myth of a miracle, but after keeping watch for a while the boys all flee. In the early morning hours, safe in their beds, they wonder how much of the world can never be understood or explained.

The light globes are made at the high school where Helene was a senior before the accident. People who never even knew her spend all afternoon in the cafeteria filling up paper bags. The first year, the art teacher ordered special sand from Arizona and the candles glowed with red light, but now the sand is trucked in from Heyward's Gravel Pit, and it's pure white. It looks like diamonds when you run it through your fingers.

There are dozens of high school girls who lock themselves in their bedrooms on the anniversary night, their hands dusted with luminous sand, prayers on their lips, their hearts heavy with sorrow. Each one thanks her lucky stars she is not Helene, even though Helene was the beautiful girl who could do as she pleased, the one every boy wanted to date and every girl wanted to be like. But that was then. Now even the outcasts—the fat, the unattractive, the lonely, the sorrowful, the lost— are grateful to be who they are, at least for a single evening. Even the most selfish girls—the ones who think nothing of snubbing their less attractive and popular classmates—offer to collect the spent paper bags on their way to school on the morning after the anniversary. The wax will still be hot; the wicks give off smoke. Occasionally a candle will still be burning, so fresh it's as though it had just been lit. Then the girls gather round in awe and solidarity, even the ones who hate each other. They close their eyes and make a wish, the same one every time: *Let it never be me.*

The one person who has never been included in the anniversary events, not the safe driving assembly at the school, or the candlelighting cere- mony on the corner of Main Street and Route 110, or the prayer vigil at the Boyds' house, is Shelby Richmond. Not that she's a high school girl anymore; she graduated when Helene would have, or more cor- rectly, the administration took pity on her and granted her a diploma after she was released from the hospital. Shelby's mother gave her a thin gold watch that she has never worn. Shelby doesn't want a gift and she doesn't want anything beautiful and she certainly doesn't want to know what time it is. She didn't go off to college the way she and Helene had planned. She was Helene's confidante, pretty enough, but not the beautiful one. She was the smart one, the one who often did homework for them both. For her, time has stopped. The girls had applied to NYU and were accepted, but it was too late for Helene, and as it turned out, too late for Shelby as well. Shelby's parents paid the first semester's tuition, but she didn't leave on the appointed day, or the day after, or the one after that. Her suitcases sat in the front hall until her parents lost hope, until the leaves started changing. They waited so long to withdraw her they lost all that tuition money for nothing.

Shelby has not done anything with her life since the night when it happened. Two years have passed, but it might as well be a moment since Helene was injured. Everything that has happened since doesn't matter. Hours and days are mere flashes: the ER room, the instant she slit her wrists after they stitched her up and declared her recovered from the crash and sent her home, the gray, hazy moment when she was locked into a psych ward, the sound of the door opening when her mother brought her back home. Shelby blinks her eyes and she's right back in the car. They'd had a disagreement that night because Shelby didn't want to go out and Helene did. Of course Helene got her way. Shelby always gave in. If she refused, Helene would find someone new to follow her around. Shelby hasn't told anyone the truth about that night because it sounds as if she were making excuses. But truly, Helene wouldn't take no for an answer. She was so annoyed when Shelby hesitated that she took off the matching bracelet to Shelby's that she always wore. Helene's bracelet had a white enameled butterfly charm; Shelby's butterfly was black. Helene was the leader. She had a charming, forceful personality, and unlike Shelby, Helene always knew what she wanted. As it turned out, she forgot the bracelet when they went out and Shelby lost hers in the accident. The chain must have snapped when Shelby was lying on the ice, gasping for breath, bleeding through her clothes until her sweater and jeans were soaked through. She's gone back to search for the charm, but there's nothing in the tall weeds along the road, only some broken glass that glints blue in the sunlight.

Sometimes when Shelby turns her head too quickly she can swear Helene is there. She doesn't trust her eyesight even though on her last eye exam her vision was twenty-twenty. Still she is convinced that something is wrong with her vision. It's been so ever since that night. When she looked up, she saw an angel. It's a moment that still burns inside her. He leaned over and covered her with his black coat and said she couldn't give up. She was shivering and her soul was in her mouth, ready to escape as a puff of air, but the angel kept her on earth. She knows it's insanity to think so. She doesn't need a psychiatrist to tell her that. She told no one in the psychiatric hospital, not even when they asked her directly: *Do you believe in demons and angels? Do you see things that aren't there?*

Why would an angel rescue her when she's worthless and Helene, who was so much better than she could ever be, was right there, in desperate need of help? All the same, every time she sees a man in a black coat she wonders if it's her angel, and every time she's mistaken. She stares at these men a little too long and they get the wrong idea. *Hey, wait up,* these men say to her when she walks on, along the highway or Main Street. She must look desperate, like someone who would be easy to command. *Come on sister, darling, babygirl.* She walks faster when this happens. She knows the difference between a demon and an angel, even in the dark. She learned that in the hospital, and she's not going back there again. On some nights she hears her mother calling her as she wanders through town. Shelby's mom drives through the streets, searching for Shelby at two or three in the morning. Her mom pulls over and gets out of her car and shouts for her, but Shelby ducks behind the shrubbery. She never answers. She's simply not worthy of her mother's love.

Nowadays Shelby sleeps most of the time, dreaming of the way it used to be, back when she didn't think about anything, when the whole

world was blue and shining, a globe no more complicated than a Christmas ball. Her diagnosis is major depression. She also has anxiety, sur-
vivor's guilt, and post-traumatic stress. She was in the ER for only one
night after the accident, but she had a three-month stay in the psych
hospital soon afterward. She had stopped talking. She refused to eat.
Then came the moment when she sat in the shower with a razor in her
hands. She was so cold but that didn't stop her. She cut across her wrist,
where the vein was blue. Her blood was so bright. She heard the door
open and her mother cry out, and she felt how cold it was when the
water was turned off. Her mother was screaming for her father to call
an ambulance, but she didn't leave Shelby. She crouched beside Shelby
on the shower floor and tied a towel around her wrist to stanch the flow
of blood. "It's okay, baby," Shelby's mom said. Someone was sobbing.
Shelby's mother wrapped herself around Shelby's shivering, naked
body.

At the hospital nobody visited except her mother. Nobody phoned.
Nobody missed her. Rumors had begun in town. She was crazy. It was
all her fault. She was bad luck and should be avoided at all costs. Girls
who had been friends with Helene and Shelby decided they had lost
both friends. It was easier that way. What was gone was gone.

A week passed, and then two, and soon Shelby stopped counting.
She was disappearing inch by inch, vanishing into thin air, and then
one day a postcard arrived. The nurse at the desk called Shelby's name
during mail call.

"Wake up, kiddo," the nurse shouted when Shelby didn't respond.
Shelby was in the TV lounge dozing from the meds they gave her and
listening to a talk show her mother liked featuring a group of women
who argued about politics and gossiped about famous people.

"Shelby Richmond." The nurse sounded more annoyed than usual.
"Get your ass over here."

Shelby went over to the desk, convinced it was a mistake.

"Take it," the nurse said, so Shelby did. "Thank you," the nurse said sarcastically, since Shelby still wasn't talking. She hadn't said a word since she woke up in the hospital the morning after the accident.

On the front of the postcard there was a delicate ink sketch of a family: a mother, a father, and a daughter. But the daughter had tape over her mouth, heavy packing tape. Shelby recognized herself as the girl who couldn't speak. Her wrists and heart were painted red. Shelby hadn't expected anyone else to know how she felt, but clearly someone did. There was no return address, no signature, only a scrawled message: *Say something.*

Shelby wondered if it was a message from a higher power, even though she didn't believe in such things. She kept the postcard under her pillow. It felt precious to her. She kept it there until the linens were changed while she was in group therapy saying nothing, and while she was out of her room an aide threw it away. Shelby searched through the garbage cans in a panic until she found it. It was perfect, not folded or torn, and she accepted that as a sign as well. Now that she's back home she's wised up. She's started speaking again, a few mouthfuls of words at a time, but mostly she retreats to the basement, which has become her lair, a wolf's den, the only place she wants to be. She cuts herself in places no one can see. The soles of her feet. Her inner thigh.

Her single bed is beside boxes of books from her childhood: Andrew Lang's fairy tales and the Misty of Chincoteague series, which turned her into a horse fanatic. She pleaded with her mom to take her to Virginia to see the wild horses in the book until Sue Richmond finally gave in and they spent the weekend scouring the dunes for the ponies that lived on the beach. Shelby can remember how happy she was, though the weather was gloomy and the horses ran from them. She thinks it may have been the happiest time of her life.

The doctors and her parents can call her condition whatever they wish; Shelby knows what's wrong with her. She is paying her penance. She is stopping her life, matching her breathing so that it has become a counterpart of the slow intake of air of a girl in a coma. She looks at her postcard every night to remind herself of what they'll do to her if she allows people to know how damaged she is and takes to silence again. They'll lock her up and then she'll disappear for good.

She hasn't seen Helene since the night of the accident. Once, Helene's dad, Mr. Boyd, who had always liked Shelby, sent a box of candy on her birthday, but she felt too guilty to open it and tossed it in the trash, uneaten. She's never wanted to see the hospital bed that has been set up in Helene's bedroom. In some sense she and Helene are still living identical lives, just as they did in high school. Shelby hasn't even bought new clothes since it happened; she still wears the same boots she was wearing that night, a wad of newspaper stuck inside the right one because the heel is tearing away.

Of course there are differences. Helene's hair has not been cut since the accident, while Shelby shaved her head the day she came home from the psych ward. She's kept it that way so that when she does venture as far as the 7-Eleven for magazines and snacks, people treat her gently, as though she were a cancer patient. Whenever someone whispers, *That's the girl who was driving when Helene had the accident*, it's even worse than if she'd had cancer. The way they look at her. They all have big eyes like in those velvet paintings. They both pity her and blame her. She and Helene were always together. Two peas in a pod. Pretty girls who glided through without a care. How can she go on living after she's ruined her best friend's life? They cluck at the skinny, bald girl in big boots. They think she wants compassion, but all she wants is to be left alone. Shelby only goes out after dark, her hat pulled down low. She wears gloves, scarves, and a fat down jacket that makes her shapeless and anonymous. And still, everybody knows.

Shelby and Helene are no longer alike. Shelby's eyes register images; she eats, poorly, all junk food, but it's not the feeding tube Helene survives on. Shelby walks, she talks, she goes down to Main Street once or twice a month—on the bus—no more driving for her, that's for damn sure—to buy weed from a guy they barely knew in high school,

Ben Mink. Ben is lanky and tall, with long hair he ties back, sometimes with a shoelace when he can't find a rubber band. He's geeky and smart. In high school, Shelby and Helene didn't know he was alive. They were in the popular crowd of achievers, planning their college visits, going to parties on Friday nights. He hadn't run with the same crowd—Ben didn't have a crowd. He used to amble around with a book under his arm, usually something by Philip K. Dick or Kurt Vonnegut. He went on a Shirley Jackson kick, reading all of her books in a twenty-four-hour period, which landed him with a prescription for Prozac. Life was beautiful, everyone knew that, but it was also bitter and bleak and unfair as hell and where did that leave a person? On the outs with the rest of the world. Someone who sat alone in the cafeteria, reading, escaping from his hometown simply by turning the page. Helene joked he was related to werewolves, because he had a scruffy beard even then. Shelby and Helene both had a fear of wolves, for one was said to have escaped from a cage in someone's basement and it had never been caught. *Run,* Helene would say when they walked through the woods, vowing that she heard howling.

For years Ben kept his sunglasses on even at night so he didn't have to look anyone in the eye. Because he believed in aliens and literature he was a target. People called him Ben Stink, if they bothered to call him anything at all. Shelby barely remembers him, but that was then. Now they're comfortable with each other, if being comfortable is possible for either of them. When they meet they sit in a nearby park, mostly in silence, two loners who can barely make it through their own lives. As dusk falls they sometimes share a joint and talk about teachers they hated most. Shelby managed to get decent grades from even the toughest ones, but now she lets her true feelings out. She doesn't have to be a good girl anymore. Whenever she talks about high school, Shelby takes out her house key and digs it into the palm of her hand until she bleeds. No miracle. That's Helene's business. Shelby's blood is strictly a penance. It's for real.

"I don't think you should do that," Ben said to her when he realized what she was doing, drawing her own blood while she sat beside him.

"You think?" she goaded him. "That's a surprise. Did you know we used to think you were a werewolf?"

Shelby guessed he'd stalk away, insulted, and maybe that's what she wanted to happen. Her aloneness, after all, is all she has. Instead Ben said, "I'm just worried about you."

"Don't be," Shelby warned him.

"I wouldn't mind being a werewolf," he said, which only made Shelby feel guiltier about all those years they'd made fun of him.

Ben was fine as long as he didn't talk, but he couldn't seem to stop himself. *Say something,* Shelby often thinks when he's blabbing on. *But not everything.* Ben now asks if it's true that touching Helene's hand can cure an illness. That's what people say. They say you can smell roses in her room, that she speaks to you without talking, that she can send a message to you that will reveal what you need to know about your future or your past. The first miracle happened on the day Helene's parents brought her home. Helene's grandmother had been unable to walk due to arthritis for more than ten years, but she got out of her wheelchair and walked straight to Helene. She never used her wheelchair again, until one day she suddenly said she needed to lie down, that she was too tired to walk. She told Helene's mom to put her in her chair and wheel her into Helene's room; then the old woman got into bed with Helene and passed right there, in comfort and peace.

After that, roses appeared on the dry stalks of the hedges in February, and in the spring the wisteria beside the driveway, always a faded purple, bloomed a pure white. A toddler with a scar on his face nuzzled his cheek against Helene's pale hand and by evening his skin was without blemish. Folks come from all over, from the Midwest and Florida and New Jersey and France. Helene is famous, that's another difference between them. There are magazine articles about the miracle of the girl in the coma. People who have been healed merely by being in her presence often give testimonials. Like Helene's grandmother, they can walk again. The asthmatics can breathe. Babies who never slept and cried all night become calm. Jittery teenagers buckle down and become A students. The roses always bloom on the day of the accident, huge, blood-red flowers that are impervious to snow and ice. Roses in February are clearly a miracle, and they've been photographed and set on the front page of *Newsday*. Helene's parents have been interviewed in *People* magazine, and this year Channel 4 sent out a news team to interview those who've been healed.

"Nobody with any brains would blame you for what happened to Helene," Ben Mink says.

Shelby looks at Ben with horror, amazed he has the nerve to utter Helene's name in her presence. She thought he was a little smarter than that. She'll talk to him, but clearly she's not about to discuss her feelings, not with him or anyone else. Feelings are best left concealed. They can bite you if you're not careful. They can eat you alive. Shelby has a tremor in her left hand. Sometimes she wakes in the middle of the night and finds she's shaking. As it turns out, people say Helene's left hand is the source of the miracles. The concept that mere touch can cure you and restore your faith disturbs Shelby. Nothing can restore her. Shelby tosses Ben a desperate look. *Not you too.*

He immediately picks up on her contempt. "Not that I expect you to believe in that shit. I know I don't."

Shelby once had a beautiful smile. That's long gone. It disappeared on that night, and at this point she doesn't even think it's possible for her to smile. She's frozen into the expression of someone who expects the worst. She taps her foot constantly now, as if she were running and getting nowhere.

"I believe in tragedy," Shelby responds coldly. "Not miracles."

"Yeah, right. Faith is for idiots." Ben seems relieved. "Statistics speak the truth."

"You have to stop thinking. It's going to drive us apart." Shelby keeps her good hand over her tremoring hand. She can feel her brain waves shift when she smokes pot. Pseudo-coma. Drift of snow. What a relief. "Let's not get too personal. I buy weed from you. Period."

On the way home, Shelby realizes she's probably spoken more to Ben Mink in the past two years than she has to anyone else. She counts the people she's come in contact with, most of them from the psych ward. Shrink. Nurse. Pathetic members of her therapy group. Parents. Clerk at the 7-Eleven. The orderly, twice her age, who told her to keep her mouth shut as he pulled down her pants. Until then her only kisses had taken place in a closet during parties at Helene's house. The orderly took her into a closet as well, a utility closet where there were mops and buckets and folded sheets and towels. She wasn't speaking then. She tried to tell him *no,* but the word sounded like a sob.

The orderly's name was Martin. He was holding her by one wrist as he forced his other hand into her underwear. He told her if she made any noise at all she would never get out of the hospital. The staff would think she was hallucinating if she tried to blame him for anything. The nurses would drug her and tie her to her bed. And if they did, he would still do whatever he wanted to her.

So Shelby didn't speak. Instead, she rose out of her body. She watched the whole thing happen. She never told anyone what he did to her on a nightly basis because she was afraid of him, but also because she was worth nothing to herself. One night when they were locked in the shower room, he told her she was never getting away from him while he fucked her up against the cold, tiled wall. He said she belonged to him, a seventeen-year-old girl still bruised from her car accident who had tried to slit her wrists and was committed to this ward. He fucked her a second time on the damp floor that smelled of Lysol. It was the same cleaner her mother used, only Sue Richmond preferred the lemon scent, and Shelby cried for the first time since the accident while he held her down. Crying did something to her. It unlocked a small part of her soul. She kept seeing her mother's face, thinking about what Sue would say if she could see what was happening, so she told her mother on her next visit. Months had passed and Shelby looked like a waif. It was impossible not to notice all the weight she'd lost, the slit across one wrist, the bruises Martin left on her. When her mother came to visit she spoke a single sentence, the first in months, the words like glass. *The orderly Martin is fucking me.* She and Sue were looking into each other's eyes and Shelby thinks that in that moment her mother saw everything inside her. Sue raced down the hall, a crow, a wild woman, a scorpion ready to sting. She grabbed the first nurse she saw and informed her that Shelby was leaving. Sue told the nurse that her daughter didn't have to pack up, all they needed was a doctor's release. They would wait by the locked elevator until the physician on call signed Shelby out. If a release didn't come through, there would be a lawsuit. They were in the car half an hour later, Shelby still wearing her pajamas. That night, down in the basement, Shelby took scissors and chopped at her hair. Then she used a straight razor on her scalp. She gazed at her reflection and it was clear: she wasn't the same person anymore.

Her mother had been in the kitchen, fixing macaroni and cheese, which had been Shelby's favorite meal. When she came downstairs and saw what Shelby had done, she sat on the basement stairs and wept. "How could you?" Shelby's mother said. "How could you do this to yourself?"

Shelby wanted to say it was easy to do if you hated yourself, but she just went to sit beside her mother on a stair, and let her mother hug her, and the truth was she felt something crack inside her while she was in her mother's arms. All the same, she didn't talk much after that. They went out to the yard to lie on their backs on the picnic table and look at stars, but they didn't speak about anything, even on the nights when they held hands. In terms of conversation, both in the hospital and afterward, Ben Mink won by a long shot. They talk for hours at a time. They talk about things that matter and things that don't.

"I believe in tragedy, too," he told her that night, as if she cared what anyone else thought. She was terrified that he was going to try to embrace her so she shifted away, but he was too smart for that. He formally shook her hand. Even though they were both wearing gloves, she could feel the heat of his hand.

February is hard. Those globes of light. The ice on the street. All of those high school girls who never knew Helene crying over her. Shelby is now nineteen, but she might as well be ninety. What happened to being young, to having her whole life ahead of her? She still doesn't like to eat, even though her mom makes nutritious meals for her every night. Sue Richmond has left her job as a librarian at the elementary school so she can focus on Shelby. She spends hours fixing meat loaf, chicken stew, macaroni, pudding. Shelby never takes more than a few bites. She stays in the basement. It's quiet and dark. She likes it there, if *like* was a word that could apply to anything in Shelby's life. The couch is lumpy, and the floor is linoleum, like a skating rink. She and Helene used to sneak down here so they could have some privacy. Helene was more daring. She brought cigarettes and beer, and once or twice she invited her boyfriend, Chris, and his entire group of friends down to Shelby's basement to goof around. Sometimes, late at night, when Shelby has smoked more weed than she should, she thinks she spies Helene on the stairs. She's got that big grin on her face and her hair is clipped up with barrettes and she wears the jacket she was wearing on the day they bought their matching bracelets at the Walt Whitman Mall. Helene bought a blue dress, perfect for going to the prom with Chris, but it was a dress she never wore. Chris broke up with her that same day. On the phone. He had applied to Cornell, and once he was there he wanted to be free. That's what set Helene off. That was the beginning of the end.

She only went out that night because Helene threw a fit and called her a baby and she finally gave in and said she would drive. It sounds like a corny, lame excuse; it feels like a lie, even to herself. All the same, it's true. By now, Shelby is so confused, all she can remember is stepping on the brake after the car hit a patch of ice and spinning around and Helene laughing, like they were in a Tilt-A-Whirl car, and then the crunch of metal against metal.

Helene wanted to throw a rock through Chris's window. She could be vindictive sometimes. She wasn't as pure as people thought. She was lazy and had Shelby do her homework. She gossiped. That night they had collected paving stones from the driveway before they set off, dug them up with their hands so there was frozen earth under their fingernails. Shelby has walked past Chris Wilson's house a few times since the accident. Chris did go to Cornell and he doesn't come home to visit. Once Mrs. Wilson ventured onto the porch to call out as Shelby was slinking by. She must have seen Shelby from the bay window in her living room; maybe she had trouble sleeping too. She was probably kindhearted, worried about the crazy, stoned-out girl on the road, but Shelby ran away, heart pounding. Off the road and into the woods. The crunch of twigs beneath her boots reminded her of metal against metal. Anything breaking reminds her of what happened. She went back to her basement, back to bed, and couldn't be woken for the next eighteen hours, not until her mother grew so worried she spilled a cup of cold water over Shelby.

Don't was all Shelby said. She didn't even shift in her sopping, freezing bed. She didn't leap up and shout *What have you done!*

Shelby's mother sat on the edge of the bed. She sang "Over the Rainbow," the song that would comfort Shelby when she was a baby and couldn't sleep. It used to sound hopeful, but now it sounded so sad that Shelby felt her broken heart break all over again.

∽

One day Sue Richmond is driving home from the market when she makes a right turn on Lewiston for no reason, something she's always avoided before. Because Sue was the librarian at the local elementary school before the accident, she knows most people in town. She's checked out books for decades of children, all grown up now, the ones who succeeded and the ones who failed. She loved her job, but then Shelby needed her. She couldn't read books to second graders when her own daughter was locked in a basement. She keeps going on Lewiston until she reaches Helene's house. Anyone would know which one it is because of the crowd outside, the line of people waiting patiently in the driveway, most of them out-of-towners, many of them carrying red roses, said to be Helene's favorite flower.

Sue has bags of groceries in the backseat, including containers of frozen yogurt, already melting, but she parks and gets out anyway. Something inside her is aching. All of a sudden she feels vulnerable in some odd way. She stands in the street crying, staring at the Boyds' yellow ranch house, the way the paint is peeling, the bouquets of roses left on the porch. Sue isn't the only one to be overwhelmed and brought to tears. Lots of people are doing it, just standing there crying. They're letting it all out, their sorrow, their desperation, their hope, right there, right now, in the presence of Helene's shrine, for that is what the house has become. There are dozens of lit candles and scores of teddy bears. Sue notices two of her neighbors, Pat Harrington and Liz Howard, and they wave to her. Sue isn't particularly friendly, she's always afraid people will say *How's Shelby?* But now she finds herself walking over to the other women. They hug her, maybe because she's crying, or because they pity her for having a daughter like Shelby, or maybe because they remember the scene Sue made on the night of the accident, before they knew which girl was critically injured and which one had nothing more than a hairline fracture underneath all the blood and bruises. Sue hit a cop who tried to hold her back. She rode in the ambulance praying when she didn't even know she knew how to pray.

Pat Harrington and Liz Howard run errands for the Boyds. They're in a group of local women who do the food shopping and help with the laundry and hand out inspirational pamphlets for the people who come for a miracle. Pat gives a healing pamphlet to Sue now. There are two printed photographs of Helene, the way she used to be—a bright, glimmering teenager—and the way she is now, lying in her bed, eyes closed peacefully. The printer has encircled the second photograph with a wreath of roses.

When Sue gets home, she goes downstairs, even though she tries to avoid the basement. She can hardly bear to see what's become of Shelby. When the state police told her that her daughter was the one who was alive, Sue knelt in the snow and thanked God. Now she isn't so sure Shelby has survived. Sue's eyes adjust to the thin light. There's Shelby dozing. The basement is smoky and the odor is foul. Like old fruit, perhaps apple cores, and there's a burning smell that makes her think of sulfur and grief. Had this been a few years ago Sue would have been suspicious that Shelby was in bad company, some trampy girls from high school or a boy who wouldn't look anyone in the eye. She would have called out, *Are you smoking down here?* The truth is, Helene was always the troublemaker. She had that bad-girl twinkle in her eye, and she always dragged Shelby along, whether it was the time they were caught shoplifting makeup at the Walt Whitman Mall or the time they took the Long Island Rail Road into Manhattan and didn't come home till two a.m. Now she wishes Shelby did have someone with her, anyone would do. She wishes Shelby was getting into trouble, kissing someone, being alive. Sue treads through the dim room, careful not to trip over stray clothing tossed about; she perches on the arm of the couch. Shelby is hunkered down in her single bed, under a blanket, staring at the TV. The light in the room is blue and wavering. It reminds Sue of a night-light. Shelby looks much the way she had as a baby, bald, with those big dark eyes.

"Mom?" Shelby seems confused. No one ever comes downstairs. "What's up?"

There's a talent show on TV where young people are singing their hearts out. Everyone looks the same to Sue, hopeful and young. The TV itself is old, with a flickering picture and bad sound.

"You like this show?" It doesn't seem like something the old Shelby would have spent ten minutes on. She'd been very discriminating back then.

"It relaxes me," Shelby says.

Paralyzes her is more like it. Even as she speaks, she's staring at the screen. It's all dots to her, blue and white, like snow.

"I think there are miracles happening at the Boyds'," Sue says.

"Watch this guy." Shelby gestures to the contestant taking the stage. "He's crap. I don't know how he made it through the first audition. People seem to love him even though he's terrible. Maybe it's his wavy hair."

"Did you hear what I said?" Sue asks.

Shelby looks at her mother. "The Boyds." She glances away. She's pretty sure she doesn't have any body language, like a zombie. "Let me guess. There are angels on the roof."

"We should go together. You should see her."

"Really? You think so?" There is a quiver in Shelby's voice, the same one that was there before she stopped talking and went into the hospital. A recurrence of Shelby's depression is what Sue Richmond fears more than anything in the world. A crack-up she supposes they call it. A breakdown. You don't know how to mourn something like that. You don't know what to think.

Shelby lifts herself up on one elbow. It takes all of her energy just to do that. Her voice is thick. The quiver is like a wrong note. "You think it's just fine that they prop Helene up in bed and have strangers come in there and kiss her hand and beg her for whatever they want? You think Helene would be happy with that? People standing around while she moans and drools? She wouldn't even sneeze in public. She'd rather have blown her brains out holding back a sneeze than embarrass herself and have to blow her nose, and now they have lines of people going into her bedroom while she craps into a plastic bag. You think we should go to that? Is that what Helene would have wanted?"

Shelby throws herself sideways in her bed, deeper under the blanket, her back to her mother.

"Maybe she likes the fact that she's helping people," Sue says softly. "Maybe that's the miracle. That her life is worthwhile even now."

"Don't you think I know what she would have liked? I knew her better than anyone!"

"You're wrong, Shelby. She's different now. You don't know her anymore."

Shelby turns to glare at her mother. Deep down, she's been afraid of that exact thing. "I know more than you do. Just like I know this guy's going to be voted off this week," she says of the singer on TV.

"She wouldn't know you either." Sue shakes her head. There's a certain tenderness in her voice, almost as if she were crying. "You're nothing like you were. You're not the same person."

"Good," Shelby declares, to hurt both her mother and herself. "Because I hated myself."

Later that same week a second postcard arrives in the mailbox. She's been waiting for another card ever since she left the hospital. Two years have passed, so she'd just about given up. Now here it is. It's a photograph of Shelby's house that has been laminated onto a blank card. The message on the back is *Do something*. Her mom brings it down to the basement.

It's addressed to Shelby, but there's no stamp, no return address. "Who would send this?" her mother asks. Shelby shrugs. She acts like she's not excited to have gotten mail, but she is. She feels a little chill of expectation down her spine. There is someone, somewhere, who knows she's alive. "Somebody writes to me, Mom," Shelby tries to explain. "They think they know me. Maybe they read about me in the paper."

Sue fetches the magnifying glass she uses to read ingredients on food labels and make certain there's no red dye or MSG involved. "I think that's you sitting there inside the house." Sue taps on the card. "Look in the basement window. There's definitely a little person on the couch."

Shelby keeps the postcards in a jewelry box her mother bought her when they went on their trip to Chincoteague Island. There's a horse painted on the box; the inside lining is blue velvet. Maybe the most recent card is a message from the great beyond. Shelby can't stop thinking it might have been sent by Helene. She knows this is impossible; all the same, soon afterward she finds herself headed to Lewiston Street, where the Boyds live. She stands on the corner, but she can't bring herself to go any closer than that. She looks through the dark. She recognizes Mrs. Harrington, who is leaving. Shelby went to school with her daughter, Kelsey, a pretty redhead who excelled at everything and is currently a junior at Brown University.

"Mrs. Harrington," Shelby calls. "Hi."

It takes a while for Mrs. Harrington to recognize the odd person approaching her. When she does she visibly relaxes. "Oh, Shelby, it's you."

"Yeah, it's me." Shelby walks alongside Mrs. Harrington. "You help out with Helene, right?"

"There's a whole bunch of us who are regulars. She's a darling girl." Mrs. Harrington has her keys in her hands. Shelby doesn't tell this nice woman that Helene always hated Kelsey Harrington. She'd thought Kelsey was a snob.

"Does she ever come to consciousness?" Shelby's voice sounds shaky and thin. Mrs. Harrington throws her a look, clearly confused. "Helene," Shelby says. "Does she ever say something or dictate something? Like a postcard?"

"Shelby." Mrs. Harrington reaches for her hand, but Shelby backs away before she can touch her. "No, honey." Mrs. Harrington shakes her head sadly. "She never does anything like that."

Shelby has secretly been harboring the hope that Helene has been pretending, that she isn't really brain-injured and in fact rises from her bed each night to walk through her house, pilfering snacks from the cupboards, watching TV, gazing into the mirror as she brushes her long hair.

"That doesn't mean there aren't miracles," Mrs. Harrington says.

"Yeah. I'll bet." Shelby runs off without another word. She must seem crazy to ask if a person who has no brain activity could be writing postcards.

Shelby calls Ben Mink to ask that he meet her in the park. Her hope that Helene will come back has faded into ash. Helene is gone. Shelby's old life is gone with her. Shelby is so jittery she can barely sit still. She despises winter and herself. All she wants to do is get stoned and check out, and Ben can provide her with her ticket to do so. Or so she thinks.

"No weed," he says sadly. "There's some FBI activity in the Bahamas. Dealers are getting busted and it's filtering up to the States. My go-to guys in Huntington and in Northport both got busted. Call me back at the end of the week."

"How can you be out?" Shelby is beside herself. "I depend on you."

"Yeah, right." He actually laughs. He thinks she's kidding.

"You're *my* go-to guy," she insists. "I need you."

"That's a mistake, Shelby," Ben says. "I let people down."

"Don't make me sit through reality," Shelby moans. The tremor in her hand is already worsening. "I don't know if I can do it. People with their petty desires and their TV shows. Everyone wants to be famous."

She was famous for a while, at least in the local *Pennysaver* and in *Newsday*. There was even an article in *The New York Times* about teenagers and car accidents and she was referred to twice. They got it wrong, as usual, and printed that she was currently under psychiatric care, when she was already out of the nuthouse, ensconced in her parents' basement.

"Lie down and close your eyes," Ben suggests. "Breathe deep. Imagine you're in Bali. Or on a beach in the Hamptons. Life's easier to get through that way."

"I would never be in the Hamptons." Shelby paces the basement. There are mice down here, but she knows they're afraid of her. She once stumbled upon three baby mice that froze until she hid behind the stairs, giving them the courage to run away. She happens to catch sight of herself in an old stand-up mirror. She has to get rid of that thing. Frankly, she's completely shocked by her own appearance. She looks like the kind of girl people back away from on the street, someone who begs for spare change while she curses the world.

"Do I seem different to you than I did in high school?" she asks.

"Sure," Ben says. "You're bald."

"I mean in some definitive way, asshole."

"That's definitive. Bald makes a statement. You're completely different."

"No I'm not." Shelby has a crack in her voice. "That would mean I'm subhuman."

"No. You're like the weird fucked-up sister of yourself, Shelby. Whereas I'm just an extension of my loser self that anyone could have foreseen. I have followed the path set out before me. You veered."

He means crashed and she knows it, so she hangs up on him. All he is to her is a drug dealer, anyway. He's become less geeky and is now good-looking, in a rangy, off-center way, better than anyone would have guessed back in high school. He's handsome, really, but so what? She doesn't care about his philosophy. Without getting stoned, it's harder to sleep fourteen hours at a time. She can feel something coursing through her. She sneaks upstairs to look through her parents' medicine cabinet. Ativan. That might work. She hadn't realized her mother was anxious enough to need a prescription like that. There's also tramadol, which she was given at the hospital. It's a muscle relaxer that they added to her Valium and lithium. She grabs that as well.

Shelby's father is sitting in the living room. She usually manages to avoid him. Lately he has kind of a looming presence. Dan Richmond used to be a man who could charm a roomful of people at a party, but he's changed. Now he goes to work at the men's shop he inherited from his father and he comes home at six. That's his life. He watches a lot of TV and doesn't talk much.

"What are you doing here?" he says when he sees his daughter. If pressed, he wouldn't be able to remember the last time she's come upstairs.

"I came to get some milk," she tells him. That sounds all-American. She goes to the fridge. "Where's Mom?"

"Nowhere," Dan says.

Shelby pours herself a glass of milk. She notices her dad is watching the same show she always tunes in to, so she sits down on the couch.

"That guy's crap," she says of the contestant she despises. He sings country-western sometimes, and eighties rock sometimes. He has no center, as far as Shelby is concerned.

"Yeah, well, he's there in Hollywood and you're here."

"I don't want to be in Hollywood," Shelby is quick to respond. She tries to sound casual, but her father's remark stings. It's just another way of saying she's a nothing. As if she didn't know that.

They watch together for a while. Shelby is tapping her foot the way she did when she was upset before the hospital, and her father is trying his best not to mention it or even notice it. Thump against the floor. Against the couch. Like she's wound up.

"I'll bet she went over to the Boyds'," Shelby finally says. "Didn't she? I told her it was stupid and vile and disgusting. I told her not to go."

"Maybe there's some truth in what people say. It doesn't hurt to see."

"Don't make me vomit."

"You'd have to be alive to do that. Living the way you do isn't being alive."

Shelby stares at her father. He looks older. He's a big, unhappy man who clearly wishes he were elsewhere.

"If I wanted to be dead, I would be," Shelby informs him.

"That's comforting," her dad says.

"It is to me," Shelby says.

She goes back to the basement. She takes two Ativan, then slips on her coat and goes out through the cellar door. She sits down on the pic-nic table, even though it's cold outside. The air is like crystals; it hurts just to breathe.

Her mother's car pulls up and parks. The headlights turn everything yellow, but when they're cut off the night becomes pitch. All the same, Sue spies her daughter perched on the picnic table. She heads across the yard. "It's freezing," Sue says.

"I'm counting stars. That should keep me busy."

Sue and Shelby lie down on the wooden table. They both look up.

"It's not the way you think it is," Sue says. "It's peaceful over at the Boyds'. She's peaceful. She means something to the people who come to see her, Shelby." No one could count all the stars. There are far too many. What's above them is endless. "It wasn't anyone's fault."

Shelby makes a sound that she hadn't expected to be a sob. She doesn't even know who she is anymore.

"I think I lost my soul," she says.

"That can't happen," Sue tells her.

"You have no idea what can happen, Mom."

Shelby takes out a cigarette and some matches. She used to be so against smoking she would go up to complete strangers to ask if they knew what they were doing to their lungs when they lit up. She was so sure of how to set the world right.

Now she goes back into the basement and phones Ben Mink. She tries not to think of her mother all alone in the backyard, counting stars. Sometime after the accident, her parents stopped talking to each other unless they needed to discuss a household chore or a doctor's appointment. It's true, tragedy can bring you closer or drive you apart.

"I'm desperate," Shelby tells Ben. "Beam me out of here."

He says he's managed to score some pot from a guy he used to know in school. He'll meet her on Main Street at nine. His parents live a few blocks from town. He rents an apartment with a bunch of guys, but he also spends nights at his parents'. They always give him a good meal and ask what he plans to do with his life. If he eats and shrugs it's all pretty painless.

Shelby hates to leave the house, but she pulls on extra socks and her old boots, then gloves and a hat. The TV is still on; the blue light from the window falls across the lawn and out into the road. Ice. Crystals. Trees without leaves. Real things. Shelby walks toward Main Street. Everything is closed except the pizza place, where a few high school kids are hanging out. Shelby wraps her scarf around her head, then loops it around her neck and keeps going. She can hear herself breathing because the inhalations are sharp, sob-like things. She can hardly catch her breath. All that smoking and the cold air and how fast she walked here. It all adds up. It makes her want to cry.

Ben Mink is standing outside the Book Revue, a regular meeting place for them. He spent a lot of time in the science fiction section in high school. He read entire books while crouched down on the floor. Now he has his hands in his pockets; he's freezing. When Shelby arrives he peers into her cloaked face. Hat, scarf, big eyes, bald. She looks like an orphan in a comic book.

"Damn it's cold," he says. "That is you in there, right?"

"Who else would meet you, Ben? As I recall, you don't have any friends. Oh, the guy you got the pot from."

"He's more of an enemy," Ben says. "You're my friend."

"Yeah, right." Shelby gets her money from stealing from her parents; very grown-up to paw around in her mother's purse and her father's wallet. She is well aware that they pretend not to know. Shelby gives Ben the cash, and he hands her a plastic baggie that she slips into her pocket. "Okay," Shelby says. "We're friends."

"I've brought something else for you." Ben presents her with a copy of Ray Bradbury's *The Illustrated Man*. "This will blow you away," he says. "Some guy is covered with living tattoos. Each one tells a story."

"You don't have to give me anything." All the same, Shelby takes the book.

"Yeah, well, I'm not going to be around much longer," Ben says.

"Really? Leaping from a bridge?"

"Don't laugh when I tell you. Promise?"

Their breath comes out like clouds. They're the only ones on the street. Ben is wearing old Doc Martens boots that crunch into the snow when they start to walk. The crunch echoes up and sounds like steel.

"I've been taking classes at Empire State College. It's independent study. An accelerated program. I started classes when I was in high school."

"A program for what?" It's so cold that Shelby thinks her fingers inside her gloves are turning blue. Maybe they'll turn to sugar candy and break off and there'll be a fairy-tale ending when one taste of her sugar-stick fingers will cure Helene.

Ben shrugs, somewhat embarrassed to have succeeded at something. "I have a BS in science."

"What does that stand for? Bullshit?"

"I didn't mention it, because I wasn't sure I would graduate. But I did and now I've decided to go to pharmacy school. I've already been accepted. I got a four thirty on the PCAT admission test." Shelby doubles over with laughter at this news. Ben grins as he watches her. She looks so pretty when she laughs. "So I'm smart," he says. "So what?"

"It's a perfect career path for you," Shelby says. "Considering your interests."

"Seriously, pharmacists can make a hundred grand a year."

"Oh, yeah, what are you going to do with all that money? Buy drugs?"

"Weren't you in the Straight and Narrow Club at school?"

The antidrug contingent that put up posters in the hallways and made a vow not to use drugs. She was so narrow-minded back then. If she met herself then the way she is now, she would have crossed over to the other side of the street to avoid such a creep.

"Fuck you," Shelby says. She can't stand the other her, the girl who thought she would always be one of the fortunate ones: good grades, good looks, good future.

"I didn't mean it in a bad way. I just like you better now. That's all."

Shelby glances at him through the slit between her scarf and her hat.

"Where do you think your soul goes when you lose it?" she asks him. He's been to college after all, maybe he's smart enough to know the answer.

"Around the corner and down the street."

They both laugh. They are at that very moment turning the corner and going down the street. There's nothing there.

"I told you it was gone," Shelby says.

"Let's go find it," Ben suggests.

"Yeah, right."

They stop long enough for Ben to take a joint from his pocket. Shelby holds her hands around it so the match won't blow out.

"Let's just walk by her house," Ben says.

"That's it? Just pass by it? Not stop or anything?"

Ben offers her a hit. "I won't tell if you don't."

They head toward the Boyds' house. It's easy really. Shelby has been here a thousand times before. She remembers a time when Ben said something to her in high school and she pretended not to hear and walked right by. She's curious about what he said and questions him. He probably thought she was an uptight snob, and she probably was. Ben swears he doesn't remember, but there's a smirk on his face. He remembers all right. He'd said, *Do you know where the music room is?* His mother had insisted he take saxophone lessons. He'd actually wanted to say, *I'll pay you a hundred bucks if I can kiss you.*

"You didn't like me in high school," Shelby says.

"Well, I didn't like anyone, so don't think you were special."

They laugh again and lean closer for warmth.

"You were popular and you followed the rules. I always hated those girls," Ben tells her.

"Right. You liked the ugly, unpopular ones."

"I liked the smart ones. I just didn't know you were one of them. You kind of hid it."

Shelby thinks that over. She's shivering as they approach Helene's. There's no one at the Boyds', no lines in the driveway, no miracle seekers, just a darkened house with peeling paint. The bushes all look black. Sparrows rustle in the leaves, but everything else is silent.

"Come on," Ben says. He grabs Shelby by the sleeve and they wheel across the yard.

"Hey," Shelby says. "Wait a minute." They're headed toward Helene's window. "I thought we were just passing by."

"This is her room," Ben says. "I've been here before. I was kind of a Peeping Tom in high school."

"Are you kidding?" Shelby is shocked. "That is so vile. No wonder I never spoke to you."

"I only saw her naked once."

Shelby glares at him. "Only once? Like that's nothing? Once is a violation. You really were a creep."

There's a rattle somewhere, a garbage can perhaps, but unsettling. Ben and Shelby crouch down beside the house so no one will see them. But there's no one around. A cat crossing the street. The sparrows in the bushes. Ben is shaking under his puffy jacket. He's had a guilty conscience all this time, and he didn't even know how bad he felt until he makes his confession. He'd been a pervert and now he has a pervert's remorse.

"I was only a kid," he says.

He sounds like he's going to crack and get all emotional, something Shelby can't stand. "Pull yourself together," she tells him. "So you spied on her. You were probably too young to know it was wrong."

"I was crazy about her."

"Helene?" Again, Shelby is stunned.

"Nuts, huh?"

They start laughing, muffled, choked giggles.

"Insane," Shelby agrees.

"Did I ever have a chance?"

"Never. Not in a million years. She was in love with that guy Chris. Truthfully, Ben? It would have never been you."

It's kind of a relief for Ben to hear this, as if a cord binding him to his past has been cut. He feels oddly grateful. He doesn't have to be loyal to Helene.

"Do you want to look?" he asks.

They're leaning into each other, but they can't feel one another. Coats. Gloves. Protection from the elements.

"You," Shelby says.

So Ben steps onto a ledge Shelby hadn't known was there. It's part of a window well cover that allows him to step up, then haul himself upward so he can look into Helene's window. Clearly he's done this before. Shelby stays where she is, knees pulled to her chest, head spinning, her hands covering her eyes. She thinks about the anonymous postcards that she keeps in her childhood jewelry box. Every day she waits even though sometimes there are months in between their arrivals. When she sees one in the mailbox she feels a thrumming inside her. She's always excited to read them, no matter the message. *Be something,* with a hive of bees made of gold ink and a girl who's been stung running into a dark wood. *Feel something.* A heart held in the palm of a hand. Inside the heart are words written in red ink: *Faith, sorrow, shame, hope.* Someone is watching over her. Someone knows what she needs.

Ben is silent as he peers into the window.

"What's it like in there?" Shelby asks.

"Her room looks the same."

Ben gets off the ledge and sinks back down next to Shelby, close, so their shoulders touch. Shelby uncovers her eyes. "How is she?"

Ben's beard is patchy, and he smells like smoke and dirty laundry.

"She looks like somebody in a fairy tale. She's peaceful."

"Really?" That's exactly what her mother said.

"She was beautiful back then, but you had more personality. You had a great laugh. I could hear it down the hall in school and know it was you. Actually I was in love with you both."

"Yeah, well, that person is gone. I've become my own evil sister. You said so yourself."

"I didn't say evil. And I like you better this way. Really. But I'm freezing my ass off."

They're sitting in a frozen patch of ivy that has broken into shards beneath their weight.

"My ass is numb," Shelby says. But she doesn't get up. She sends a silent message to Helene. *Say something. Call my name and I'll rescue you.*

"When I get my first job, I'm getting a Volvo. Ever see their safety records? Man, nothing can hurt you in one of those. A truck can hit you and you walk out of there in one piece, every limb intact. You'd be safe with me."

"Are you coming on to me?" The realization that he is dawns on

Shelby all at once. She swears a lightbulb goes off in her head, but her skull is so cold she thinks it might shatter.

"I'm sitting in the fucking ivy with you," Ben says. "It goes way beyond that."

Shelby moves closer. She's not interested in Ben, but she's comfortable with him. Maybe that's enough for now. When she whispers her breath is damp and hot. "Should I look?"

"You can if you want to. I'll tell you one thing—that's not her in there. So I don't recommend it."

Shelby thinks over all he's said. "How long did you stalk her?"

"It wasn't stalking her. I told you, I was crazy about her."

"Did you stalk me?"

"What do you think I'm doing right now? Maybe you're not as smart as I think you are. It's like twelve degrees and I'm out here on the Boyds' lawn with you."

Shelby starts out laughing and then it becomes something else. Ben covers her mouth with his gloved hand so that Helene's parents won't hear anything. "Shelby," he says.

Shelby hears the way he says her name and she knows that somehow he's fallen in love with her. She's so stunned she stops crying.

Ben says, "Okay?"

Shelby nods and he lets go.

"I really am freezing," Shelby tells him.

Ben stands and helps her up. Shelby could have looked in the window. She could have stepped up and held her gloved hand to the glass; she could have climbed into the room, gotten down on her knees, touched Helene's warm hand, and begged for forgiveness, the way people do on a regular basis, greedy for a miracle. Helene might have blessed her, she might have changed everything that is about to happen and released her from the punishment of being herself. Instead, Shelby follows Ben across the lawn. They go back the way they came, conscious of the sound of their boots in the snow. Crunch. It's like a tree being chopped down, like a heart beating. The sky is black. There's the scent of hyacinths cutting through the cold. That was Helene's favorite flower, not roses.

"I need something hot to drink," Shelby says.

"Being bald probably lowers your total body temperature," Ben remarks. He's taken every science course available at college, and yet he knows nothing about human emotions. Love is a mystery. It's like an alien abduction. You think you're on earth, and there you are among the stars.

Shelby doubles her scarf around her head. "Being an idiot probably lowers yours," she shoots back.

She smiles, or at least Ben thinks she does. He would do anything she asked. Even something stupid like robbing a convenience store. He'd leave everything behind and follow her to some far-off destination. He'd look for a miracle if he could.

"Probably," he agrees. "I bet it does."

But he hadn't been enough of an idiot to actually open his eyes when he was at Helene's window. He thought about those times he'd stalked her. Even then it was Shelby he wanted. He was just too afraid of what she'd do if he got caught spying on her. Helene was simpler. One night while he watched, Helene was on her bed, chatting on the phone. She was undressed, lying on her back, one bare leg thrown over the other. All she had on was a bracelet. She was almost too beautiful to be real. His eyes are closed now, and he imagines her as she was. He hears the echo of her voice as she talked on the phone to Shelby, cooking up some plans for the weekend. Her skin was snow-white; her hair was the color of roses. That's the way she'll always be to him. Some things are best remembered the way you want to remember them, like this road, these stars, this girl right beside him as they walk into the center of the cold night, looking straight ahead.

CHAPTER

2

On the day Shelby and Ben Mink move to New York City, Ben drops a bookcase on his foot and breaks three bones. They wind up sitting in the ER at Bellevue Hospital for so long someone barges into their apartment with the help of a crowbar and steals their TV, actually Ben's TV, since Shelby owns nothing. Naturally, it's Shelby who forgot to double-lock the door. Ben doesn't blame her. He doesn't raise his voice even though he now wears a soft cast and can expect to have pain for up to thirty days. He simply says, "Welcome to city living," and begins to unpack everything that hasn't been stolen, mainly clothes and pots and pans his mom gave him, along with his great-aunt Ida's dining room table and chairs, a set so ugly no one in his right mind would steal it. Ben's kindness only serves to reinforce Shelby's notion that he's all wrong for her. Before it's even begun she knows she's made a mistake.

She's moved into a cramped studio apartment on Tenth Avenue with

Ben because she was haunted in her hometown on Long Island. Ben is well meaning, with a kind and open heart. For some reason he's fallen in love with her, so when he asked her to come to the city she said yes before she thought things through. She still doesn't understand what he sees in her, but she doesn't bother to ask. They'd been thrown together by fate and boredom. They began their relationship by reading chapters of *The Illustrated Man* to each other. Shelby blames Ray Bradbury for tricking her into having sex with Ben. His stories made her feel something around the edge of her heart. Still, the intimacy of being scrunched into a single bed in the basement with Ben felt all wrong. She thinks of sex as something nasty, quickly over and done with on a bathroom floor while someone holds you down and treats you roughly. Ben was tender, which was upsetting. Shelby didn't know how to respond. This was her parents' house after all. Once, while in bed, Ben was whispering something about being in love with her and she was thinking about the snow falling down, Shelby had heard her mother's tread on the stair, probably as she carried down a basket of laundry. The washing machine was only a few feet away. Panicked, Shelby had shouted out, "Don't come down here!" as if she were packaging cocaine or running a house of prostitution. Her mother had run back up the stairs and shut the door.

"It's okay," Ben had said, "I want to meet your mom." He'd patted Shelby on the back to calm her, which only served to make her want to push him away.

Ben had pulled on his clothes. He wasn't kidding about doing the proper thing. He'd gone out the back door, through the yard, around the house, then up to the front door, where he rang the bell and introduced himself to Sue. Shelby and her mom still laugh about the fact that he was wearing Shelby's boots, which he'd put on by accident. He'd been forced to hobble around the house while Sue Richmond served him tea and cookies.

All that spring they were together. Sometimes they talked and sometimes they just had sex. Shelby liked to keep the lights off so she couldn't see the way he looked at her, love-struck and dumb. Ben is a romantic. He's a sap. *It's only sex,* Shelby always thinks. It's so different from what the orderly made her do on the bathroom floor, where he said nasty, dirty things about how he owned her ass while he fucked her. That wasn't sex, it was assault. When she rose out of her body to escape him she thinks that may have been the moment she lost her soul. Somewhere in the hospital her soul is flying above the patients in their beds, trapped inside the ward where Shelby spent those awful months.

Ben found the apartment, signed the lease, and hired the moving van. Shelby finally agreed to live with him because she is fairly certain she is a victim of space and location and time, and all she needs is to get out of town in order to escape her past. But it isn't working out that way. She's still spooked in Manhattan. She has an eye for tragedy and sorrow. Show her a rose and she'll see only the wasp in the center of the bloom. On the city streets she finds herself haunted by the smallest thing: a child with a purple bruise on his cheek peering up at her from a stroller. An old woman with papery-thin skin and a huge, ill-fitting coat who cannot go forward without a walker. A cat in an alley, with one torn-off ear. Does no one else see all this pain floating around Manhattan? Shelby sits on the bed in their new apartment and she's just as haunted as she'd been when she was living in her parents' basement. She takes Ativan morning, noon, and night. When Ben gets home from pharmaceutical school up on 125th Street, she pretends nothing's wrong. She's a Stepford wife and they're not even married. They smoke dope and order Chinese food delivered and Ben talks about his day and Shelby doesn't listen. It's all fine as long as Shelby doesn't look into the eyes of the deliveryman from the Hunan Kitchen, who always seems in the grip of some great and quiet sorrow, no matter how much of a tip she gives him. She takes the fortune cookies from the bottom of the bag and throws them into a glass bowl she keeps in the closet. She has no desire to know what her future might hold.

"Who made it your job to feel guilty for every bad thing that happens?" Ben says fondly when she begins a litany of the awful things she's seen in a single day. A man with no shoes. A girl crying as her father drags her along Fourteenth Street. A woman begging people for help in a language no one can understand. They both know Shelby wouldn't have looked at Ben twice in high school, but she wonders why he doesn't flee from her. He thinks she's beautiful, which convinces her that he has not only lousy vision but terrible judgment as well. Shelby still shaves her head and she only wears black; she's so skinny her veins are luminous under her skin, like the old ladies on the street with their walkers and their plastic bags filled with belongings and trash. Ben, on the other hand, has begun to care about his appearance. He wants to look professional. He bought five white shirts that will need ironing. As for Shelby, she has never used an iron and she hopes to keep it that way.

Tonight as they sit on the fire escape, they're stoned enough not to care about the heat. It's ninety-nine degrees, hotter than the human body. The sky is falling and the evening is wet and thick. It's the kind of humid night when people shoot each other for no good reason. Shelby has wrapped herself in a damp sheet. The desire for an air-conditioned environment has recently led her to apply for and then surprisingly get a job at a pet store in Union Square. It's disgusting, boring work—cleaning out cages and unpacking boxes of dog food—but fortunately the store is ice-cold. It's Shelby's first job ever, if she doesn't count babysitting in high school. She still can't believe people actually trusted her with their children. Helene used to come over and sneak out before the parents came home. That is her entire occupational experience other than living off her parents and mooching off Ben Mink. Her parents think the job is some kind of breakthrough, which is just pitiful. Her mother went so far as to send her a greeting card. *Congratulations. We're so proud of you!* There was an illustration of a little girl wearing a crown on the card, holding a magic wand and standing on tiptoe as if she were a good little fairy. Shelby can't bear to look at it. She wishes it had been another postcard from her anonymous correspondent. She's come to depend on those well-wishes and their strange and beautiful artwork. She crams the card from her mother into the old jewelry box she has where she keeps the postcards. Shelby had thought distance from her hometown would make a difference, but she still feels she's responsible for everything bad that has ever happened in the world. She has bad karma. Unfortunately, she's fairly certain that bad karma is something you're born with and can't ever change.

"I wonder how it feels to cure someone," Shelby muses as they have their fire-escape dinner. "Do you feel like a magician or like a god when you save someone? Or maybe you just feel like you're a plumber fixing pipes."

"You should go to school," Ben suggests. "I see you as a healer." He has a long, skinny body, even more evident now that he's shirtless. Shelby thinks he's lost weight since he started graduate school. Even though he'd been a screwup as a kid, he's surprisingly serious about his studies now. He's a nerd, falling in love with science just as he had with Shelby, suddenly and for reasons that are impossible to fathom. Plus he's better-looking all the time, and Shelby doesn't know how that's even possible.

"I'd be a terrible student," she remarks. She blew off NYU, and now she'd be two years behind. She's pretty sure it's too late for everything. "Plus I'm too poor."

She's earning minimum wage. She eats noodles and tofu and spicy eggplant for dinner only because Ben is foolish enough to take care of her. Caring about things doesn't come easy to Shelby. She can hold her hand over the lit burner of a stove for the longest time and not feel a thing. Sometimes she sticks pins into her flesh just to make certain she's alive.

"City College is nearly free. You can get a scholarship for the rest.

And you won't be poor when I get my degree. We'll be borderline rich. That's the whole point of becoming a pharmacist. People always need drugs."

It seems Ben has plans for the future. Shelby assumes he'll dump her by the time he succeeds at anything. She's stoned most of the time, and she's haunted, but she isn't stupid. Ben latched on to her when he was a loser; once that changes, everything else will too.

"You've got a lot to give, Shelby. You can save the world."

"Right." Shelby feels a deep bitterness inside her. He doesn't know her at all. She ruins whatever she touches.

On this evening the air smells like sulfur. Lacy pieces of black dirt float through the air as if the two of them are trapped inside an upside-down snow globe. Ben can think whatever he wants. Shelby has absolutely nothing inside of her. She's a black hole. A sinkhole. A whole lot of nothing. She's told Ben that, but he doesn't want to believe her. Who would have imagined he'd turn out to be such an optimist? Maybe that's the reason Shelby has sex with him whenever he wants her. She has to give him something in return for his devotion. She makes certain to imagine she's somewhere else when they're in bed so she won't be haunted by his desire and the sounds he makes, as if he's drowning and expects her to save him.

Shelby hasn't told Ben anything about her job. She doesn't tell him much. She keeps things inside. She usually wears a hooded sweatshirt; that way everything in her mind is packed away where it belongs. At work, she prefers stacking dog food to manning the cash register. Fewer interactions with people equal fewer complications. She likes to feed the birds. Already, the parrots know her and do little dances when they spy her; the parakeets go wild when she approaches their cages. She loves birdsong; it clears her head. Or maybe it fills it. With all those chirps and trills ringing out, she doesn't have to think about what she's done and how she can never be forgiven.

The one area she can't stand is the puppy department. The poor things are so cheerful and hopeful. She avoids that section, as she avoids her co-workers, who are equally friendly, although more bored than hopeful. They order pizzas delivered at lunch and give each other nick-names as if they're in a fraternity. Juan is called G-man because he's determined to one day join the feds, a whacked-out dream for someone in charge of lizards who sells weed on the side. Maravelle Diaz is known as Mimi because she sings and has a five-octave range reminiscent of Mariah Carey. Their supervisor, Ellen Grimes, who manages the store as if it's a small, corrupt country, is called Hellgirl or the Grimester be-hind her back of course. Shelby was dubbed E.T.—the bald head, the big eyes, the silence—her nickname is a no-brainer. G-man called her that the very first day. Shelby refused to answer at first, but after a while it's easier not to fight it. *Hey, E.T., give me a price on the birdseed! E.T., stack the Science Diet.*

Shelby does as she's asked no matter what they call her; there's less human contact if you don't argue or give your opinion. At lunch she goes off on her own. She usually picks up a packet of cheese and crack-ers at a deli, then goes to Union Square Park. She's there even on rainy days, and there happens to be rain on the day she becomes a thief. It's summer and hot, and the sudden shower is a surprise. While the rain pours down, she skitters toward an overhang of the subway, squeez-ing up against a wall. Union Square smells sweet and green on days like this. Petals and leaves from the Greenmarket are scattered about, and the scent of mint mixes with the hard smell of hot concrete. People dart about, trying to get out of the rain. Everyone is walking so quickly Shelby can't pick up on anyone's despair. The truth is, she feels empty without it. Maybe she's empty if she doesn't latch on to sorrow. She's beginning to wonder if perhaps she's haunting herself.

Shelby's favorite sweatshirt is red, like Riding Hood's cape. She finds herself thinking about wolves and how they've always been hunted, caught in traps and hung upside down on ropes, blood dripping from their mouths and noses. She often dreams she's running through the grass in the dark and something is following her. She's too afraid to turn around in her dreams and see what's behind her. When she wakes, she's drenched in sweat. She gets out of bed, then climbs out the window so she can be alone on the fire escape while Ben sleeps. She gazes upward as the sky turns pink. If she's not careful she may cry thinking about wolves and accidents and ice. She wants to think that Helene is watching the same pink sky through her bedroom window, that she weeps for the beauty of the world, even though she knows that Helene no longer has the ocular ability to shed tears.

On the day when she's ducking the rainstorm in Union Square, Shelby hears a slight huffing and puffing. She thinks of ogres under a bridge, of the werewolves she and Helene used to imagine were lurking in the woods. Shelby glances beside her to see not a monster but a homeless person. He's a kid, with a blanket tossed over him to protect him against the rain even though it must be broiling under a woolen blanket. His belongings are stored in garbage bags balanced on a rolling wooden platform. Atop the platform are two dogs. One is asleep; the other is the thing that's huffing and puffing.

The kid rises out of his stupor. "What are you looking at?" he growls.

The kid seems older when he speaks. He has a cut on his lip that looks infected. Shelby glances away. She's always on the lookout for ghosts, but this guy is definitely real. Shelby feels guilty eating her cheese and crackers. She puts the package on the sidewalk.

"Are you going to eat that?" the homeless guy says.

Shelby slides the cheese over, and the kid, or whatever he is, eats her lunch.

"What about the dogs?" Shelby asks. "They're probably hungry."

The kid throws her a look, and after considering he tosses the huffing and puffing dog half a cracker. "Dogs in America are too fat. Don't think I'm starving them, because I'm not. Why would I do that? Everyone loves dogs."

"What are their names?"

The kid shrugs. "Dog," he says of the filthy, white, huffing and puffing one. "That one's Puppy," he says of the sleeping one. The second dog's eyes don't even flicker. For a moment he seems dead.

"Is he sick?"

"The secret is Benadryl. Quiets them down. People want to give you more when you've got two dogs depending on you."

"You do that?" Shelby is distressed by this news. She has realized the kid thinks she's homeless too. Maybe it's her wardrobe, the holes in her boots, the old sweatshirt. "What are their real names?" she asks. When he doesn't answer, she presses on. "Seriously."

The kid glares at her. "I already told you!"

Shelby has broken her own rule. She never speaks to people she knows, let alone strangers. It's time for her to get back to work, yet she feels she won't make it through the day. She gets out what's left of the joint she began that morning. She takes a few hits before passing it to the homeless guy. He smokes greedily, and although he doesn't say thank you, he does give her a piece of advice. "You can rent them, you know. Twenty bucks for four hours. It's a good deal." Shelby looks at him blankly, not understanding his meaning, so he adds, "The dogs."

"Rent them from you?"

"Are you nuts? If they were my dogs wouldn't I know their names?"

The animals are so filthy Shelby wonders if she might get fleas merely by being in the same vicinity. The sleeping one is a Lhasa apso— like thing, and the other is a French bulldog. It has a furrowed expression, as if it was considering something of major importance that is far beyond human scope. They both make Shelby feel itchy.

"Maybe some other time," she tells the kid.

She returns to the pet store to stack twenty-pound bags of cat food. She's amazed anyone in New York City needs that much cat food. How many cats can fit into one apartment? Seven? Eight? Twenty? When she leaves work at the end of the day, the rain is over and the sidewalk is steaming. She spies the dogs and the platform cart, but as she crosses the park and gets closer, she notices the person they're with is different. Now it's an older man with long braids. He has a sign—*Money for Dog Food*—and a basket filled with dollar bills.

～

The heat gets worse. That night Shelby and Ben wrap themselves in wet sheets and sit on the fire escape. Neither wants dinner.

"We're in togas," Ben says cheerfully. "Amor in aeternum."

He's been studying Latin, which he says is important for anyone working in pharmaceuticals. Unfortunately Shelby has glanced through his textbook and therefore knows he's talking about love. More and more he thinks she's someone she's not. They have tangerines and water instead of dinner. It's too hot for food. The street looks beautiful when the neon lights of the bar across the street are switched on, as if blue bath oil has been poured over everything. Colors drip over the black street. Shelby is grateful for every horn that honks; the noise takes up space in her head. Emptiness is dangerous. When it's quiet she starts to hear Helene's voice. She used to just catch a glimpse of her in the basement, now she hears her whispering. *Why didn't you save me?* When she looks in mirrors and windows, her friend surfaces in the glass, her hands out, wearing the blue dress she never got to wear to the prom. Every day, every minute, Helene is with her.

In bed Ben takes it a step farther and actually tells her he's in love with her. This time it's in English, not Latin, so she can't pretend not to know what he's talking about. "Ben," she says. "Love is a false construct. It's how people convince themselves that life is worth living."

"I only know how I feel," he tells her.

When Shelby falls asleep, she dreams she's in a big green field. A man is calling to her. *Do something,* he tells her. It's the writer of the postcards. She fears he wants more from her than she's able to do. Isn't leaving home enough? She sees the person's shadow, but not the man himself. The grass grows taller, and the whole world smells like mint. Shelby's hair has grown back in her dream, long golden-brown hair, the way it used to be. There are black butterflies rising from the grass, one after another, until they fill the horizon.

When Shelby wakes she finds herself wishing she were still inside her dream. It takes all her energy to get out of bed and make coffee. She opens the closet and sees that Ben has bought an ironing board that he crammed in beside the coats. He has taken to pressing his white shirts, secretly, while she's asleep.

On her way to work she stops at the park. There is the platform; there are the dogs. This time a girl is with them. She has tattoos on her face, blue lines and swirls. Shelby gazes at the sky and notices the clouds are white on one side, blue on the other. If you slit them open with a knife something strange would likely fall down. Snow in the summer, postcards with no postmark, advice from above. The floppy, sleeping dog is balanced on the shopping bags, and the bulldog is on the sidewalk; it looks more alert than the tattooed girl and, frankly, much smarter.

The homeless girl senses someone near and opens her eyes. "I need money for dog food," she announces. It's as though she's a robot with a single skill. She knows how to beg.

Shelby slips one of Ben's dollars into a hat. He gives her spending money every week, and though she feels guilty, she accepts his generosity.

"What are the dogs' names?" Shelby asks. It's like a magic spell. If she knows their names she will be free of them.

"Fuck you," the girl says. "I don't give out that kind of information for a dollar."

Stunned by the girl's venom, Shelby takes off. She heads across the street to find her co-worker Maravelle waiting at the door of the pet store.

"What the hell did you do that for?" Maravelle asks. They've never said more than two words to each other, so Shelby is taken aback. "I saw you give her money. Those dogs are just props. Do you think they see a lick of that money? I used to give them a dollar or two until I noticed they always had a different owner. Those people aren't begging for dog food."

"I'm supposed to take advice from someone who works in a pet store?" Shelby remarks archly.

"Honey, you work in a pet store," Maravelle reminds her, her mouth twisted into a smirk. She's a beautiful woman who's not about to take crap from a bald girl who stacks dog food.

Shelby feels shamed by her own rudeness. The truth is she likes Maravelle's snappy attitude. "I wouldn't work here if I had your voice." Maravelle sings all day long, even when she's ringing up people at the register. "Why don't you get out of here and sing professionally? Be the next Mariah Carey."

"Because I have three children and I'm a realist. I know I'm not as good as Mariah."

"I think you're good." This may be the first compliment she's given in years.

"Not *as* good. That's the thing. Don't give those people any more money," Maravelle warns. "They just drink and drug it away."

All the same, Shelby goes to the window to keep an eye on the girl with the dogs. The scene is so upsetting that she stays in the store at lunch in order to avoid them. She has a slice of the pizza her co-workers have delivered.

"Well, what do you know! You actually consume food. Go on, E.T.," Juan from the lizard department says to her. "Have two pieces if you want."

When Shelby leaves work she sees that the shift in the park has changed as well. Now the dogs are back with the kid Shelby first saw. Maravelle comes up beside Shelby, matching her stride. "You really think my voice is that good?"

"I do."

"Yeah, well, what do you know? I'll bet you've never even listened to Mariah Carey."

True enough. Shelby is more a fan of sad singer-songwriters. Her current favorite duo is called The Weepies. She loves The Decemberists. She prefers music about lost love, lost souls, and lost opportunities. But she does know a beautiful voice when she hears one. "I don't ordinarily give out compliments," Shelby assures her co-worker. "But you can sing."

Maravelle nods. "I've never heard you say a nice word to anyone. So I appreciate the comment."

Unless Shelby is completely crazy, the French bulldog is staring at her from across the street. "Don't your kids want pets? If you gave those rats a good shampoo, they'd be cute. Your kids would love them."

"Do you know what my life is like? I'm a single mother with three kids. I don't have time for that. If you're so worried about those dogs, you take them."

Shelby makes a face. "I can't take care of anything."

"Why don't you try to do something?" Maravelle says.

"What did you say?" Shelby feels a lump in her throat. She wonders if Helene is talking to her through other people, repeating the postcard messages she receives, whispering about her failures.

"I said N-O. I do not want any pets. Not now and not ever. Although those things do look sad," she says of the dogs.

As they cross the street together, Shelby and Maravelle come up with a plan. They work well together, almost as if they're friends. As decided, Shelby hangs back when Maravelle begins to sing in the middle of Union Square. Even though she's used to hearing her at the pet shop, Shelby is amazed at the sheer power of her voice. Those beautiful birdsong trills are thrilling in the open air. A hush comes over the park, and people draw close, forming a crowd. Someone tosses some money down, and soon enough others follow suit. The homeless kid, annoyed that his space has been invaded, has started to shout. He sets off to harass his competition, declaring that he'll have her arrested for disturbing the peace.

This is the plan, to distract him so that Shelby can sneak over to the rolling platform. Once there she quickly unties the rope around the bulldog's neck. He gazes at her, as though he's been expecting her. "I'm doing something," Shelby tells the dog. He doesn't blink. The drugged-out, shaggy one startles when she picks him up. Something's wrong with him; he can only open one eye, but he starts to doze again as soon as he's in Shelby's arms. He weighs next to nothing. "Let's go," Shelby says to the bulldog. She thinks of him as the smart one, and indeed, he follows without a leash, with a bowlegged but dignified gait.

When Ben gets home from school, he drops his briefcase smack down on the floor and stares at the dogs on the couch. "Seriously?" he says. "Two of them? Where'd they come from? The ugly dog department?"

Shelby has already ordered dinner delivered from Hunan Kitchen, making certain to choose all the dishes Ben likes most, including the spicy tofu that Shelby hates along with General Tso's chicken, their shared favorite.

"They were being tortured." Shelby's already bathed them in the kitchen sink, and the odor of wet dog permeates the apartment. In the morning she'll use the allowance Ben gives her to buy leashes and collars and dog food. Tonight she feeds them white rice mixed with chicken, which they inhale.

"Let me guess." Ben accepts a plate of food and collapses on the couch next to the one-eyed dog. "One is Yin and the other is Yang? Or Heckle and Jeckle? Spock and Kirk?"

"The one next to you is Blinkie. The other one is General Tso." The names come to her then and there.

"You named them without me?" Ben actually sounds hurt.

"Well, if anything happens and we break up, they'd be my dogs." Shelby doesn't realize how cold this sounds until she sees Ben's expression.

"Is that your plan?" Ben puts down his plate, not noticing when Blinkie snags a piece of tofu. His sight is good enough to steal food.

"Ben." Shelby throws up her hands. "I don't have a plan. Isn't that obvious?"

She surprises him that night in bed when she embraces him. She's never the one to initiate sex, but she moves on top of him and begins to kiss him, so deeply it seems she loves him, and maybe she does, although what does love matter in a world where it's so easy to hurt someone?

⟲

All through the summer Shelby walks the dogs along the riverside before work. Since Ben asked her if she had a plan, she can't stop thinking about the fact that she's an aimless nothing. On the street people stay away from her because she still shaves her head and she wears her hoodie even when it's ninety degrees. Clearly, she looks like someone who's about to snap. But she'd already done that and all she got out of it was a stay in the hospital, where they told her to squeeze frozen oranges to bring her back to reality when she was having a panic attack. As if reality was what she wanted.

Shelby writes to colleges, but she's so conflicted she throws the catalogs into the trash as soon as they arrive. And then one day she leaves the dogs at home and walks up to Hunter College and signs up for two classes, Latin, because she figures then she'll know what Ben is talking about, and Principles of Biology. Maybe a science class will help her make sense of the world. She tells Ben that she'll be out on Tuesday and Thursday nights.

"You do have a plan," he says. "Does it include me?"

Shelby feels bad for him and goes to sit on his lap.

"I'll take that as a yes," Ben says.

She kisses him as though her life depended on it, even though she knows it doesn't. It depends on equal parts probability and luck. That's why she keeps throwing the fortune cookies into the glass bowl. No one can predict what will happen. On the night of the accident Shelby fastened her seat belt, something she did only three times out of ten. Helene was perched on the edge of her seat, too excited over their rock-throwing adventure to bother with her seat belt, which she fastened nine times out of ten. Whenever anyone says that people get what they deserve, Shelby turns away. If that were true, she knows where she'd be right now, asleep and far away, cold to the touch, a dreamer who will never wake or rise from bed or kiss her beloved or lie to him and say, *Yes, it's true, the future is ours.*

Shelby wonders if when you make one choice that's out of the ordinary, all the rest of your life will change, an emotional domino effect. A few weeks after classes begin she's called into the office at work. Ellen Grimes has recently been fired; there have been rumors of embezzlement and a trio of accountants has spent the last two weeks in the office, behind closed doors. Shelby assumes she's also about to be fired as part of the downsizing. Clean out the waste before it cleans you out. Frankly, if she were in charge, she would fire herself. She's been at the pet store for four months, time enough for people to see that she's a black hole and a malcontent. She smokes weed in the storeroom with Juan. She wears her smock inside out. She gives herself a fifty percent discount rather than the usual twenty when she's buying kibble for the General and Blinkie, and she does the same for any customer she senses has fallen on hard times. Shelby is the perfect person to get rid of, so she throws a couple of squeaky dog toys in her backpack before the meeting, thinking it's the last freebie she'll ever get from this place.

The general manager of the entire chain is waiting for her, a man in a suit and tie who stands when Shelby enters, as if she's someone worthy of his good manners. Shelby sits down. She's ready, willing, and able to be fired, and her mouth falls open when she's told that she's the new manager of the store. The company likes her integrity and her dedication. They're impressed that she's gone back to school.

"I don't deserve it," Shelby tells the general manager. "I've only been here for a few months. And I just started school. I'm sure I'll be at the bottom of the class."

She may be a nothing, but she's honest. Doesn't this company see that she's worthless? Lately she's been dreaming about the field again. She loses her way in the tall grass and she doesn't even care that she's lost. There are blackbirds above her and the wind comes up and that's when she spies Helene. That's who's been following Shelby in her dreams. Helene is running, calling out to Shelby, but the funny thing is she's speaking a different language, one Shelby can't understand. Shelby is always disappointed when she wakes up and sees Ben making coffee and the dogs on their doggy bed, another item she marked down for herself at the pet shop. She wants Helene to be there in the apartment, speaking English, telling Shelby that she forgives her.

The manager's job pays $250 more a week. She'll no longer need an allowance from Ben. The thought of herself as independent gives Shelby a little shiver of pleasure. She hasn't felt that for so long she doesn't know what it is at first and wonders if she's coming down with the flu. Shelby will have to do more office work, meaning less time with the customers, which is a definite plus. And she's good at math, even though she hates it. She can figure things in her head without knowing how she does it. The answer just pops up and presents itself to her. The problem is that Maravelle has been working at the store for two years and supports three children. She's the one who should be promoted.

"Maravelle should have the job."

That's what would happen in a fair and just world, but Shelby can tell from the expression on the general manager's face they're not functioning in a world like that.

"Do you know how much time she took off last month?" The general manager isn't a pet person, he's an accountant. He isn't a people person either.

"Her kids had the chicken pox." Maravelle has twin ten-year-old boys, Teddy and Dorian, and a thirteen-year-old girl named Jasmine. She has photos of them taped up on her cash register. In spite of herself, Shelby knows Maravelle's life story. There was a bad boyfriend, and drugs and abuse, and then one day Maravelle took her kids and walked out to start a new life. Shelby respects that kind of nerve. She and Maravelle usually take their lunch break together. They're such opposites, Juan, the king of all nicknames, has taken to calling them Beauty and the Beast. They simply call him Asshole.

"Bottom line, she's absent too much. She's not being promoted. If you don't take it, I'll hire from outside."

The general manager stands; he'll shake her hand or he'll dump her. Shelby knows that much. So she accepts his offer. She's self-destructive, not stupid. She doesn't mention the meeting to anyone, but word gets around fast. At the end of the day, Maravelle comes looking for her.

"I can't believe this! I've been here way longer than you!" Maravelle is pretty and talented, but she got pregnant at sixteen and her life took a detour that keeps on veering from the path she thought she'd be on. "Thanks a million, Shelby," she says with real bitterness.

"They were going to hire from the outside if I didn't take it." Shelby hasn't had a friend for so long, she supposes Maravelle is the closest she's got. "Look, I'll give you half the money."

"I don't want half the money!"

"Seriously, I mean it. I'll share fifty-fifty!"

"You just don't get it, Shelby. It was about me deserving it." Maravelle looks as though she's about to cry. "It was the chicken pox, wasn't it? All that time I took off?"

Shelby nods.

"To hell with everything," Maravelle says as she stalks away.

That night Ben and Shelby go to the Half King to celebrate. It's owned by one of Ben's favorite writers, a fearless journalist he admires, not that Ben has time to read anything other than pharmacy texts these days. They're sitting at a table on the street, so they can bring the dogs along. The General stays close to Ben, who is messy, and therefore more likely to drop food, even though the bulldog is one hundred percent devoted to Shelby. Frankly, if the General had been a man instead of a bulldog, Shelby would probably run away with him.

"Every time I see Maravelle I feel guilty," she tells Ben.

"You just feel guilty period, Shelby. If you want to make things right with Maravelle, then do something," Ben says.

Shelby puts down her veggie burger and narrows her eyes. Is this merely good advice or the suggestion of some higher power or Helene speaking to her through Ben?

"Such as?" Shelby has again begun to tap her foot whenever she's anxious, which she did when she had her breakdown. Leave it to Shelby to be upset about a raise. Ben had picked up a bunch of tulips for her after she'd told him the news. She told him she hated tulips before she realized it would hurt his feelings.

"Do something that would be meaningful to her," Ben suggests. "Something that will show her you're a true friend."

"But I'm not," Shelby says.

She's certain that it's guilt, not friendship that drives her to buy two tickets for a Mariah Carey concert at Madison Square Garden, one for Maravelle and one for her daughter. They cost a fortune.

"Scalpers have to make a living," Ben says when he hands over the cash.

Ben has paid for the tickets, but Shelby is the one Maravelle hugs when she's called into Shelby's new office and is given the envelope containing tickets for two seats in the tenth row. "You're the best," Maravelle says. She does a little jump for joy. "Not that I'm so easily bought off. But this is a good beginning."

"It's a beginning and an end," Shelby tells her. "My bribery goes no further."

Later in the week, when Shelby and Ben are in bed, he starts talking about money. Not exactly romantic. He thinks it's great that Shelby is getting a raise. Look at how expensive the concert tickets were. Then he drops what Shelby considers to be a conversational bomb.

"Think of how much people pay to have weddings."

Shelby sits up in bed. She can feel the pulse in the base of her throat. She's read that people who are about to be shot feel that pulse and nothing else. "Who's talking about weddings?"

"No one. It's just that people pay a fortune for so much excess, like an eight-layer cake that tastes like white bread, when they could easily elope and spend the money on a trip to Mexico."

"Are you planning a trip to Mexico?" Shelby is wearing black cotton underwear and a T-shirt. She's pale and bald and her feet are thin and long and now she's the manager of a chain store when she doesn't even believe in chain stores. She's a mom-and-pop-store kind of person. She starts thinking about her father, who runs the family business. Maybe she's inherited her entrepreneurial skills from him. Ben is staring at her in some strange, hopeful way. Is he asking her to marry him? "Are you talking about a honeymoon?" she says in a thin voice.

"It's a what-if situation."

Shelby grabs Blinkie off the floor and holds him between her and Ben. When Blinkie falls asleep he rumbles. Ben is quiet and dreamless. Or at least that's what he's told Shelby. Perhaps he's dreaming of Mexico, of aquamarine water and white birds, perhaps she's beside him in his dreams and that's why he calls out to her. Shelby's name bursts out of his mouth even though he's still asleep, but she's already on the fire escape waiting for the morning. She's much too far away to hear.

⌒

Shelby has decided to go home for Christmas. She plans to bring the dogs, but not Ben. She says she doesn't want her parents to get the wrong idea.

"What idea would that be?" Ben's gotten a haircut, and his white neck looks naked and vulnerable. "That we're a couple?"

"My father's crazy," Shelby says, dodging the issue of the meaning of their relationship. "He'll interrogate you."

"Let him. I don't mind."

"I do. Let's just go to our own homes."

Ben rents a car and drops her off at her parents'. It's Christmas Eve and the houses in the neighborhood are strung with lights that flicker and cast red and blue patterns into the snow. There are no lights at Shelby's, however. The place almost looks deserted. Snow has piled up, and it appears no one has shoveled the walkway.

"Are you sure your parents are here?" Ben squints as he tries to look through the front window.

Shelby points. There's her mother opening the front door, waving cheerfully. Shelby waves back. "Told you so." She slips on her backpack, opens the car door, and ushers the dogs out.

"I'll pick you up tomorrow at three," Ben calls as Shelby navigates through the snow. "I'll bring one of my mom's pies." Judy Mink is known for her baking. She made a wedding cake for her next-door neighbor that was photographed for *Newsday*. Unfortunately, Shelby hates pie.

She leaps through the drifts, carrying Blinkie. "Hello, stranger," Sue Richmond says cheerfully as Shelby stomps her boots on the front porch. Shelby's mom takes Blinkie and gives him a hug. "He's so ugly he's cute."

"Ben?" Shelby says.

They both laugh, then go inside. There's no Christmas tree. No decorations. Shelby looks through the pile of cards on the coffee table. A few are from neighbors, others are from her father's business associates. Then there is a postcard with an intricate drawing of a maze. At the center of the maze is a question mark. Shelby turns it over to read the message.

Want something.

Shelby thinks she sees a tiny photo of herself clipped from a newspaper article about the crash pasted onto the card. The writer knows her so well. When she lost Helene, she lost her desire for life. Who is she to deserve something? How dare she want anything at all? She has a sort of burning feeling in her chest.

"I never really liked decorating the house," her mom is saying. "It's too much trouble. Who has time for that kind of thing? I always hated tinsel especially. You can never clean it up. Your dad got to the point where he forbade using it back when you were little."

Shelby gazes around the room. Something is wrong here. "Where's Dad?"

Sue is studying Blinkie. "This dog's eye is infected."

Nothing like changing the subject. Shelby goes with the flow. "The vet said he needs the eye removed. It costs a thousand bucks for the surgery, so I'm saving up."

Shelby wishes she could heal Blinkie herself, that she had the skill and knowledge to take away his pain.

Sue decides to pay for the surgery as Shelby's Christmas gift. Shelby insists she'll pay it back, she even signs an IOU, but Sue tears it up. "I'm just glad there's something you want," Sue says.

Shelby is taken aback. "Did someone tell you to say that to me?"

"You mean like your father? He said he's not giving gifts this year. He says it's commercializing the holidays. Meanwhile he's still at the store."

"No. I mean like Helene." That sounds so crazy Shelby adds, "Or anybody."

Sue links an arm through Shelby's. "Sometimes I think my mother is talking to me in my dreams. Who's to say the dead don't still speak to us and guide us? Maybe Helene does, too."

It doesn't feel like Christmas Eve with just the two of them in the dark house. Yet Shelby is glad to be home.

"What kinds of things does Grandma say when you dream about her?"

"She tells me to dump your dad."

They both laugh.

"Anything else?"

"She says I'm lucky to be here with you and that I should get off my ass and start dinner."

Shelby takes the dogs out. She sees a snow shovel and decides to make a path from the street to the house. By the time her dad's car pulls up, she is more than halfway done.

"I usually hire the kid down the street to do that," Dan Richmond says.

"I guess you forgot." Shelby is so cold she no longer feels her fingers or toes. "Like you forgot this was Christmas Eve."

Business is bad at Shelby's dad's menswear shop. People go to the mall or to some of the newer shops. It was his father's store, and he's always treated the inheritance like a curse.

"Yeah, well, some of us work," he says.

They can see Sue at the window. She's lighting a candle, the way she did when Shelby was little, an old tradition said to bring wanderers home.

"What made you fall in love with her?" Shelby asks her father.

"I'm not answering any trick questions," Shelby's dad says, and then Shelby knows her parents are married, but not really, and that her dad probably can no longer remember the reasons why. She wishes her mother had listened to the voice of her dead mother. People get divorced, they don't have to stay together just because their stupid daughter had a car accident and a nervous breakdown and can't seem to do anything right.

"Why don't you just take off?" Shelby says to her father. "Close the store. Start a new life. Let her start one, too."

Dan gives her a look. "My kind of person doesn't do that sort of thing, Shelby."

That's the difference between them. Her kind of person does.

In the morning, Shelby is given her presents—a black sweater, a box of chocolate truffles, and unbeknownst to her father, a check for a thousand dollars so that Blinkie can have his surgery. She's brought her parents a fondue pot. "I thought maybe you and Dad made fondue when you were first together."

"I love fondue," Sue says, hugging her.

When Ben comes to pick her up, he is carrying one of his mother's apple-cranberry pies. He greets Shelby's mom with a hug and accepts a cup of coffee. As usual, Shelby's dad is MIA. "My mom had twenty-two people over last night and I think she had twenty-two turkeys," Ben reports. "Not to mention all the pies."

"You don't celebrate Christmas," Shelby reminds him. "You're Jewish." She has taken the postcard and slipped it into her coat pocket.

"But we celebrate eating," Ben says. "Good food is part of a family get-together."

At Shelby's they'd had vegetarian lasagna and orange sherbet.

"Hey, Mr. Richmond," Ben says cheerfully when Shelby's father comes in from the garage, where he's been sneaking a cigarette. "How's business?"

"It sucks," Shelby's dad says.

"Dan!" Sue doesn't approve of that kind of language in front of the kids, as she calls them.

"He asked! Do you want me to lie?"

"That's the great thing about pharmaceuticals," Ben says. "Business is always good. People always need drugs."

"Well, Shelby would know about that," Dan says darkly.

Shelby gives her father a cutting look. "Merry Christmas to you, too."

Ben defends her. "Not anymore. She's back in the Straight and Narrow Club."

"I won't go that far," Shelby says.

"Shelby's great," Ben says. And they all look at him, a little surprised.

When it's time to go, Shelby and Ben pile into the car with the dogs and the bags of presents. Ben's mom has given him a collection of Kurt Vonnegut's books—even though he's read *Cat's Cradle* a dozen times—along with a cutting board that will never fit on their countertop and a coffeemaker they will never use. She sent along Jo Malone cologne for Shelby, a fresh grapefruit scent that Shelby will regift to her mom on Mother's Day. Ben has to get the car back to the rental company before five and there's bound to be traffic, so they get going even though Shelby's mom keeps suggesting they spend the night.

"Your dad seems a little off," Ben says.

"He's unhappy. But instead of leaving he's just making my mom's life miserable. He thinks that's more honorable."

"They'll work it out," Ben says reasonably.

Shelby studies Ben as he drives. Maybe if she watches him closely enough she'll understand what makes one person kind and another, herself for instance, mistrustful and hopeless. The more she thinks about her father the more she knows she and Ben are not meant for each other. They stumbled into each other's lives one cold winter when they were both desperate for warmth, and if they stay together she will be the person who comes home late on Christmas Eve.

CHAPTER
3

Maravelle's grandmother in Florida has fallen ill. Because she's in her eighties and frail, Maravelle's mother has already flown down to Orlando, and Maravelle hopes to join her, if Shelby will help her out.

"Fine, go," Shelby says when Maravelle asks for time off. "I'll find someone to cover for you. Take as much time as you need." Shelby is known to be a soft touch when employees need time for personal reasons. Juan's mother is getting radiation treatments, and Shelby lets him come in at noon every day so he can take his mom to the hospital.

"My kids will love you," Maravelle says.

"Kids?" Shelby says, wary. "I don't like kids."

"You'll like mine."

"Why would I have anything to do with them?"

Maravelle grins. "You're my babysitter, baby."

Shelby might have used school as an excuse, she's taking Advanced

Biology, but it's spring break, there are no classes, and if she doesn't take a few days off from work she'll lose her vacation time. Not that this is the vacation she had in mind. She was thinking she would sleep late, go to movie theaters during the day, and spend evenings at the Strand bookstore on Broadway looking for Ray Bradbury books she hasn't yet read.

"I need you to watch them," Maravelle insists. "You're the only one I trust."

This is probably the moment Ben had mentioned, when Shelby can show Maravelle she's a true friend. This is beyond concert tickets. This is her life. As soon as she says yes, Shelby is furious with Ben. He always thinks she's more human than she is. That night as she packs, Shelby won't talk to him. She tends to blame him for whatever goes wrong.

"Don't worry. There's nothing to taking care of kids," Ben assures her.

But Ben has nephews and nieces and is kindhearted. Shelby is nasty and ill-tempered. She shudders at the thought of babysitting. "I don't even know how to talk to a child."

"Talk to them like you talk to me," Ben advises. "But without the curse words. They repeat what you say, like parrots."

She's agreed to three days with Maravelle's children. And in Queens, a place she only travels through by train when visiting her parents. Because she has the dogs, Shelby takes a cab out to Astoria, which costs a fortune. It takes forty minutes with the meter ticking before the cab reaches the street of triple-deckers where Maravelle rents a ground-floor apartment. Shelby gets out and stands on the sidewalk, then walks up a weedy path. The bell doesn't work and she has to bang on the door. Maravelle appears and embraces her. "You made it to Queens!"

The boys have ducked behind the door and peer out. Jasmine, a pretty girl who resembles her mother, clearly disapproves as soon as she gets a look at Shelby. "She can't take care of us!" Jasmine declares. "She's bald! I'm not going to be seen with her."

Shelby really doesn't care how she looks, but Jasmine's reaction reminds her of how concerned she'd been about her appearance back in high school. She used to get up in the dark so she'd have time to brush her hair a hundred strokes and apply her makeup. Nowadays, she doesn't even look in a mirror. She's afraid no one will be staring back at her.

Maravelle shows Shelby around, but since it's a one-bedroom apartment, there isn't much to see. The bathroom is so overstuffed with towels and toiletries that things keep falling off the shelves. Maravelle sleeps on a foldout couch in the living room, and the three kids share the bedroom.

"You literally have no privacy," Shelby says.

"Well, for the next three days, neither do you."

Shelby unpacks, which takes about two minutes. She's got underwear, T-shirts, and a whole lot of kibble. The twins hang around staring at Shelby's dogs. The surgery to remove Blinkie's eye was a success; at a thousand bucks it should have been. He now has a permanent wink.

"He looks creepy," Teddy says after his initial study of the dog. Teddy is the take-charge twin. Sometimes his daring gets him into hot water at school and Maravelle is called in to the principal's office.

"That dog is none of your business," Maravelle tells him before she turns to Shelby. "That other eye's not going to drop out while you're here, is it?"

Shelby notices the kids are always getting something out of the refrigerator. It's like they never stop eating. "Do I have to cook for them?"

"No pizza and no junk," Maravelle informs her. "I made out a menu for every day, and I already went grocery shopping. All you have to do is get them ready for school and on the bus, and be here waiting for them at two. Then make their supper."

"We don't get home till three," the quieter twin, Dorian, reminds his mom.

"I want Shelby here at two, just in case you're early. Don't butt in," Maravelle tells him. "Go out and play."

The twins do so. There's a small yard out back, where they've set up a kind of swing. They're pretty cute boys, Shelby thinks, if you liked children. But Jasmine is another story. She's sitting at the kitchen table, sulking. Just one of the girls.

"The kids can go in the yard and to the playground on the corner. No farther," Maravelle continues with her rules. "And Jasmine has to come directly home. No friends. No hanging out. She's got homework."

"Stop talking about me," Jasmine says.

"And no makeup," Maravelle tells Shelby.

Jasmine storms away. The back door slams.

"You're a hard-ass," Shelby says, impressed.

"What happened to me is not going to happen to Jasmine."

"Sex?" Shelby says.

Maravelle throws her a look. "A baby at sixteen."

The responsibility of Maravelle's life is mind-boggling. "I don't think you should leave your kids with me."

"Well, I don't have anyone else, so stop talking like that. You'll be fine. You'll probably wind up wanting kids of your own by the time you're through."

Shelby tries to think of a way to get out of her promise, but before she knows it, Maravelle hugs her children, grabs her suitcase, and is gone. Now Shelby is in charge. She makes boxed macaroni and cheese that the kids say is inedible. After a single bite Shelby agrees and heats up a pizza she finds in the freezer. She lets them watch whatever they want on TV just so she can be alone. She goes out to the yard and lets her dogs sniff around. She takes one of the cigarettes she keeps with her for times of extreme anxiety. She can almost see the stars come out. Queens is not Manhattan, but it certainly isn't the suburbs. Sirens blare in the distance. The back door opens and Jasmine comes out.

"You smoke?" Jasmine says.

"No." Shelby stubs out the cigarette on the concrete steps.

"You were too smoking. I saw you."

"Aren't you supposed to go to bed soon?"

"You don't know anything about taking care of kids. And you'll probably get lung cancer."

General Tso trots over to Jasmine, interested, but Jasmine shrinks from him.

"He's not the one with one eye." Shelby claps her hands. Blinkie follows the sound and hops over. "This is Mr. One Eye."

"You're weird and you have weird dogs," Jasmine informs her.

"You're rude."

They don't disagree with each other.

"You have to wake us up at six o'clock tomorrow," Jasmine tells Shelby. She knows an incompetent when she sees one. She's got a big grin on her face because she can foresee how miserable Shelby will be.

"Don't you wake yourselves up?"

"And just so you know, you're going to have a lot of trouble getting my brother to go to school."

"Which one?" Shelby can't tell the twins apart, except one is quieter. She and Jasmine go inside. Jasmine double-locks the door. One of the twins is sitting on a kitchen chair.

"That one." Jasmine points. "Dorian."

The kids trail off to the bedroom, and Shelby collapses on the couch. She doesn't bother pulling it out into a bed as Maravelle told her to. She doesn't bother to take off her clothes. She's already realized that when the alarm rings in the morning, she had better be ready.

Shelby doesn't exactly follow Maravelle's instructions. She's not Martha Stewart. She can't remember the last time she made breakfast for anyone. So she improvises, substituting toast for French toast, pouring glasses of soda instead of orange juice. So far, no complaints.

"Now you've got to pack us a lunch," Teddy says.

Shelby still hasn't let the dogs out in the yard or had a cup of coffee. She tosses juice boxes, apples, and string cheese into three paper bags.

"Cookies," Teddy reminds her.

Shelby finds the Chips Ahoy! and throws in some of those too.

"Five minutes," she calls. "Then you're out of here."

She's a drill sergeant in dirty clothes. She fills the kettle, desperate for coffee. She thinks about her own mother, and how she tried to do everything right despite how difficult Shelby was. She wishes she could tell Jasmine she'll regret all of her attitude.

Jasmine exits the bedroom wearing her jacket and carrying her books.

"See you later!" she calls.

"Hey! Your lunch!" Shelby shouts.

When Jasmine comes to grab her lunch bag, Shelby notices that she's wearing eye shadow, blush, and lipstick. That was on the list. No makeup.

"Wait a minute," Shelby says.

She and Jasmine stare at each other. It's like that moment in battle when you're either going to start something up with an enemy soldier and have to kill him or look the other way and let him slink off into his foxhole.

"Okay," Shelby says after a moment's reflection. "Have a nice day."

Jasmine flees from the apartment, waving good-bye as she runs out the door.

Shelby has won over one of the enemy. Maybe everything will be fine. She'll get rid of the kids and have coffee and laze around, maybe even go back to sleep.

Teddy and Dorian have their backpacks and their jackets, but they haven't left.

"He won't go," Teddy informs Shelby with certainty. He's got a twinkle in his eye, as if he'll enjoy the difficulties Shelby will soon face.

"Yeah, well, good-bye," Shelby says to them both. "Be back here at three."

She escorts the twins out the front door and closes it behind them, then, alone at last, she takes her dogs into the yard to do their business. When she returns, the kettle is whistling. Shelby pours water through a filter full of coffee, extra-strong, and splits a can of dog food between the General and Blinkie. Only the General isn't there anymore.

"Hey, General," Shelby shouts. "Breakfast!"

He's in the front hall.

"What are you doing here?"

Usually he's a chowhound, but now the General gazes at her, then barks at the closet. He has a soulful, meaningful bark.

Shelby opens the closet. There's Dorian.

"You're kidding me! Now you've missed the school bus."

Shelby heads into the kitchen to have her coffee and think over what she's supposed to do. She still hasn't changed her clothes or taken a shower. Dorian trails into the kitchen, followed by the General.

"His food is in a bowl on the counter," Shelby says.

Dorian gives the General his breakfast, then gets in a few tentative pets while the bulldog eats.

"I think he likes me," Dorian says.

"Didn't you hear your mother say I was in charge and you had to go to school? Now what am I supposed to do?"

Dorian takes a bowl of cereal for himself and sits at the table. He eats the cereal without milk.

Shelby can tell she'll have to interrogate him. If she doesn't do it carefully he'll clam up for good.

"Do you like school?" Personally, Shelby had hated school, but Dorian nods yes.

"Is somebody bullying you?"

"Nope."

"Do you feel sick?" Shelby asks, even though he's eating a huge bowl of Frosted Flakes that Maravelle had said was only for the weekend.

"Nope."

"Well, if you don't want to tell me what the problem is, tell the General."

The General is at Dorian's feet, wagging his butt, hoping for a Frosted Flake or two. Dorian gazes into his eyes.

"To get to the bus we have to walk past a monster," he tells the General.

Shelby pours another cup of coffee. Someone else would have told Dorian there were no monsters and insisted he stop being such a baby and get his ass to school. But Shelby gulps her coffee, then grabs her sweatshirt. "Come on," she says. She isn't like most people. She opens the silverware drawer and takes out a butcher knife.

"What are you going to do?" he asks.

Dorian is a skinny, serious boy who can eat a bowl of cereal in no time flat and is still young enough to tell his secrets to a dog.

"I'm going to kill the monster."

They walk two blocks, then take a right. They're nearly to the bus stop when Dorian hesitates.

"Is that where he lives?" Shelby asks.

Dorian nods.

There's a deli and a gas station and an auto parts shop and a yard that looks like a dumping ground for old cars. The traffic on the avenue is so noisy Shelby leans close in order to be heard.

"I don't see him."

Dorian nods to a high chain-link fence on the other side of the street, circling the junkyard filled with tires and the rusted-out hulls of cars.

"You want to wait here while I go kill him?" Shelby says.

"Are you going to kill him with the knife?" Dorian holds tight to his paper bag lunch. Something about him makes Shelby want to cry.

"I might and I might not," she tells him.

Shelby runs across the street. She can't wait to get the kid to school and go home and go back to bed. If she pretends the monster is real and kills it, maybe Dorian will cut the crap and take the school bus. It's up to Maravelle to get him to a therapist. Shelby turns back to the kid to wave, just to let him know everything is okay.

Then she hears the monster.

The snarling makes her think of a bear growling deep down in its throat. The thing facing her is the size of a small bear too, only it's white; filthy and bloody, but white. It's chained to a pole, so as it runs toward her, it's stopped short when it reaches the end of its chain. It's up on its hind legs, and she swears it's taller than she is. The kid is right.

Shelby's heart is pounding as she runs back across the street.

"Did you kill it?" Dorian's got his hands over his eyes.

"Not yet," Shelby says.

Dorian slips his hands down and stares across the street. A shiver passes over his face.

"Give me your lunch," Shelby says. Every beast has a soft spot after all.

Dorian hands over the bag, and Shelby runs back across the street. She's getting more exercise than usual due to this monster. He's still barking when she takes out a cookie and pitches it over the fence. The monster backs away, as if she's thrown a stone, so she tosses over another Chips Ahoy! He catches that one and swallows it whole. Shelby unwraps the string cheese and sends that over the fence. The monster gobbles it. He's no longer barking. He's staring at her. Shelby sees that he's a Great Pyrenees.

She runs back across the street. More exercise when she'd planned to spend the morning sleeping.

"Is he dead?" Dorian asks.

"As it turns out he's not a monster. He's a dog."

"I don't think so."

Dorian seems poised to run. He is convinced that a monster will get him if he takes another step.

"Dorian, I know about dogs. Come on. I'll show you."

It takes a while, but Dorian is finally convinced to cross the street with Shelby. He stops at the curb.

"He's just a dog that they keep chained up," Shelby explains. "When you chain something up, you turn him into something he shouldn't be."

Dorian nods. "You're right. He looks like he's broken." All at once, with that one sentence, Shelby understands how you could fall in love with a kid. "Look at his foot," Dorian whispers.

In fact, the dog is limping. Shelby can see how skinny he is. He's being starved.

"I'm going to walk you to school," she tells Dorian. "You don't have to worry about anything being broken."

She does so, but instead of going back to the apartment, Shelby heads to the deli and sits near the window. She has a cup of coffee and a buttered roll. She's staring at the junkyard, thinking about how the kids pointed and laughed at her when she took Dorian to his classroom. Someone shouted out "Baldy!" She usually doesn't care if people insult her, but now she's worried that Dorian may be ridiculed and embarrassed because of her.

When she's done with her breakfast, Shelby goes to stand outside so she can study the big dog on its chain. One of the guys from the deli is out having a cigarette break.

"Hey." He nods at Shelby.

"Hey," Shelby replies.

The deli guy notices her gazing across the street.

"It's a damn crime," he says. "I throw stuff over to him. Like when I'm making chicken salad I throw over the bones."

"Chicken bones kill dogs," Shelby informs him.

"Yeah?" The guy might have said more if he hadn't noticed the butcher knife stuck in Shelby's waistband.

"Chicken bones fragment," she tells him. "They can pierce the esophagus and intestines."

"You a vet?"

"I'm nothing." Shelby has one of her last cigarettes. She's decided she's going to quit. She wants something all right. She wants everyone who has ever been cruel to a dog to be tied up on a chain for twenty-four hours, no food, no water.

"One time I saw the guy over at the junkyard hit him with a metal pole when he wouldn't stop barking. There was blood everywhere."

"Monster," Shelby says before she stalks away.

Jasmine doesn't come home after school. Shelby is still wearing the same clothes she arrived in. Her shower never materialized. Teddy and Dorian are having a snack before they get to their homework. Shelby is doing her best to follow Maravelle's schedule, which doesn't include a missing girl who wears makeup when she isn't supposed to and who, now that she's gotten away with lipstick and rouge, probably figures she can do as she pleases with Shelby in charge. When asked where their sister is, the twins both shrug. They are clearly sworn to secrecy.

At last the phone rings and Shelby jumps for it. She's hoping it's Jasmine, but it's Maravelle.

"How are my babies?" Maravelle wants to know.

"Good," Shelby lies. Real panic is setting in. "Doing homework. How the hell do you do all this, Mimi? Plus a full-time job? You're super-woman."

"Jasmine's doing homework? Is that what you said? That doesn't sound like her."

"I'm having some trouble with her." Shelby backtracks. "She's definitely not perfect."

"Put her on and I'll let her have it."

"I would, but she locked herself in the bathroom. Let me put the boys on." Shelby grabs the twins and puts one hand over the phone receiver. "Don't mention Jasmine," she warns them. "Got it?"

The boys nod, and Shelby puts Teddy on the phone. He'll be the better coconspirator. "You have no idea where your sister is?" she asks Dorian. After this morning he's her buddy.

"She might be at the park on the corner with Jessie and Maria. We saw her there and she said not to tell you."

"Oh, great." Shelby rushes to the door. "Stay here, and don't you or Teddy go anywhere."

She locks the door and races to the park. She spies a bunch of kids hanging out near the basketball hoops. There's Miss I'll Do Whatever I Want. Shelby could strangle Jasmine.

"Hey," Shelby shouts. Jasmine glances up and instantly looks mortified. The last thing she wants is some bald lady confronting her friends. "Get over here!" Shelby tells her.

Jasmine says something to her friends and ambles resentfully toward Shelby.

"Hurry! Your mother's on the phone."

When she hears that, Jasmine runs home even faster than Shelby does. Before they go into the house, Shelby grabs her arm. "I told your mother you were locked in the bathroom. Stick with that story."

Fortunately Dorian is still on the phone when they get into the house. Jasmine grabs the receiver out of his hand.

"Hi, Mami," she says. "Everything's okay. I just hate Shelby."

Shelby retreats to the backyard, where the boys have gone to throw a tennis ball for the General. Blinkie whines to be held, and Shelby hoists him onto her lap.

Jasmine comes outside when she gets off the phone. "I had to say I hated you," she says. "Otherwise it wouldn't make sense for me to have locked myself in the bathroom."

"That's just fine. Say whatever you want, just come home on time so your mother doesn't kill me. I told her I would take care of you, so while I'm here, just do what I tell you."

"Were you bald in high school?" Jasmine asks.

"No. I was pretty. I had long brown hair."

"What happened to you?"

Shelby tries to explain her situation as best she can without the details. "I stopped caring about things."

"Not everything. You care about your dogs."

"Stop trying to psychoanalyze me," Shelby says.

"Stop trying to tell me what to do."

They both fall silent.

"I'll come home on time tomorrow," Jasmine says.

"It's not because I care whether or not you do."

"How late can I stay up?"

The schedule says ten o'clock.

"Midnight," Shelby tells her.

You have to give the enemy some leeway.

"Fine," Jasmine says.

The next morning is smoother. Everyone leaves for school. Dorian heads out with Teddy without mentioning the monster. Jasmine, wearing eyeliner and lipstick and big hoop earrings, has vowed to be home by three and asks if Shelby can help her with a science report.

Shelby finally takes a shower. It's the best shower she's ever had. She stands under the spray until the hot water is gone. She uses Maravelle's green-tea-scented soap and Neutrogena body oil. After she's dressed, Shelby clips the dogs' leashes on and walks down the avenue. She saw a hardware store yesterday and now returns to buy a pair of work gloves and wire cutters. Ben calls her later in the day.

"Still hate kids?" he asks.

"Not as much," Shelby admits.

"I bet they love you."

"Only an idiot would love me," Shelby blurts.

There's silence on the other end of the line. Shelby has been push-ing Ben away from the start of their relationship. All at once she realizes if she pushes too hard he may no longer be there.

"Ben," she says. "I didn't mean you." When there's no response, Shelby says, "Are you there?"

"I'm here," he tells her, but she can't help but wonder for how long.

After the kids are safely home, Shelby helps Jasmine with her ecology report, grateful that she herself is taking a bioecology class this semester and therefore knows more than she ever expected to about recycling. When they're through, Shelby is so exhausted she falls asleep on the floor and doesn't wake until past dinnertime. She was supposed to have made meatballs with tomato sauce. That's what's on the schedule. In-stead she goes into the kitchen to look through the restaurant section of the local paper.

"How's House of Chen?" she asks Jasmine.

"We don't go there," Jasmine tells her. "It's too expensive."

Shelby orders pork fried rice, spare ribs, orange-flavored beef, white rice, and General Tso's chicken. She gets an order of egg rolls for the twins.

"I'm not going to like this," Teddy assures her after the delivery guy drops off the food. Shelby has already dumped the fortune cookies in her backpack. No reason for these kids to think the future will be handed to them on slips of paper.

"Me either," Dorian agrees.

"Good," Jasmine says. "More for me."

They all eat huge plates of food. After dinner, while Shelby is rins-ing the silverware, Dorian comes up to stand beside her at the sink.

"The monster didn't bark at me today," he says.

"He's a Great Pyrenees. His breed of dog was used in the mountains in France to rescue people. They would go through snowdrifts and find people who were lost in avalanches, just like Saint Bernards."

"So they're saints, too?" Dorian asks.

"Kind of."

"I liked the food," Dorian says.

Shelby knows there's no point feeling this way about someone you're only spending a few days with.

"Thanks, Dorian," she says.

Dorian stays in the kitchen while Shelby washes the dishes.

"So maybe I'll rescue him," she says casually. "What do you think?"

"Good idea," Dorian agrees. "I was thinking the same thing."

When the boys are in bed and Jasmine is in her pajamas, lying on the couch with Blinkie and the General, Shelby borrows one of Maravelle's jackets and slips it on. It's black leather and fits her perfectly. She has the wire cutters and gloves. At the last minute, she grabs the container of leftover orange-flavored beef.

"I'll be back before you know it," she tells Jasmine. "Don't open the door."

Jasmine is suddenly interested. "Where are you going? Do you need me?"

In her pajamas, without any makeup, Jasmine looks like a little girl. She has Blinkie sitting on her lap as if he were a stuffed animal.

"Thanks, but this is a one-person job."

She runs all the way.

There is the big dog, at the end of his chain, watching the street. He sees her and stares.

"Don't make any noise," Shelby tells him.

She begins to cut through the fence. She's breathing too hard because she's nervous. Maravelle will kill her if she ever finds out Shelby left Jasmine in charge so she could commit a felony or a misdemeanor or whatever breaking and entering to steal personal property is considered.

Shelby rolls the fence back. She's seen it done on TV. Then she climbs through. The big dog looks at her, but doesn't lunge. Shelby waves the container of orange-flavored beef, then pours some on the ground. The dog comes to devour the Chinese food. While he does, Shelby cuts his chain from the pole. He looks up at her, drooling. He has streaks of blood on his fur along with dirt and oil and lots of drool. He makes her think of a screwed-up piece of modern art.

"Pablo Picasso," Shelby says. She grabs the end of his chain. "Let's go, Pablo."

Shelby crouches back through the fence, and the dog follows behind. She can feel his weight on the other end of the chain. As soon as they're through, Shelby sprints off and the dog runs behind her. When they get to Maravelle's, she takes him into the yard. There she bends over, hands on her knees, and tries to catch her breath.

Jasmine has heard something; she cracks open the back door to take a peek, then rushes out, Blinkie in her arms. "Oh my God! You're crazy!" she cries out. "You can't bring that thing here!"

General Tso races through the open door, barking.

"Grab him," Shelby shouts, afraid the big dog will snap up the General in one bite, but it's too late. The General runs up to the Great Pyrenees, yapping. The big dog leans down and sniffs him. The General gives off a few more soulful barks, then sniffs back.

"My mother will kill you," Jasmine says.

"She won't know. And stop staring at him. He's been abused, that's why he looks this way."

They go inside, all of them.

"She will seriously kill you," Jasmine says in a hushed voice.

Shelby grabs a bowl and fills it with kibble. The Great Pyrenees eats it up in a few gulps.

"Do you think he'll attack Blinkie?" Jasmine asks.

"He seems pretty calm."

Jasmine lets Blinkie down. The big dog stands back while Blinkie licks out the bowl.

"His name's Pablo," Shelby says.

"I think you're the craziest person I ever met," Jasmine announces.

"Thanks," Shelby says.

"I didn't mean it in a bad way." Jasmine is studying Shelby. "I just think you'd be prettier if you weren't bald."

The next morning Shelby is in the kitchen having a cup of coffee when Dorian and Teddy come out of the bedroom. She's got this schedule thing down now.

"Holy shit," Teddy says. He's definitely going to cause Maravelle grief someday. Shelby can tell from the grin on his face. He's drawn to trouble.

Pablo is on the kitchen floor. He looks like a white mountain.

"You did it." Dorian pats Shelby on the back. Both boys ignore their breakfasts even though Shelby has made microwave waffles, something they're allowed only on weekends.

"Is he alive?" Teddy asks.

"Oh, yeah. He's eaten a big bowl of kibble and been in the yard. You should see the size of his poops."

Shelby had gotten up early to give the dog a bath out in the yard, using dishwashing soap and two buckets of warm water. Pablo is still dirty, but he definitely looks better without the blood. He's damp and has the blankety smell of a wet dog. He'd been very patient about Shelby washing him. He's a big, resigned creature. *Pablo,* she said to him as she toweled him off, *how did you get such a good heart?*

"Our mother hates dogs. She says they shed," Teddy tells Shelby as he takes a few bites of his waffle. "And they shit." He gives Shelby a look to see if he'll get a rise out of her when he uses bad language. He doesn't, so he shrugs. Then, as an afterthought, he asks Dorian, "Isn't he the monster?"

This is Shelby's last full day with the kids. Tomorrow Maravelle will be back. Shelby adds six cookies to each of their lunch bags and cans of orange soda, even though she's supposed to stick with juice boxes. Jasmine comes out of the bathroom, dressed and ready for school. She's wearing pale coral lipstick, but no eye makeup. Shelby guesses it's a draw between them.

Jasmine grabs a waffle and heads off.

"Come right home after school," Shelby calls to her.

"Yeah, yeah, yeah. See you later. See you, Pablo," she adds.

"I like Pablo," Dorian tells Shelby when he stops at the counter to grab his lunch.

"He's the strong silent type," Shelby says.

Dorian gives Shelby a hug, which nearly undoes her. "Thanks for fixing him," he says. "He looks good."

Shelby decides to meet the bus after school. She doesn't want to take any chances on a mix-up or a lost kid on her last afternoon in Queens. She stops at the deli for a café con leche and a bag of chips.

"Hey there," the counterman she met on the street calls to her. "I guess you don't mess around."

"I don't know what you mean." Shelby fits a takeaway cover onto her café con leche. But when she reaches into her jeans pocket for some money to pay, the counterman stops her.

"The coffee's on me. You saved me a fortune in stale rolls. I used to give him two or three a day. You did a good thing."

Shelby shakes hands with the counterman, then heads outside. It's a good thing she's leaving. She's getting too attached. But for today she just plans to enjoy the fact that she rescued something. Across the street someone has already patched together the hole in the fence. No one would even notice there's been any damage, except the new fencing is green. When Shelby spies the kids getting off the bus, she puts both arms over her head and waves. At that moment, standing on a corner in Queens, waiting for three kids who are racing toward her, she is exactly where she wants to be.

CHAPTER

4

Sue Richmond is coming to visit and there's no way to put it off. Shelby has kept her mother away from the apartment with a string of excuses for as long as she possibly can. She's afraid her mom will be shocked by her living conditions, but Sue won't take no for an answer this time because she wants to celebrate. The occasion is Shelby's twenty-first birthday, which Shelby would just as soon ignore. All this week she's been preparing for her mom with a cleaning frenzy. But even after she's swept and mopped and attacked the teeny bathroom with a vengeance, the apartment still looks terrible.

"Your mother's coming to see *you*, not the apartment," Ben says. He wishes he could join them for lunch, but he works uptown in the school's clinic. He brushes Pablo's hair from his black slacks. He is not a fan of the Great Pyrenees: there's the shedding, the cost of his food, the way Pablo sprawls across the couch. "Small apartments should have small

dogs" was Ben's initial response when Shelby brought Pablo home.
Their place is three hundred square feet. There's hardly any storage
space, so coats and boots are shoved under the bed. Pots and pans line
the small countertop, the washed and the unwashed side by side. There's
a big garbage can filled with kibble that takes up most of the small hallway. But there are no decorations on the walls, no prints, no paintings,
nothing to hide the peeling paint; it's as if this place was nothing more
than a pit stop when in fact Shelby and Ben have lived here for nearly
two years.

When her mother arrives, Shelby buzzes her in. It's a cold March
day and Sue is out of breath by the time she gets up the four flights of
stairs.

"I guess you don't need to exercise when you have to climb all the
way up here," Sue says, collapsing on the couch next to Pablo. "Hello
there, big boy," she says to him, stroking his boxy head. Shelby notices
that the couch is worn, with frayed threads on the arms. "This is a cute
apartment," Sue says as she gazes around. "It's compact."

"It's the size of a closet," Shelby says.

"A closet would have shelves." Sue laughs, and Shelby does too. Her
mother wants to see the best in everything and everyone. She's brought
along two shopping bags full of presents. There are chocolates and a
soft alpaca shawl and a new set of sheets, all very much appreciated. "I
know you usually prefer black, but the green looked so springy."

"Definitely springy," Shelby says of the shawl. She already knows
she'll never wear it.

"You're only twenty-one once," Sue says cheerfully. "It's a big
day. I think you've made this place very homey," she adds, even though
Shelby is fairly certain her mom has spied the mousetraps in the cor-
ners. Her dogs don't bother to go after the mice; they just watch them
as though they were some form of entertainment. Shelby gets Havahart
traps so she can bring the ones she captures down to the riverside.

They go to a French restaurant on Ninth Avenue because Shelby knows her mother wouldn't approve of the Hunan Kitchen as festive enough for the occasion. Hunan is more of a takeout place with two plastic tables set near the window. The bistro is funky with a touch of elegance. They order beet salads and glasses of white wine and sit in uncomfortable rattan chairs. Sue thinks the place is charming. "I'm so glad I get to take you out!" she says. Shelby keeps her mouth shut. She doesn't want to be a downer, but all this birthday means to her is that she's lived four more years than Helene.

"I can't believe you're a biology major," Sue says. "I always knew you could do anything you wanted to."

"It's not like I'm going to be a doctor or anything," Shelby says. But secretly she has been thinking about vet school. It's stupid, she'd never be smart enough; all the same she could do some good for the creatures that need her.

"I forgot to give you this," Sue says, pushing an envelope across the table.

It's a birthday card with a photo of a basset hound. Inside the message reads: *Have an Arfing great birthday*.

"Very funny," Shelby says. She opens the card to discover five one-hundred-dollar bills. "Mom," she says. She knows her parents are having money problems. "You don't need to do this."

"Your father sold the store, so I wanted you to share in the good luck."

Dan Richmond has always said the family store he inherited from his father would only be taken away over his dead body.

"Are you kidding me? He sold it? When was he going to tell me? After my death?"

"It's going to be a Starbucks," Sue tells her cheerfully. "They bought out his lease, and your dad got a job at the Walt Whitman Mall. The men's department at Macy's."

Shelby is fairly certain that Walt Whitman has been turning over in his grave ever since the mall on Long Island was named for him. She and Helene used to go there every Saturday. Shelby thinks of the day they bought their matching bracelets. They had saved up for months. Babysitting money, allowances, chores. They'd been so proud of themselves.

"And Dad's okay with all of this?" she asks. "What about the family legacy and all that?"

"Did you want to run a men's clothing store?"

"No," Shelby says.

"Take the money," Sue tells her. "That's the legacy."

So Shelby does. She leans over and kisses her mom. "It will be good for emergencies. Like if I ever have to leave Ben." She's said aloud what she's been thinking about for a long time. They're not suited for each other. They're like strangers on a train, only they live in the same apartment and sleep together, but they don't know each other in any deep way. *How would you want to die? What would you do for love?*

Sue studies her. "Is something wrong between you two?"

The tables are jammed together, ensuring that customers have zero privacy. There is an older couple sitting next to them who have suddenly stopped talking. Obviously, Shelby's conversation with her mother is more interesting then anything they have to say to each other.

"It's a *what-if* situation," Shelby says. "Like if I catch him having an affair."

"Your dad's having an affair," Sue says.

"What?" Shelby's ears are ringing. She must have heard wrong.

Their onion soups are delivered, so Sue doesn't speak until the waiter leaves them more or less in peace. The couple next to them are rapt. They don't say a word.

"Someone at Macy's. She got him the job."

"How do you know this?"

Sue gives Shelby a look. "You know these things, Shelby. Plus Sheila Davis next door told me. She saw them walk out of the store and get into your dad's car and drive away. Anyway, it's nothing new."

"What's that supposed to mean?"

Sue shrugs. "It's been going on, Shelby. He considers himself to be a ladies' man. I think it makes him feel better about himself. Do you think he wanted to take over his father's store?"

"What the hell did he want?"

"He wanted to be a singer."

"Seriously?"

"I thought he looked like Paul McCartney."

"Dad?" Shelby can't help but laugh.

"Before he was bald." Sue is laughing as well.

The couple beside them order the onion soup. They tell the waitress it looks good. "It is, isn't it?" the woman asks Shelby.

"First-rate," Shelby says to her. "Like it's from Paris."

"Oh, and you got this." Sue opens her purse and hands over a post-card. "I'm forgetting everything today."

"Great. My stalker." Shelby's started to wonder why this person has never come forward. Lately it feels like someone is playing a game with her. He knows everything about her and she knows nothing about him.

"Your angel," Sue says. "This time I saw him. He drives a black car."

"I doubt he's an angel. Probably just some lunatic who read about me in the paper."

On the postcard there is a drawing of a woman wearing a blindfold. It's a beautiful little drawing actually, something worth framing. The message is *See something*.

It's then Shelby notices that her mom's hand is shaking. Just the way Shelby's hand tremors when she's anxious and upset. Shelby has been so busy feeling sorry for herself, she hasn't seen what her mom is going through. Her mother is truly unhappy. Shelby reaches to take her hand. "I'm sorry," she says. "Dad is a shit."

"We just got stuck in a marriage that is sadder than being alone. If you don't love someone, don't stay. I mean it, Shelby. Even if you need more than five hundred dollars to get your own place. Even if you hurt Ben."

What Shelby sees is that her mother loves her, that she's driven in from Huntington to have onion soup that is not particularly good, and that she's bold enough to ask the waitress if she can put a candle in the éclair they share for dessert. No one else would sing "Happy Birthday" to Shelby in a restaurant on Ninth Avenue or tell her that, despite everything she has been led to believe, love is the only thing that matters.

One bright day, when the leaves on the plane trees have turned green in Union Square and Shelby is on her way to work, the crowd in front of her swells, then moves aside. Shelby has been keeping her eyes open. She sees that a man has collapsed in the crosswalk, hitting his head. Blood sends people skittering away. Shelby should keep going like everyone else. Instead, she runs over to the fallen man.

She isn't the sort of person who gets involved. She's never been a doer of good deeds. But she thinks of the last postcard on her birthday. *See something.* And she does, she sees the way this man is splayed out on the concrete. She can't help but think of Helene trapped in the car, her face pale, her lips the color of hyacinths. Shelby dreams of ice on cold nights, it's blue or black or red with blood. She dreams she is down on all fours, fingers freezing, the cold going up through her bones until a black coat is covering her.

"Call 911," Shelby tells the person next to her in the crowd of onlookers. She sounds as if she won't take no for an answer, and even though the stranger she barks orders to is on his way to work, he does as he's told. Shelby kneels on the concrete. There's a pool of blood from a gash in the fallen man's head that she tries her best to avoid. "You're going to be okay," she tells him. The concrete feels cold, like ice.

She knows it's the right thing to say. She learned this from the nurses when she was in the hospital. They told her they had a list of steps when dealing with new patients. *Be calm. No matter what. Even if someone is in a psychotic state and threatening to jump off the roof. No need to worry. No need to shout. Tell them they're going to be okay.*

The fallen man has a long dark beard and knotted hair; he's wearing a gray overcoat, faded corduroy slacks, army boots. For an instant his eyes flicker.

"Talk to me," Shelby says. "What's your name?"

The fallen man mumbles something, but not in English.

Shelby turns to the stranger who dialed 911. He's a good-looking young man who's stayed on to wait for the EMTs. "What language is he speaking?" Shelby asks him.

"He's speaking Russian."

They're in this together now and they know it. They can hear sirens, but the morning traffic is heavy, sure to slow down the ambulance. The young man crouches so he can take the fallen man's pulse, then he unbuttons his coat and listens to his heart. Shelby notices the fallen man's nails are long and curved, a dull yellow color.

"Malnutrition and nicotine," the stranger says when he sees her staring at the long, misshapen nails. "They need to be clipped."

"Are you a doctor?" Shelby asks.

"A vet."

"Seriously?" Shelby's secret dream for herself. She looks at the stranger with newfound respect. He grins and introduces himself as Harper Levy. "Your name sounds like a folk song," Shelby tells him.

Harper gently raises the fallen man's eyelids. "This is strange. The white film looks like a third eyelid, which is what canines have. I would guess he had a seizure. The fall is probably a by-product of that."

Shelby's falling for him as he speaks. The ambulance pulls up, and the EMTs immediately fit the fallen man with an oxygen mask. They ask Shelby and Harper Levy questions neither can answer. There's no ID in the fallen man's pockets.

"We don't know him, but we think he's Russian," Harper Levy says.

Shelby is pleasantly surprised to be included in a "we."

Harper talks to one of the EMTs as the fallen man is lifted into the ambulance. When he comes back to Shelby, he says, "We have to get tested for HIV and vaccinated for hep and tetanus. My grandpop always said no good deed goes unpunished. It will probably take hours."

Shelby realizes they both have blood on their hands and clothes.

"They'll survive without me at the pet store," she says. "Since I'm the manager, I can't fire myself."

"Is that what you do?" Harper seems surprised. A smart girl in a shop.

"For now," Shelby says.

"Well, we've got to go to Bellevue. That's where they're taking him."

Harper phones in to the animal hospital where he works to cancel all of that morning's appointments. As they walk uptown, people edge away from them. Shelby decides to take off her bloody sweatshirt and throw it in a trash can. Harper takes off his jacket, a really nice one he reveals that he got on sale at Barneys, and dumps it in the trash as well. They're both wearing white short-sleeved T-shirts.

"Twins." He's staring at her in a way that makes her forget where they are. "What are the odds?"

On the way to the hospital Shelby tells him a few basic facts. She's a student at Hunter College and her favorite food is Chinese, so much so that Shin Mae, the owner of her local takeout shop, knows her order by heart. Shelby leaves out the fact that she lives with Ben Mink. She tells herself that would be too much personal information. But she knows this isn't exactly true. She wonders what her father tells the women he meets. That he's single, or unhappily married, or filing for a divorce? That he's misunderstood, sex-starved, a selfish bastard who can only think of his own needs?

"I just finished a Chinese cooking class," Harper informs her. "I make fantastic wontons."

He cannot be as good as he looks. So Shelby gives him her ultimate test question for a man she might consider. "Do you have a dog?"

"Two pit bulls. I adopted them when their owner went to prison."

Is it possible the perfect man can be found on the street beside a pool of blood?

"Those dogs are loyal," Harper says. "Even though their owner treated them like shit, when I say his name they still jump up and run to the door looking for him."

They arrive at Bellevue and wait for the triage nurse. By now Shelby is head over heels. Why did she never feel this way with Ben? She is light-headed, walking on air.

"What do you put in the wontons?" she asks Harper, so intent on his answer it's as if he's invented the cure for cancer.

"Water chestnuts, spinach, mushrooms, carrots."

"I hate water chestnuts."

"I could use bamboo shoots instead."

Shelby feels little sparks of energy in her chest, her throat, her heart. Her head has nothing to do with this.

At last, it's their turn. Their names are called together, as if they're a couple.

"Do you think he'll live?" Shelby asks Harper as they head down the hall. There are sick people everywhere, in wheelchairs and on benches. Shelby is embarrassed to be so healthy.

"Last week a Rottweiler who'd been hit by a car was brought in," Harper tells her. "His breathing was so shallow I thought for sure I'd lose him during the surgery. But he came through just great. He tried to bite me the next day."

After the triage nurse takes down their information, Shelby and Harper Levy go their separate ways to be tested and inoculated. Shelby and the nurse discuss communicable diseases and the upsurge in measles.

"Next time, wear gloves," the nurse suggests when she reads the report. "The old man is up on the third floor. They're checking for seizures."

"There won't be a next time," Shelby assures her.

"I thought you were a med student," the nurse says.

"Me?" Shelby laughs. A big bruise is forming where she'd been inoculated against tetanus and hepatitis. "I'm nothing."

After the nurse is done with her, Shelby scans the ER for Harper. When she doesn't see him, she feels a wave of disappointment. She decides to check in on the fallen man. Near the elevators, two orderlies are speaking Russian. Shelby goes over to them. "I need a translator."

"Med student?" the younger of the two asks.

Shelby shakes her head. "I just need help to talk to a Russian patient."

The older orderly says something in Russian, then both men look at Shelby and laugh.

"We can't help. We're working," the younger one tells her.

"Five minutes," Shelby says. "You'd be doing a good deed."

"I do good deeds all the time," the younger orderly tells her. "All day long, that's my business."

Shelby follows him into the elevator. Two elderly women in wheelchairs are in there with them, along with their caretakers. Shelby taps the button for the third floor.

"What did the other guy say that was so funny?" she asks.

"He said you'd be cute if your head didn't look like an egg."

"I'll pay you ten bucks to help me," Shelby says. They've reached the third floor. The door opens. "Okay. Twenty."

"I don't want money. I'll tell you what I want." The orderly grins at her. "Grow your hair."

Shelby is mortified. She feels like slugging him. "What do you care about my hair?"

The orderly shrugs. "That's my price. I want to do a good deed. For you."

They stare at each other. One of the women in a wheelchair starts to complain that she's hungry. They can't hold up the elevator forever.

"Okay, fine," Shelby agrees.

They step out and head down the hall, peering into rooms. No fallen man.

"Maybe he doesn't exist," the orderly suggests. "Maybe he died."

At last they find him at the far end of the hall. They approach the bed, and the orderly reads the chart.

"This lists all the tests they're going to run. He's got a broken wrist and a fractured shoulder. So far he's stable even though his vitals don't look great. They think he might have rabies. That could have caused seizures."

"Is that spread through blood?" Shelby doesn't want rabies.

"Saliva. You're fine as long as you don't let him bite you. You're a good-deed doer too."

"No." Shelby shakes her head. "I'm not."

The fallen man is tied to the bed with restraints.

"Ask him how he's doing," Shelby instructs the orderly.

"I can tell you just by looking at him. He's not doing too good."

"Talk to him in Russian. That's why you're here."

The fallen man appears to be unconscious, but when the orderly speaks a few words in Russian, his eyes flutter beneath his closed lids.

"He's responding," Shelby says.

"What do you care?" the orderly asks.

"I don't." But the truth is, Shelby feels the same about this stranger as she did about her dogs when she rescued them. "Keep talking."

The orderly continues speaking, and the fallen man groans, then mutters something. The orderly signals Shelby to follow him from the room.

"It's better to leave some things alone," he tells her. "Go have lunch. The burritos in the cafeteria are good. Ask for the chicken."

"What did he say?"

"He said he's a wolf, let him die."

"He's not a wolf." Shelby is currently taking a class in comparative zoology along with advanced biology.

"He says he's a wolf. Let him die. You wanted to know? Now you know. He asked me to shoot him, as a matter of fact. I told him we're in New York. We don't do things that way."

"He's delusional."

"Maybe. But now you have to let your hair grow. You promised you would. Then you'll be beautiful, Miss Egghead, and you'll have me to thank."

"How do you say *wolf* in Russian?"

"Volk."

After the orderly leaves, Shelby goes back into the room. She can hear the fallen man's ragged breathing. She knows she's not supposed to get involved. But the idea that he's something other than human, that he's a wild animal, makes her go closer. She thinks about how it feels to rescue something, how fast she ran when she took Blinkie and the General, how her heart was pounding when she freed Pablo. She is a do-gooder and she didn't even know it. She sings the song her mother sang to her long ago. "Over the Rainbow." She sings until she realizes the wolfman has fallen asleep.

Outside the hospital, Harper Levy is waiting on the sidewalk. "You disappeared," he says.

"He said he was a wolf."

"I could have helped him if he had been. Canidae, same family as the domestic dog."

They walk toward Union Square, but they won't go to work. Instead they'll have coffee and sit in the park. They don't want to go their separate ways. They hang on, as if the day is a dream and they don't want it to end. When Shelby does get into bed beside Ben later that night, she dreams of wolves and of a white world of snow and ice. She dreams her hair is so long it reaches her waist, and every morning when she wakes she brushes it a thousand strokes, all because of a promise she made to a stranger.

CHAPTER

5

It takes months to break up with Ben. He just doesn't take a hint. Shelby stays out late, she spends nights at Maravelle's, she stops talking to him for days on end, and he still doesn't get it. By now Shelby's hair has begun to grow out. It's short and spiky, and she looks fierce, like a terrier. She's afraid to tell Ben the truth. She thinks about the nights they walked through Huntington in the snow. The way he was there for her when they first moved to the city and how generous he's always been. She waits until his graduation, which is probably a terrible idea, but she doesn't want to disrupt his studies. They have been together for more than four years. They're at the point in their relationship when most couples would be making a permanent commitment, but instead Shelby tells him it's over at the restaurant on the Upper West Side that his mother chose to celebrate his graduation. He is a full-fledged pharmacist now, and his parents are proud. The restaurant is called Coral

Reef, and everything inside is dark, as if they have fallen to the bottom of the sea. As soon as they're seated, Judy Mink takes Shelby's hand and says, "So. You two. What's next?" Clearly she's hoping for a daughter-in-law. Ben's father, Arthur, immediately suggests they order drinks. He never looks at Shelby. She doesn't blame him for disliking her. By the time the day is over, he'll probably hate her.

Shelby says she's feeling dizzy, which is true enough, and Ben, a gentleman as always, walks her to the toilets. She had planned on telling him after dinner, but she can't act as if nothing is wrong for another minute. She pulls him inside the ladies' room. If she waits any longer she'll explode. She's been living a lie and she hates herself even more than usual.

"Hey," Ben says with a grin when she locks the door. He thinks she wants to have sex with him here, a kinky graduation present. He leans to kiss her before she can back away, then says, "Don't you think my parents will wonder what happened to us?"

He's so tall and kind and stupid Shelby can barely stand it. She doesn't tell him she's been seeing another man for some time, or that she was unsure of the relationship from the beginning, or that the thing that any other woman would want—a commitment, a ring—is what she dreads. He has never heard what she's tried to tell him a hundred times before. Every time she turned away from him in bed, every time she walked out of the room while he was still telling a story. He doesn't understand now when she says they're over.

"Over? Because my mother made that stupid remark? She didn't mean anything negative. She likes you. She likes us. She probably wants to plan a wedding or something."

Shelby shakes her head. It's not easy to look Ben in the eye. When she forces herself to do it she has a sinking feeling, but she dives right in. "We're breaking up. Your mother will get used to our not being to-gether."

"My mother?" Ben says. "What about me?"

"You know what I mean. Everyone will get used to it. It will just be something in the past."

"Why now?" Ben asks.

"It's just time." There's a knock at the door when another customer wishes to use the facilities. Shelby calls out, "Go away."

Ben looks stung. He's wearing a black suit he bought for the occasion. His mother took about a thousand pictures of him in his cap and gown, and he didn't complain. Now he's in a tiny public bathroom with Shelby. The place is so small his elbows push up against the walls. "This is the time? While my parents are sitting out there ordering the striped bass?"

"This isn't love," Shelby tells him finally.

"Oh yeah?" He says it with real bitterness. He doesn't sound like the Ben that she knows. Shelby feels a shiver of fear when she sees the look on his face. She's probably ruined him, turned a sweet, loving person into a cynical bastard. "How do you know?"

Because I'm not worth it, she wants to say. Because you knew me at my worst point, when I was bald and desperate. Because I was never good enough for you. Because my mother told me love is everything.

"I just know," she answers.

"Well, thanks for including me in this decision," Ben says. "It just means our breakup is exactly like the rest of our relationship. All about you."

They manage to get through dinner, but Shelby can swear Mr. Mink knows. He raises his glass to her and says "Good luck" for no particular reason. "Of course she'll have good luck," Judy Mink says, patting her husband's arm, perhaps thinking he's had one too many. But he hasn't. And he's right. Shelby will need luck after what she's done tonight. Ben doesn't talk to her in the cab ride downtown. Shelby wants to hold his hand. She wants to tell him he was her friend when no one else was, that he reminded her she was alive. Maybe they can still be friends. Probably ninety-nine percent of people breaking up say that, and it's probably true for less than three percent. From the wounded, angry look on Ben's face, it's likely they're not in that three percent. They may be the couple where the wronged party hates his ex-partner forevermore.

Shelby keeps the apartment. It's Ben's really; he found it and paid for most of the rent, but that's how Ben is, gracious. All the same she hears him cursing as he packs up his belongings. She hears her name flung around as if it was a curse as well.

"Maybe you should be the one to stay," Shelby says. He is taking almost nothing. Not even his great-aunt Ida's dining room table. It's an eyesore, but a family eyesore, not that Ben cares. Now that it's over and he's finally seen Shelby for who she is, it seems he can't leave fast enough.

"Don't worry," Ben tells her. He's done. He's ready to go in less than an hour. She can see in his eyes that loving her has changed him. "I'll get something better."

The summer is bliss. Monday evenings spent with Harper in his office. Chinese dinners that he cooks at her place. Great sex that leaves her wilted and without a thought in her head. Harper told her right away that he was married, but he and his wife are unhappy and will soon be separating. It's not a true marriage in any real sense. He's assured Shelby that she has nothing to do with their breakup; he's been unhappy for eight years and they've only been together for ten. Harper has made it clear that he and his wife were ill suited from the start; she's always been too dependent, and it was just a matter of time before their relationship imploded.

Time, however, is the one thing he doesn't have when it comes to seeing Shelby, at least not yet. So she takes what she can get. This is nothing like her father's sleazy affairs. Unlike Shelby's parents, who have been very married for almost thirty years, Harper doesn't love his wife. He loves Shelby. When he tells her so, she tells herself she is saving him from a life without love.

Shelby likes meeting him at the animal hospital on Monday nights. She is more convinced than ever that working with animals should be her career path. She's assisted Harper during some of his appointments, taking time to smooch between pet patients. Lately Harper has allowed her to sit in during surgeries, and Shelby has never felt as alive as when she's been in the operating room.

"You surprise me," Harper said to her after her first viewing. It was a simple procedure, a tumor removed from an old basset hound. Shelby thought the entire event was beautiful, the dog saved from pain, the bright blood, the calm in the operating room. "Some people faint the first time, most people get dizzy, everybody flinches, but not you."

"I liked it," Shelby told him.

"Liked?" Harper said.

Shelby shrugged. "What's not to like about a miracle?"

The time spent with Harper passes quickly, as the best times often do. Shelby knows she's changing as the months go by. Her hair is chin-length now, angled, and she looks chic, despite her ragged clothes. She's not as skinny as she used to be when she was made out of angles and pain. Occasionally she dabs on lip gloss and some black eyeliner. Now when Harper tells her she's beautiful she half believes him. Her perfect day is the one when he picked her up in a rented car and they drove to Jones Beach to go swimming in the salty waves, then sunned in the sand with thousands of other beachgoers. She felt alive. She wonders if she might love him. She's aware of the way her heart pounds when she's with him. Sometimes Ben's image rises in her mind while they're in bed, and Shelby says *I'm sorry* out loud before she can stop herself. Harper laughs and says she is the sorriest girl he ever met. Sometimes she dreams of Ben. He sits on the edge of the bed in her dreams and watches her sadly. *Hey, stupid,* he says. *Miss me yet?*

Shelby's mom asks when they're going to meet Harper, and Shelby

always says, *Soon*, but Harper is always too busy. He has so little time
for her. Less and less it seems.

"He sounds like your father," Shelby's mom says when Shelby
comes out for a visit. "He's always working too." Shelby's mom serves
her lemonade and hands her a postcard. "This arrived last week."

There is an inked drawing of a box with something trapped inside.
Eyes peer out. Shelby turns the card over. *Save something*. She keeps
staring at the box. What is it looking out at her?

"Did you see him leave the card?" Shelby asks her mom.

"He comes at night," Sue tells her. "I think he doesn't want to
bother me."

Shelby laughs. "He just wants to bother me."

"Oh, I don't think that's what he wants," Sue says.

"Then what?" Shelby runs her fingers over the drawing. There are
little animals inside the box. Sad eyes. Foxy faces.

"I think he wants the best for you," Shelby's mom tells her.

Then summer is over, gone as quickly as it arrived. The days are crisp
and filled with brilliant orange light. At sunrise a shimmer of color spi-
rals over the asphalt. Shelby usually walks her dogs along the river, up
to five miles on her days off. But today she's in a cab on her way to
Central Park. It isn't easy to find a cabbie willing to take a fare with
dogs, especially a huge Great Pyrenees, but finally one stops. He's curious about Pablo. "I never saw anything like him," he tells Shelby as she
herds the dogs into the back of the cab. "I thought he was a polar bear."

"They used this breed to find people in the French Alps," Shelby
says. "They were search and rescue dogs."

Shelby gazes out the window. *Save something*. She thinks about that
when she's at the animal hospital on Mondays, and then when everyone
leaves and she and Harper stay on to be together, she tries to convince

him to start over. They'll go to California and change their names. He'll never have to go home again. That's why she's going to see him on an off day, since they never get together on the weekends. Shelby looks casual, wearing jeans and an old sweater and hiking boots. She wants it to seem like a coincidence when she runs into Harper, rather than the desperate act of someone who is willing to humiliate herself by plotting out an accidental meeting on the path she knows he walks on Sunday mornings.

If this is love, it makes her do stupid things. From the start Harper has been saying he's waiting for the right time to leave his wife, but nearly a year has passed and that day has yet to come. She wants more than Mondays, and those weekends when his wife goes to see her parents in Buffalo. She has never been to his apartment, never gone out to a restaurant with him, never seen his dogs. Maravelle has met him only once, and then accidentally, as he was leaving to rush home before his wife returned from a visit to her parents. Maravelle and Jasmine had arrived so they could take Shelby with them to Rockefeller Center to see the tree. Harper hugged them both; he'd heard so much about them he felt he knew them and he wished he could stay, but he was already out the door.

"A cheater," Maravelle said when he'd left. "You should stay away from him."

Shelby trusts Maravelle's intuition, but hasn't followed her advice. She's under a spell and she can't snap out of it. Shelby and Harper have sex in the locked lounge of the veterinary office on a fake leather couch. Shelby is sometimes catapulted backward in time to the hospital and all that sex she didn't want. But this is different. This is love. All the same, she can't imagine what Maravelle would say if she ever found out. *Do you think you're worthless? Is that all a man has to do to get into your pants? Give you one night?* Maravelle would never sneak around like a woman who's been hexed by some sort of dark magic. What will Shelby do next to win Harper? Perch outside his window? Beg for his love? Haunt him as if she were his personal ghost?

Harper lives on Eighty-Ninth Street, so Shelby asks the cabbie to drop her at Fifth and Seventy-Ninth, so she can walk behind the Metropolitan Museum. If they ever were to get married, she would like to have the ceremony in Central Park, so the dogs could be there. Fall would be nice, or spring. Actually, a winter wedding would be beautiful, a bower of snow, a perfect and cold blue sky. The dogs are excited to be in the park. This is not their usual walk. Shelby unhooks the General, who likes to walk ahead of the pack. Shelby respects him for that. She had been looking for a man who has some of the qualities the General has. She thought she'd found them in Harper Levy. But what does it mean when a man won't leave his wife? Is he loyal or disloyal? Trustworthy or a lying manipulator? The General looks over his shoulder to make sure they're behind him. Blinkie is so slow Shelby scoops him up to carry him. Everything smells like leaves and smoke. Light spins down through the leaves.

She has to get the timing right so she can bump into Harper when he walks his dogs. She hates women who do things like this. She hates the *other woman*, even in movies, but that's what she's become. Shelby heads to the park entrance at Ninetieth Street. She can see the white circle of the Guggenheim Museum. Her pulse is pounding. Here she is with her dogs, walking through the leaves, irresistible, perfect for him. What more can Harper want? However, despite the fact that he's told her he takes this walk with his dogs faithfully every Sunday, he doesn't appear at eight, or at eight fifteen, or even eight thirty. Shelby's dogs mill around, and the General gazes watchfully at the steps to Fifth Avenue. If only he were a person and not a bulldog, Shelby could marry him and forget about Harper.

There are more people out now. It's a beautiful day. Shelby knows she doesn't belong on the Upper East Side. People here are well dressed and she's not. Her hair is now long enough to clip up, and she looks younger than her age, like a dog walker or a personal assistant for one of these elegant East Side ladies passing by. The brownstones seem like castles; it's as if she's entered a fairyland, but she doesn't know any of the secret passwords. Sick of waiting, Shelby crosses Fifth Avenue and heads down Eighty-Ninth Street. She knows Harper's address. He hasn't hidden much from her. Except for his wife. He says it's too depressing. He's only told Shelby that they met in college and fell into marriage the way people fall over their own feet.

Shelby stops in front of his building. Her dogs are confused, and thinking they may have arrived somewhere, they start up the steps, but Shelby pulls them back. Her heart is beating so fast she thinks she might be having a heart attack. She has it all: pain down her left arm, shortness of breath, dizziness, nausea. Harper lives on the sixth floor. Maybe his is the window with the beige curtains, or the one with slatted shades. Shelby realizes she shouldn't be standing outside the door, but before she can walk on, a pretty young woman with two large dogs comes through the door. The woman is Sarah Levy, Harper's wife.

There is a photo of Sarah in Harper's office at the animal hospital, and yet Shelby has never thought of her as three-dimensional, which she most certainly is. A real live woman in a navy jacket, corduroy slacks, a tweed cap. Her hair is so pale it shimmers. She's beautiful, with a light sweetness of spirit. She chats with the doorman as she clips leashes on the dogs, then heads toward the park.

Shelby follows without thinking. Thinking has little to do with this whole endeavor. She is walking so fast that Blinkie has to trot to keep up. She feels hot inside her sixties-era sweater. She bought it at a thrift store on Twenty-Third Street and thought it was so cute with its Mary Quant squares of black and white; now she realizes it looks like a rag. By the time Sarah reaches Fifth Avenue, so has Shelby. They cross together when the light turns. They walk down the steps to the park so near to one another that Pablo almost collides into the pit bulls. Their names are Axel and Jezebel, Shelby knows. Before Harper adopted them from a client who was sent to prison, the dogs were kept in a studio apartment on the Lower East Side. They didn't know how to walk up stairs, and

Harper had to teach them by putting bits of liver on each step. How could Shelby not have fallen in love with a man who had the patience to do that?

"Sorry," Sarah Levy says when her dogs bump into Pablo. She laughs and pulls her dogs out of the way. "You have quite a troupe there. Do you do dog walking?"

"Nope. They're all mine." No one can tell her pulse is going crazy when Shelby speaks. "I'm kind of a soft touch when it comes to dogs."

"My husband's like that. That's why I have these two monsters."

They're walking along together as if they've known each other forever.

"You must be a softie, too. You're the one walking the dogs, not your husband," Shelby says.

Shelby sounds so pleasant. Not the sly bitch that she really is. She has managed to say *Where the hell is Harper?* without even mentioning him.

"He plays tennis on Sunday mornings."

Bullshit, Shelby thinks. He's never mentioned tennis. He probably hasn't played since high school. She wonders what he's really doing. He calls her his Monday Girl, and now she wonders if there's a Sunday Girl. Perhaps he told Shelby he walked the dogs as an alibi for time spent with someone else. Her brain freezes at the thought. It's not as warm out as she had assumed. She should have worn gloves.

Sarah lets the pit bulls off their leads, and Shelby allows Pablo and the General to run with them. She scratches Blinkie's ears.

"Poor little guy," Sarah says of Blinkie.

"Enucleation," Shelby says. "He was already blind, but his cornea was infected, so the entire eye had to be removed."

"You sound like a vet! Just like my husband."

"My dream is to go to vet school." Shelby has no idea why she's just confessed her deepest desire to Harper Levy's wife. She's never said it out loud to anyone before.

"I wish I were a brain," Sarah says. "I paint."

Shelby feels little jittery pinpricks in her arms and legs. She's having vicious thoughts that include leading Sarah into one of the underpasses and tying her to the wall with a dog leash. "You're creative," she tells Sarah. "That's better." Is she insane? She's seen one of Sarah's paintings on the wall in Harper's office. It's a still life, a snow-covered field, a stream, a gray boulder, and a blue sky dotted with clouds. Surprisingly good. Shelby has often found herself staring at it, wishing she could walk into that landscape.

"Except I can't even do that right now. I use oil-based paints, and the fumes aren't what you want to be breathing in when you're pregnant."

The General is leading the gang of dogs into the underpass. On the other side is a field. Shelby doesn't say anything. She just breathes. So Harper is a liar. Or maybe he thinks omission doesn't constitute a lie.

"I never walk through there," Sarah says as the dogs romp ahead, through the underpass. But now they have no choice but to follow the path of the pack ahead of them. "But I guess we're safe with all these dogs. Right? No one's going to kill us in broad daylight."

"Right," Shelby says. She's got the leash clenched in her fist.

They walk inside the underpass. There is writing on the wall and spray-paint art. Shelby prefers Sarah's landscape.

"Congratulations on being pregnant." Shelby's hands are freezing; she sticks them in her pockets. Sarah is wearing leather gloves. Nice ones. "I happen to hate kids."

Sarah laughs. "No you don't."

"My best friend has kids, but they're the only ones I like."

"You'll love your own baby," Sarah Levy says.

She sounds so sure of herself. How would she like to see a video of her husband and Shelby fucking in his office? The office smells like Lysol, and there are dog calendars scattered about. Sometimes they do it on the floor, even though Shelby always wonders what else has happened on the tan throw rug.

"I prefer dogs," Shelby says. She lets Blinkie down once they're through the tunnel, and he trots off.

"It's a girl," Sarah says.

"Excuse me?"

"My baby is a girl. I haven't even told my husband. He said he wanted it to be a surprise. But I had an ultrasound. I couldn't stand not knowing." Sarah has big, beautiful eyes. "I don't know why I'm telling you all this."

"I don't either," Shelby says.

They both laugh, then Sarah begins to cry. "It must be hormones," she says. She fishes a tissue out of her pocket. "Sometimes I can't tell my husband anything. I feel like he's judging me and weighing his response." She blows her nose. "I just want someone to be happy when I announce the news."

"I'm happy," Shelby says. "I'm glad you're having a girl."

Sarah throws her a grateful look. "Thank you."

"You're welcome," Shelby says.

They are walking through the grass, off the path, following the dogs. Harper told Shelby that he definitely would not be with Sarah after the first of the year. He said so last Monday, when they were having Chinese food at his desk. Orange-flavored beef, chicken in plum sauce, mushrooms and broccoli.

The dogs have grown tired. Sarah clips on the pit bulls' leads. Shelby does the same with Pablo and the General, but Blinkie is still wandering around.

"Do you mind holding them?" she asks Sarah. Shelby ambles across the grass. She could grab Blinkie and run, leaving Sarah holding on to the leashes. When Harper came home, there her dogs would be and then he'd know that she understood that he's a liar. But when it comes down to it, her dogs are more important to her than Harper is. That should tell her something.

Shelby scoops up Blinkie and heads back, takes her leashes and thanks Sarah. Together they walk toward the Ninetieth Street entrance.

"So what are your favorite girl names?" Sarah asks.

The park is much more crowded now. There are kids everywhere, or maybe Shelby doesn't usually notice toddlers and babies in strollers.

"My friend's daughter's name is Jasmine."

"That's pretty," Sarah says. "I love that." They'd reached Fifth Avenue. "Are you going down Eighty-Ninth?"

"Nope. Downtown."

"I'm going to think of her as Jasmine." Sarah pats her belly. "Thanks for the name. Thanks for being happy for me."

Shelby stays where she is. Sarah crosses Fifth, then turns and waves. Shelby waves back.

Then Shelby starts downtown. No cab will stop for her until Fifty-Ninth Street.

"I have to charge you extra for the animals," the cabbie says. He's nothing like the first driver.

"Fine." Shelby gets in. "Go down Ninth Avenue." She directs him to the veterinary hospital. She promises him an extra twenty bucks if he'll watch the dogs for five minutes.

"But just five minutes," the cabbie says. "Otherwise it costs more."

Shelby goes to the entrance. She knows the maintenance guy, Leandro, who cleans the cages and watches over the kennel on weekends. When she taps on the glass, he waves and buzzes her in.

"It's not Monday," he says to her. Everybody is aware of her schedule. Everyone is aware of what she's done. He seems concerned. "Are you sure the doc is expecting you?"

And then she knows. He's got someone else back there.

"Oh, yeah," Shelby assures Leandro, a nice man, about her father's age. His worried expression isn't changing, but Shelby takes off running down the hall. She can hear them before she opens the door. The murmurs of lovemaking; a girl's thick voice, and then his, a voice she would recognize anywhere. Shelby walks in, braced for it; still she's stunned to see him fucking a girl on the couch. She's young, with masses of long black hair; maybe she works in the billing department, or perhaps she's one of the veterinary students interning for a semester.

Harper gazes at Shelby, and for a moment it's clear that he doesn't recognize her. She just stands there as the girl pulls on her shirt. Then Harper's eyes light up. He looks like he's already thinking of ways to spin the situation to his best advantage. "Shelby, this is not what it looks like."

She can't believe he's just said that. That's dialogue from a movie that she doesn't wish to see, let alone star in. "Really? Then what is it? You're doing to me what you do to Sarah. Lying."

Harper is pulling on his jeans. "Shelby. Don't be like that."

"Do you know her?" the black-haired girl asks.

"I'm Monday night," Shelby tells her competition. "I assume you're Sunday morning."

"What is she talking about?" the girl asks, a break in her voice.

Every Monday for over a year it's been the same. After she assists while he attends to sick dogs and cats, after surgery, after she mops the bloody floor and washes her hands, they come here. The couch, the desk, the calendars, the photos of Sarah. Shelby breathes in the scent of Lysol. How did she ever overlook that wretched smell? It reminds her of the hospital, of the floor of the bathroom, of the way she was treated like an object not a person.

Harper comes to take Shelby's arm. "We can talk later."

Shelby wrenches away from him. "I think we're over."

"You're never happy. It's never enough with you, Shelby." Harper sounds wounded, as if he's the one who's been betrayed.

"By the way," Shelby tells him, "it's a girl."

Harper looks at her, confused.

"Sarah's planning on calling her Jasmine."

"You saw Sarah?" Harper runs a hand through his hair. His expression has darkened. Shelby has moved outside of the box he put her in. One night a week, separate from his real life.

"She couldn't have been nicer," Shelby tells him. "I think we could have been friends. We'd have a lot to talk about." She wants to hurt him, at least a little.

"Listen to me, Shelby, you leave her alone."

Harper is no longer his usual charming self. *See a charmer and you're bound to see a snake nearby,* Maravelle told her, and it's turned out to be true. Maybe this is just a part of her punishment. She dumped Ben, she was thoughtless and mean, maybe she deserves to have wasted her love on a liar. All the same, she wants to salvage something out of this mess, so she does. She grabs Sarah's painting off the wall. She's always liked it.

"What do you think you're doing?" Harper has moved from faux-betrayed to furious.

Shelby knows what she's doing, so she ignores him.

"What's going on?" the girl on the couch asks.

"She's a maniac," Harper mutters. "That's what's going on."

The painting is heavy, but Shelby manages to get it down the hall. Leandro helps her by opening the door into the street. "You okay?" he asks. He's a big, gentle man, and Shelby smiles up at him.

"I am," she assures him. "Thank you."

The painting fits neatly into the trunk of the taxi. It will probably be another ten-dollar charge, but Shelby doesn't care. She wants to look at a field, a stream, a boulder, a blue sky, a landscape of pure white snow. Whenever she does, she'll think she couldn't save Helene, and she couldn't save Sarah, but she can save herself.

CHAPTER

6

The tattooed girl is in the deli, stealing an apple. Shelby is there by happenstance, since she's rarely in Union Square these days. She doesn't work at the pet store anymore, and only stopped in to see Maravelle. When she first resigned, they didn't want to let her go. They offered more money. They kept saying she was too big an asset to lose, when all she did was boss people around in a way that made them think the decisions they made were their own. So she made a deal: Maravelle would be promoted to manager and Shelby would train her, without pay.

Now Shelby is picking up a Swiss on rye with mustard, lettuce, and tomato to scarf down on her way to class. It's her last semester. She has zero downtime in her day. She's gone from a pot-smoking failure to a workaholic. She is a tutor at school and works in a lab. She doesn't know how it happened. It's like a magic spell, one where there's a transformation and everything that happens is invisible. One minute she's a lost girl sitting in a deserted park in her hometown smoking weed, and the next she's got a 3.8 average at Hunter College and is seriously considering vet school. Her biology professor suggested she apply for a fellowship, which she was stunned to receive. Now the City of New York actually gives her money each month. When she quit the pet store her employees took her out to a club in the East Village, where they danced on the bar and all got extremely drunk. She danced for hours with Juan, who has qualified for the New York City Police Academy and quit the week after Shelby did.

The tattooed girl's face is covered by blue patterns. People glance at her, then quickly look away. She's disturbing, like a cannibal queen let loose in New York. Ever since Shelby stole the dogs she's felt a weird connection to this girl, as if they were soul sisters. What would have happened if fairy-tale logic prevailed and they'd changed places that day? Then it would be Shelby out there begging in Union Square, and the tattooed girl would be lugging a tote bag filled with zoology textbooks.

Shelby glances over as the tattooed girl slips out, the bell above the door jingling. "Make it two sandwiches," Shelby tells the deli guy.

She knows what it's like when someone is compelled to show her pain. When Shelby shaved her head it was a public penance, there for the whole world to see. She now has straight, gold-brown hair reaching to her shoulders. Jasmine has told her she can't believe how pretty Shelby has become. And yet when Shelby looks in the mirror she still sees the bald girl she was for so long.

Shelby waits for her sandwiches, pays, then goes looking for her doppelganger. The girl is in front of Barnes & Noble, hunkered down, eating the apple. Maravelle always says give a beggar what he wants and all you do is teach him to beg harder. But Maravelle believes in rules, and Shelby never has.

The tattooed girl was probably sixteen the first time Shelby saw her. She doesn't look so young now. She's probably lucky to still be alive.

There are abscesses on her mouth and on her arms. She's wearing light sneakers, even though it's a chilly November evening, along with torn jeans and a black hooded sweatshirt. Shelby stops and hands her one of the sandwiches, wrapped in white paper.

"What the fuck is this supposed to be?" the girl says. The blue patterns are asymmetrical on either side of her face. It makes Shelby dizzy to look at her.

"Swiss on rye." Shelby sees the uptown bus pulling away. She'll have to wait for another and will probably be late to class.

The tattooed girl grabs the sandwich. "It better be good," she says.

Shelby thinks about the girl's comment all evening during her zoology class. It's almost funny how entitled she was. Shelby goes up to her professor after class and apologizes for being late. She's a better student than she ever would have imagined. "You are definitely a workaholic," Maravelle says when they talk on the phone later that night. Shelby is in bed with the little dogs and Pablo is sprawled on the couch. Pablo is seriously in love with the couch. He doesn't even want to get off when it's time to eat. "My problem with Jasmine is that things come too easy to her. She gets As in nearly everything without even trying. She's slacking off and this is the year she applies to college."

Maravelle often complains about her daughter. Jasmine wears too much makeup, she pays no attention to her studies, she dresses like a slut. Frankly, Shelby doesn't think a short skirt and boots equals slutdom, and one C does not a loser make. Maravelle is convinced that Jasmine has a secret boyfriend, one of the older guys from the park. Maravelle's mother has come to live with her and help out with the kids, and that's driving her crazy too. It's a whole lot of people in a one-bedroom apartment. Maravelle and her mother both sleep in the living room now, Mrs. Diaz on the foldout couch and Maravelle on a blow-up mattress. This is one of the reasons Maravelle is going out to Long Island, to look at a house in Valley Stream. The other is Jasmine. "I've got to get her out of Queens. I don't like the way guys in this neighborhood are looking at her."

"Guys are going to look at her no matter where you are," Shelby informs her friend. After all, Jasmine is gorgeous. "But maybe a move is a good idea."

Jasmine has confided to Shelby that she does indeed have a boy-friend, but she's made Shelby swear she won't tell Maravelle. Now Shelby is riddled with guilt, keeping this secret from her friend. The boyfriend, Marcus Parris, is older, not in school. From what Shelby has heard, he has a bad attitude, and that is likely his best quality. He texts Jasmine half a dozen times a night to make sure she's not cheating on him. Maravelle has her suspicions. She found a gold necklace he gave Jasmine for her birthday stuffed into a drawer.

"Maybe I should shave her head while she's sleeping," Maravelle says to Shelby. "Then she'll look like you used to and all the boys will stay away."

When Maravelle finds the house of her dreams, she insists that Shelby come to give her opinion. Shelby takes the Long Island Rail Road to Valley Stream, where Maravelle is waiting in her mother's car. Mrs. Diaz and her two sisters, one in Puerto Rico, one in Fair Lawn, New Jersey, have offered to help Maravelle with a down payment.

"Miss Suburbia," Shelby says with a little smirk. "What's this?" she says of the car Maravelle is driving. "A Volvo?"

"That's Ms. to you," Maravelle says. "It's a Subaru. The Volvo comes next."

The house is in a nice neighborhood. It's a brick colonial with wooden shutters and a manicured front lawn and a big backyard. There's already a basketball hoop over the garage.

"Let me guess," Shelby says. "The boys love it."

"Love it to death. And my mother is overjoyed. There's an apartment over the garage for her. We can live together without actually having to live together."

They go up to the porch, and Maravelle takes out the key. "Ta da," she says, unlocking the door.

"Don't we have to meet the Realtor or something?"

"We don't need a Realtor, baby. I bought it! Well, me and my mom and my aunties, but my name is on the deed."

There is a big oak tree on the front lawn. It's leafless now, but come next fall it will drop all its leaves and be a real pain in the ass. Shelby knows the downside of suburban life, but she doesn't mention all the work that awaits Maravelle. *Get out the rake, the lawn mower, the snow shovel, the grass seed.* "Nice tree," she says.

When they step inside, there's still paper rolled out to protect the hardwood floors and ensure that potential buyers don't scuff things up.

"Is it gorgeous or what?" Maravelle chirps.

It probably is to somebody and that somebody is Maravelle. Why should Shelby burst her bubble? There's a gas fireplace and a good-size dining room. In the kitchen there are new appliances and white floor tiles that Shelby knows will be hell to clean when the boys stomp around in muddy sneakers.

Shelby goes to the window and gazes into the yard. It reminds her of where she grew up, out in Huntington. There's even a picnic table.

Jasmine is going to hate it.

Maravelle comes to stand beside her. "Pinch me," she says. Shelby does, and Maravelle squeals. "Hey, bitch!" Maravelle rubs her arm and grins. "This house is due to you, you know."

Shelby gives her friend a look. She refuses to take responsibility for Valley Stream.

"You made them give me the manager's job," Maravelle says gleefully.

That's true, but Shelby won't admit it. They go out the kitchen door to the patio. It smells like rain and grass.

"You know Jasmine's not going to want to move here, right?" Shelby says.

"She'll get used to it. The high school is three blocks away. I don't have to worry about the kids taking the bus. My mother can walk to the supermarket."

Shelby sits cross-legged on a retaining wall and lights a cigarette. She knows there's no safety in this world, even if you're on Long Island. What happens in Queens can happen here too. Still, she keeps her opinions to herself.

Maravelle comes to sit next to her. "What do you really think?" Shelby is brutally honest. That's why Maravelle likes her. Maravelle is brutally honest too. You can't have many friends if you act that way, but you can depend on the ones you have.

"I'd kill myself if I lived here," Shelby says. "But I'm proud of you."

Maravelle leaps up, arms out, and twirls on her tiptoes. "Suburbia, I love you!" she shouts.

The last few leaves are falling from a grapevine that grows along the side of the garage. Shelby can't help but imagine what a mess it's going to be when the grapes are overripe and scattering everywhere and angry bees buzz through the air, drunk on the juice. Maravelle won't be dancing around then.

"You did good," Shelby says. "Your kids will be safe and everyone will live happily ever after."

"Will you go furniture shopping with me?" Maravelle is really excited about this home ownership situation.

"Not on your life. But I'll visit you and bring Chinese food from the city because it's probably terrible out here."

They get back into Maravelle's car and head for Queens along Sunrise Highway. There's a lot of traffic in Valley Stream, especially around the mall. The fact that it's called Green Acres is a joke. Parking lots, cars, chain stores filled with stuff no one needs. Shelby hates malls. She hasn't been in one in years. She sighs and gazes out the window. She thinks about the town where she grew up and how excited she and Helene were that they'd be moving to New York City when they graduated.

As if she could read her friend's mind, Maravelle says, "Don't say anything negative. Don't tell me this isn't my dream come true."

Maravelle was Shelby's friend when Shelby was bald and smoking pot four times a day. She was Shelby's friend through bad breakups with two boyfriends. More important and for reasons Shelby will never understand, Maravelle trusts Shelby with her children. Why should Shelby ruin her day by telling her that a teenage girl who doesn't want to be in suburbia can put her mother through hell? She did it, after all. It was easy.

It happens two weeks later, on the eve of the move. Maravelle calls Shelby at ten o'clock at night, frantic. The boxes are all packed, the movers are coming in the morning, and Jasmine has taken off.

"Wait until midnight to get hysterical," Shelby advises. The witching hour, the time of night that scares parents most. Jasmine will be back by then.

Except that she's not.

Maravelle calls all of Jasmine's friends, waking some of their parents, but Jasmine isn't with any of them. Maravelle then races through the quiet neighborhood, searching the park, a place no one with any sense would go after dark. She calls Shelby on her cell phone from the corner deli near the school bus stop. Shelby can barely understand her over all the crying.

"She's trying to scare you," Shelby says.

Shelby certainly wouldn't wish the scares she gave her own mother on anyone.

"Well, she's doing a damn good job of it," Maravelle says. "I'm going to kill her when I get hold of her."

Shelby is on the couch with big Pablo snoring beside her, hoping to be phoned with good news. She has always considered the view from her window to be beautiful, a mix of tar, cobblestones, rooftops, water towers, but now the outside world looks wicked. While she waits to hear from Maravelle, Shelby is drinking green tea and smoking a cigarette. She figures the habit that's good for her will cancel out the one that's bad. The police have told Maravelle they can't do anything until twenty-four hours have passed from the time her daughter is reported missing. Just long enough for a murder or kidnapping. Long enough for Jasmine to wind up stuffed into a green garbage bag and dumped onto the Grand Central Parkway. Shelby can't imagine what Maravelle must be going through. The responsibility of loving someone is too much for anyone to take, which is why she's done her best to avoid it.

Not long after midnight, a cab pulls up to Shelby's building. Pablo starts barking, which revs up the other dogs. Shelby hushes them. She perches on the back of the couch and spies a young woman with a backpack getting out of the taxi. It's Jasmine.

Shelby phones Maravelle, pronto. As soon as she answers, Shelby says, "Forget the police. She's here."

"Oh, my God! I'm driving over there right now."

"She'll run if you do." Jasmine rings the bell downstairs. Shelby darts to the wall so she can buzz open the door. "She needs to feel like some outside adult will listen to her. So I'll pretend to be an adult. You know she'll tell me stuff she won't tell you."

"Okay, Shelby, but understand this: I'm leaving the most precious thing in my world in your hands."

Fuck it, Shelby thinks as she hangs up. She has never wanted to be involved with people. People are dangerous, unreliable, stupid, greedy, needy, breakable. Look what happened to Helene, to Ben Mink, to

Harper Levy's wife. The dogs go nuts when there's a knock on the door. Fortunately the upstairs neighbor is a waiter who doesn't get home till dawn, and the couple beneath her have such huge drunken fights they're in no position to complain about noise.

Shelby tries to plan a great opening remark, but when she sees Jasmine's tearstained face, she simply puts her arms around the girl and hugs her.

"I hate my mother," Jasmine says.

It's as good a beginning as any. The dogs are thrilled to have company, especially Blinkie, whom Jasmine used to think of as creepy and scary. He leaps around until she picks him up. "Oh, Blinkie," Jasmine says, as if he's the only one in the world who could ever understand her. She hides her face in his fur and sobs.

"You must be starving. I have Chinese food," Shelby says.

Shelby always has Chinese food. She now stores her unread fortune cookies in a plastic container she keeps on the kitchen counter, behind the toaster.

"Why don't you ever eat those?" Jasmine asks.

"No one should know the future," Shelby says. "What if it's horrible?"

"What if it's great?"

"Like life on Long Island?" Shelby jokes.

Jasmine groans and throws herself onto the couch while Shelby reheats broccoli with black bean sauce and General Tso's chicken. "I don't know if I can eat," Jasmine says when the plates are brought out.

Shelby starts right in on her food. How did she come to be responsible for the well-being of someone's child?

"The taxi driver was so creepy," Jasmine says. "He told me if I didn't have a place to stay I could stay with him. He made me sick to my stomach." All the same, she has begun to eat, daintily at first and then as if she were starving. "Do you have soy sauce?"

Shelby gets some soy sauce. She starts the discussion gingerly. "Let me guess. You hate Long Island."

"You try living there."

"I did until I was nineteen. How do you think I got this way?"

They both laugh, but Jasmine doesn't stop laughing. It's the kind of laughter that quickly becomes hysterical. Shelby can tell it's going to turn into crying before it does.

"I have a life," Jasmine sobs. "I have friends."

"As in the creepy boyfriend?"

"Marcus is not creepy. And he loves me."

"Love is for when you're older," Shelby says.

"Like your age?"

"I am not the love expert," Shelby admits. "Learn from my mistakes."

"My mother thinks she's the expert. She thinks she rules the world."

"Well, I hate to tell you, but she does rule your world. You'll make new friends on Long Island."

"Oh yeah, sure. Now you sound like my mother."

A mistake. Shelby tries another tactic. She's best as bad-girl sister who knows the score. "Don't you get it? You'll be the new hot girl everyone wants to date. People are so bored with the friends they have, you'll be a queen. Queen Jasmine from Queens. You'll meet other guys. Better ones."

"Hah," Jasmine says, but Shelby can tell from the look on her face, she's begun to make a dent.

"I bet you a hundred bucks you get asked out the first day you're in school there."

Jasmine is eating in earnest now. Shelby fetches them two Diet Cokes. The apartment is so small a person sitting on the couch can see every inch of the place, including the kitchen and the sleeping alcove that's entirely taken up by Shelby's bed.

"We could go to Pier 1 and get some awesome stuff for your new room. Red silk curtains."

"I like blue," Jasmine says. "Aqua."

Shelby tries not to smile. She's hooked Jasmine with shop therapy. "There's a huge mall near your house. Green Acres."

Shelby hates shopping. Most of the things in her apartment are cast-offs—the couch is from some ex-neighbors who skipped on their rent, the table and chairs belonged to Ben Mink's great-aunt. True, she got the rug at Pier 1, but only because there was an eighty-percent-off sale and the rug was fluffy and white, the perfect accessory to go with dog hair.

"Would you go shopping with me?" Jasmine asks. "My mother likes everything to match."

Shelby brings out an extra quilt and some sheets so they can make up the couch. This means tying Pablo to the dining room table with his leash so he won't try to share the couch with Jasmine in the middle of the night.

"Thank you for understanding." Jasmine hugs Shelby tight. She's still a little girl even though she looks like a grown woman. She's five foot seven with perfect coffee-colored skin and high cheekbones. Maybe she's relieved to get away from her neighborhood and her jealous boy-friend.

Shelby goes to the bathroom and runs the water full blast so she can phone Maravelle without being overheard.

"What the hell took you so long?" Maravelle has had a pot of coffee, and her nerves are shot. "Put her on." Now that Maravelle knows her daughter is safe, she can allow herself to be furious. "I'm going to punish the crap out of her."

"I'll get her there in the morning," Shelby whispers.

"I can't even hear you!"

"I don't want her to know I'm talking to you. She'll feel betrayed."

"She'll feel betrayed! She likes you better than she likes me."

"Yeah, well, I'm not her mother. And I used to be bald, therefore I can't be a full-fledged adult." Shelby gazes at herself in the mirror. She thinks of what Ben said long ago, how Helene's hair was still long, how it was still the color of roses.

Maravelle laughs. "Well, I love you anyway, bald or not. Just don't lose my daughter."

The funny thing is, Shelby can't sleep. She keeps getting up and checking on Jasmine. Jasmine is curled up with Blinkie beside her, but Shelby still feels anxious. Someone could climb up the fire escape and grab Jasmine. Shelby stays up all night so she can save her if need be. At seven, she makes coffee and feeds the dogs.

Jasmine lifts her head. "Hey," she says sleepily. "I dreamed I lived in a castle."

"Was it in Valley Stream?"

Jasmine grins and throws a pillow at Shelby. "There was a white horse in my dream. See if you can find me one of those. Then I'll be happy."

They take the train out to the island, then grab a taxi to the mall, where they have the driver wait while they shop. When they arrive at the new house, they're carrying two huge shopping bags. They have cornered the market on candles, velvet pillows, wall hangings.

Maravelle must have ESP because she's waiting on the lawn when they arrive, no coat, no sweater, nothing, even though it's chilly. There are empty boxes from the move stacked by the curb, ready for the trash pickup in the morning.

"You finally made it," Maravelle says, her hand on her hip.

"We had to go shopping," Shelby informs her.

"Why don't you bring all that inside?" Maravelle tells Jasmine, and Jasmine, grateful not to be confronted, dashes into the house.

"You rewarded her for running away?"

"Yep. And now you owe me two hundred and twenty-four dollars."

"Good luck collecting." Maravelle hugs Shelby. "Thank God for you, crazy girl."

"How do you do all this, Mimi? I was so worried I couldn't sleep all night. Why does anyone become someone's mother?"

"Sometimes I think I'm messing the whole thing up." The shock of the evening has taken a toll.

"You're not." Shelby is very sure about this. "What Jasmine really wanted was a horse, so you should be thankful I just let her get pillows and vanilla candles. You could have a palomino in your backyard."

"What would I ever do if something happened to her?" Maravelle says.

"Let's order Chinese food," Shelby suggests. It's her answer to everything. She doesn't want to think about any what-ifs. She just wants hot and sour soup, and then she wants to get back on the train and get the hell out of Long Island. "You can treat."

The experience of Jasmine's running away lingers. Shelby feels haunted by her own ragged emotions. Is this what love does to you? Makes you feel accountable for things you can't control? All week she wakes in the middle of the night, worried about the future. She opens the closet door and looks at the jar of fortune cookies. She takes one, then quickly tosses it back in the jar.

One afternoon when a cold rain is falling, Shelby heads for the deli in Union Square. Since she quit work, she's missed the place. There's a chill in the air, so Shelby orders a container of chicken noodle soup.

"Make it two," she decides at the last minute. Maybe that tattooed girl is out there; maybe she's hungry and cold.

It's the time of year when the trees are still bare. Shelby is wearing a heavy sweatshirt and boots. The brown paper deli bag is threatening to tear under the weight of the two containers of soup. The tattooed girl is indeed there, huddled beneath the overhang near the subway. She's got on striped leggings and an army jacket. As Shelby approaches, she spies a little white cat perched on the girl's shoulder, just sitting there, as if it weren't raining. Shelby's allergic to cats, she doesn't even like them, she's a dog person, but she feels something inside her that is like an electric shock.

"Hey, I brought you something," Shelby says to the girl. She crouches down and takes out one of the containers of soup; the cardboard is burning hot. She places it on the cement while she fishes around in the bag for a plastic spoon. The air is foggy and gray. The cat is most likely drugged. That's why it ignores the rain. It's tiny and drenched.

"Is that a kitten?" Shelby asks.

The tattooed girl grabs the soup and opens it. Some hot liquid spills on her hands. "Shit. Why is this so hot?"

"Does that kitten belong to you?" Shelby feels the breaking thing inside her that always leads to trouble.

"Why don't you kiss my ass, bitch?" the tattooed girl sneers. "One cup of soup doesn't buy you anything."

That's it. Shelby grabs the kitten and runs. She runs so hard and so fast she nearly slips on the wet pavement. Her pulse is pumping and there's a thud inside her ears. She hears the tattooed girl screaming at her, but she doesn't care. She doesn't care that she'll be so allergic from having the cat tucked inside her sweatshirt she'll have to get herself a bottle of Benadryl. There is nothing that could stop her, really. Not a bullet, not a police car, and certainly not a beggar girl.

Shelby runs to Seventh Avenue, to Penn Station. You rescue something and you're responsible for it. But maybe that's what love is. Maybe it's like a hit-and-run accident; it smashes you before you can think. You do it no matter the cost and you keep on running. It's dusk now, and the puddles are filled with neon. It's only thirty minutes by train to Valley Stream. *Don't make a noise,* Shelby whispers to the cat when the conductor comes around. *Soon you'll be sleeping on a velvet pillow. You'll be looking at the rain from behind the window where there are blue silk curtains. You'll be glad there was a thief like me.*

CHAPTER

7

It's May and the world is green and lush, even in Valley Stream. There are daffodils in the gardens and birds in the willow trees. Shelby takes the train out for Sunday dinner, even though Maravelle's mother, Alba Diaz, hates her. Shelby knows this because whenever she walks in the house Mrs. Diaz, an opinionated, no-nonsense widow in her fifties, hightails it into another room. She'll come out for dinner, but she won't speak. Not in English at any rate. Not when Shelby's there.

"Come on, Abuela," Jasmine always says to her grandmother on these occasions. "Shelby won't bite you."

"Oh, I'm not afraid of that," Mrs. Diaz says, her glance burning through Shelby. "If anything I'll bite her."

Maybe she hates Shelby because she thinks Shelby is a bad influence, or maybe it's because Shelby gave Jasmine the cat, Snowball. Mrs. Diaz hates cats as much as she does Shelby.

"Mami, please," Maravelle always says. "Behave yourself."

As for Shelby, she keeps her mouth shut until Mrs. Diaz retires to her room.

"Geez Louise," Shelby says. "She is tough."

"You have no idea," Maravelle says. "I couldn't go on a date so I did it behind her back. I went crazy wild."

So of course Maravelle worries about the beautiful Jasmine, closing in on seventeen. That's why Shelby has been summoned out to Long Island on a Saturday rather than for the usual Sunday dinner and why she can't take the train back to the city until Maravelle returns from her first date in nearly ten years. Mrs. Diaz works evenings at the intake desk in the ER at the local hospital, and Maravelle doesn't want the kids home alone. She found evidence of a romance. First there was the gold necklace, then gifts of perfume and cologne. Then she found a man's sweatshirt in Jasmine's bureau drawer. She's afraid of what she'll find next.

That afternoon they go to the mall so Maravelle can look for something to wear. Her date is with the lawyer who handled the transaction when the house was bought. Maravelle thinks he warrants a new dress. The mall is Shelby's idea of hell, walking along with Dorian and Teddy, both now fourteen and ridiculously tall, over six feet. Jasmine and Maravelle duck into stores with names like Dressbarn and Forever 21. No one is twenty-one forever, Shelby knows that for a fact. She has turned twenty-five and will soon be graduating from college. A little late, but better late than never. Teddy is browsing through the Gap. He's a clotheshorse and looks great in everything he puts on. He's got a lethal grin and the girls are all wild about him. Unfortunately, he's lazy and he can be selfish. As far as Shelby can tell he's hanging out with a rotten crowd. Guys in fast cars pick him up without bothering to come to the door. "See you later," he'll call, but he won't introduce his friends to his family. Dorian is more low-key; he's the captain of the swim team and excels in just about everything. He and

Shelby are having frozen yogurt. It's filled with fruit and little mushy white things that have no taste.

"This stuff is terrible," Shelby says. "Why don't people just eat ice cream?"

"Because this is good for you," Dorian says. "Low carb."

"Right, like I care about that." Shelby loves this kid. He's still a tender sweetheart even though he looks so grown up.

"What if I told you something I don't want my mother to know?" Dorian looks into his yogurt cup as he speaks.

"Are you using drugs?" If anyone were to get into trouble she'd always thought it would be Teddy.

"No!" Dorian looks seriously offended. "It's not about me."

"Teddy," Shelby says.

They can see Teddy looking through racks of T-shirts. The boys are equally good-looking, only Teddy happens to know it. He has the kind of charm that makes people notice him.

"No," Dorian assures her.

"Okay. Go ahead. I won't tell."

"There's a guy bothering Jasmine."

"Your mom moved here to get away from that crap. Is it someone she's serious about?"

Dorian shakes his head. "Used to be. He's the guy from Queens she was dating. Marcus Parris. Jaz broke up with him but he keeps going after her. He's coming out to the house when my mother isn't around even if Jaz tells him not to. The other day she went out to scream at him. He got out of his car and grabbed her and she ran back into the house. The car's out there almost every day. He's got a blue Toyota. The windows are tinted black."

"Oh great," Shelby says. "A gangster."

"And now Teddy's hanging out with him."

Shelby watches Teddy through the window as he flirts with a salesgirl at least ten years older than he is. "They're friends?"

"Teddy thinks so. Marcus is using him to get to Jasmine."

Maravelle waves from the doorway of Dressbarn wearing a slinky red dress. Shelby gives her a thumbs-up.

Dorian is tapping his feet, anxious. "I don't want to get the cops or my mother involved. Am I supposed to beat Marcus up or something?"

"No. Definitely not." That's all anyone needs. Dorian getting into the mix. "Let me think," Shelby says.

It's not easy to think with the noise and crowds. Malls are all pretty much the same. They really could be anywhere. Maravelle and Jasmine signal to Shelby again. Shelby makes her way through the crush of shoppers. Maravelle has on a black and white dress that looks great on her. But it seems like something she'd wear to a parent-teacher conference, not on a first date.

"This is the one, right?" Maravelle asks.

"Sure," Shelby says. She's busy thinking about the gangster and the fact that she's going to keep something this big a secret from Maravelle.

Maravelle gives her a look. "You're not lying?"

"Actually I am. Get the red one."

"I told you the same thing!" Jasmine says. "Why do you only believe Shelby?"

Maravelle gets dolled up, and they all watch through the window when she goes to meet her date. He comes to open the car door for her. He looks like he's about fifty, more dating material for Mrs. Diaz than for Maravelle.

"He's not for her," Jasmine mutters. "I don't know why she's bothering."

"What about you?" Shelby says, playing detective as smoothly as she can. "Anyone special in your life?"

Jasmine is in the midst of SATs. "I'm way too busy at the moment," she says primly. No mention of Marcus. For a moment, Shelby feels stung. Jasmine has always confided in her, but not this time. Then she realizes that Jasmine may be scared; she's protecting Shelby from knowing too much. Once Shelby knows what's going on she'll have to do something. But she does know, so she begins to plan.

Fortunately there's a basketball game at the high school, so the kids will be out of the house if the stalker shows up at his usual time, right after supper. When everyone is gone, Shelby positions herself at the front window. She plans on letting the guy from Queens know that if he ever bothers Jasmine again she will call the police. This is not an idle threat. The little white cat, Snowball, sits beside Shelby on the couch. Snowball is spoiled and snooty, but Jasmine loves her. Shelby has looked for the tattooed girl in Union Square, but lately there's been no sign of her. Maybe she's taken off for a city where life is a little easier, Portland or Seattle, or maybe she overdosed one rainy night on a subway platform. Of course it's possible that she turned her life around and went back to New Jersey or Connecticut; maybe she rang the bell of her parents' house and said, *I just want to come home.*

Dusk is sifting down when the blue Toyota pulls up. Shelby can hear the music blaring. The windows of the car are indeed tinted black. Shelby pulls on one of Dorian's sweatshirts, then, on impulse, takes the broom from the coat closet. As she goes outside she pulls her hood over her head. She doesn't want to look like someone's mother. Or even like someone's mother's best friend.

The truth is, she wants to protect Maravelle. She knows how upsetting this would be to her. Maravelle met the kids' father when she was sixteen, younger than Jasmine is now. He was married at the time, and soon enough he did to Maravelle what he'd done to his wife. *If a man lies to one woman, he'll lie to you,* Maravelle once told Shelby. By the time she found out he was both a drug dealer and a cheater, she had three children. Her worst fear is that Jasmine will make the same mistakes she did.

The leaves of the grapevine running along the garage smell sweet. Shelby has the broom under her arm, wooden handle pointing out so it appears lance-like. She crosses the street, pulse pounding in her ears. It's a quiet neighborhood and dinnertime is finishing up in most households. Dishes are being washed and put away. Down the block, some children play in a yard and their lilting voices echo. The music's bass line from inside the car is throbbing. It sends shivers down Shelby's spine. Her breathing has quickened; it's fight or flight. Because of the tinted windows she doesn't know who she's up against. She walks over to the car and raps on the driver's window. Nothing. She does it again, heart pounding so hard it hurts. Her whole chest is burning.

"I want to talk to you," she shouts to the window.

Her voice doesn't sound the way she wants it to. It's too soft.

Shelby expects him to buzz down the window, but instead he opens the door and gets out. Marcus is older than she expected, in his twenties, nearly Shelby's age. His hair is closely shorn and there's a tattoo of a crown across his throat. He's dressed up for the occasion, wearing a leather jacket and expensive jeans. But the car upholstery is torn, and smoke billows out when he opens the door. He's been sitting there smoking weed. No way on earth he is getting anywhere near Jasmine, no matter how pissed off he looks.

"This isn't a parking lot," Shelby says. "I suggest you move along."

Marcus is compact, wiry, fueled by drugs. He's also handsome in a hard-edged way. "Yeah? I don't see any No Parking signs."

"People who loiter get tickets." Good Lord, she sounds like the mean teacher in high school. No wonder he's sneering at her.

"Be smart, lady," he says. "Leave me the fuck alone."

Marcus turns his back on her. He gets back in the car and slams the door. Shelby can see his shadow through the black glass. What the hell does he mean by calling her *lady*? He's leaning back against the head-rest. But he still seems coiled, ready for what happens next if Shelby dares to annoy him. She raps on the glass again, this time with the edge of the broom. As she does, Shelby feels the burning inside her chest flame, a sign she is about to do something stupid. She keeps tapping until he finally opens the door again.

"What?" Marcus shouts.

"I don't want you to come here anymore. If you contact her I'll call the police."

It dawns on Marcus Parris that Shelby is talking about Jasmine. This time he gets out of the car in a rage. Shelby takes a step back. Without thinking she holds the broom in front of her.

"You think you can tell me what to do?" her opponent says with real menace. "You can't stop me from seeing her." He looks Shelby up and down. The sweatshirt, the broom, the heavy black boots. "I'm a friend of the family and you're nobody. Who are you anyway? The cleaning lady?"

"I'm the person who'll put you in jail if you bother her again," Shelby says. "And you are not a friend of the family. The family fucking hates you."

Marcus smiles at her then, broadly, so that his dimples show. Shelby can see how Jasmine might have fallen for him, how he could have sweet-talked her, given her that gorgeous smile of his. She was likely head over heels before she had time to pick up on any of the warning signs, how possessive and controlling he is.

"You're crazy," he says to Shelby. "You'd better stay out of this."

"She's done with you," Shelby tells him.

"She belongs to me."

When Marcus turns away, Shelby hits him squarely on the back.

He spins to face her and spits out, "You are one fucking crazy bitch."

Before Shelby can respond, he punches her. Shelby gasps, stunned as she wheels backward. At first she feels nothing but shock, then there's the hot sting of pain as blood rushes from her nose, so much of it she can't believe it's coming out of her. She puts the broom between them and stabs at the air with the handle, trying to ward him off.

"You think that's going to stop me?" Marcus Parris smirks. Shelby is nothing to him, a fly, an annoyance, no more than that.

They're in a bubble of hatred, so it takes a while for Shelby to hear the wail of the siren. The cop car pulls up across the street and two officers are over to them so quickly it seems to Shelby that the whole world has speeded up. They grab the guy from Queens and shove him up against the car. There's a thud when he tries to wrench away, and then Shelby sees the glitter of handcuffs. She's dizzy and her face is throbbing. She thinks she may fall, but then someone's arm is around her. It's a woman. Mrs. Diaz.

"Keep your head down." Mrs. Diaz hands Shelby a tissue so she can try to stanch the blood pouring from her nose. "Are you faint?"

Shelby nods.

One of the officers comes over. "We're going to call an ambulance."

"I don't need it," Shelby insists.

"Hi there, Mrs. Diaz," the officer says when he recognizes Maravelle's mother from the ER. "It's a good thing you phoned. She should get checked out."

As it turns out, when Mrs. Diaz pulled up from work, she saw the encounter in the street and immediately dialed 911. Then she went into the house to grab an ice pack, which she now hands to Shelby. "Hold this against your nose."

"Is it broken?" Shelby asks. "It was my one good feature."

The cop and Mrs. Diaz give Shelby the once-over. "Just bruised" they agree. "It was a warning punch," the cop tells her. "You're lucky. He had a gun in the glove compartment."

The guy from Queens, now restrained, is being held in the back of the police car. The officer takes down Shelby's account of what happened.

"He's been stalking Mrs. Diaz's granddaughter and she's under-age."

"But you're the one he assaulted, so I assume you want to press charges."

"Yes," Mrs. Diaz says. "She does." The last thing Shelby wants to do is get more involved with the stalker, but Mrs. Diaz tells her, "If you take him to court and get the restraining order, then Jasmine doesn't have to. Isn't that right?" she says to the officer.

"We could do it that way," the cop says. He's young, about Shelby's age.

"Fine," Shelby says. "I'd like to press charges."

Shelby and Mrs. Diaz stand on the sidewalk as the officer returns to his car to fill out some paperwork.

"I've seen that man parked out here before." Mrs. Diaz shakes her head. "That's why I try to come home around this time. Lucky for you," she says matter-of-factly.

"Very lucky for me," Shelby agrees.

The officer returns and has Shelby sign several documents, and then he asks her to come into the station to speak with the sergeant and give her sworn statement. Mrs. Diaz drives her there in a Subaru that is spotless inside and out. She waits in the parking lot while Shelby goes in to be questioned. Shelby is shaking and cold. Mrs. Diaz told her to give her address as Maravelle's. That will be the address the stalker cannot approach without being immediately arrested. They'll sit Maravelle down and tell her the whole story soon enough, but for now it is Shelby who must take care of this mess. She realizes she still has the broom in her hand. She's been carrying it all this time, like a visiting witch. When the sergeant asks why she has her legal address in New York City and yet she wants the restraining order in Valley Stream, she says she is the maid. "I'm at that house a lot." At least that much is true.

It's dark when she comes out of the station. Mrs. Diaz flashes her headlights so Shelby can find her car. Shelby's nose is puffy and swollen but the blood has stopped. All the same, Mrs. Diaz insists they stop at the ER.

"Totally unnecessary," Shelby says.

Mrs. Diaz doesn't listen. "Which one of us works at a hospital?"

Because Mrs. Diaz is a beloved employee, the triage nurse has Shelby examined in no time. She is given a prescription for painkillers and told to keep ice on her swollen nose.

"I told you I was fine," Shelby tells Mrs. Diaz.

She intends to take the train back into the city, where her dogs are waiting for her, but Mrs. Diaz insists she spend the night. When they get to Maravelle's house, Shelby phones her neighbor, the waiter who works nights, and asks him to take the dogs for a walk before he leaves. She'll be back in the morning. Then she sits out on the porch, waiting for the kids to return from the basketball game. To Shelby's surprise, Mrs. Diaz opens the screen door and brings out two tumblers of rum and water on a tray. Both glasses have plenty of ice. They sit side by side on the wicker couch.

"This is better for you than a Vicodin," Mrs. Diaz says.

Maravelle's date pulls up, and she gets out of the car and waves to them.

Mrs. Diaz looks displeased. "That man is not for her. He's too old."

"You should date him," Shelby suggests.

Mrs. Diaz laughs. "I'd teach him a thing or two."

"What are you two doing?" Maravelle asks as she comes up to the porch. "I've never even seen you talk to each other." She looks more closely. "What happened to your face, Shelby?"

"That Marcus boy from Queens happened," Mrs. Diaz says. "Only he's a grown man."

They tell her everything, including the part when he asked if Shelby was the cleaning lady. Maravelle embraces her friend. "This is the kind of thing you can never repay," she says.

"I'll think of something." Shelby grins. There is still blood caked on her face, and Mrs. Diaz offers her a napkin.

It's the end of the evening, and soon Jasmine and the boys are shambling down the street, goofing around, teasing one another. "Our team won," they call when they notice everyone out on the porch. They stop horsing around when they see Shelby's condition and race up the porch steps.

"What happened to you?" Jasmine says, upset. She kneels down beside Shelby to get a better look. "Oh my God! Is your nose broken?"

The grown-ups have decided there's no reason to make Jasmine any more worried than she has been. The monster's been sent away, fended off with a broom. Shelby wants Jasmine to enjoy her youth in a way she didn't, so she says the first excuse that comes to mind. "I fell off a bike."

"Shelby, you don't ride a bike," Teddy says, suspicious.

"Yes she does." Maravelle has pinched Shelby's drink and takes a sip before Shelby can grab it back.

"It's something you never forget how to do," Shelby adds.

"Apparently you do," Teddy says, with a grin. "If that's really what happened."

"She fell headfirst." Mrs. Diaz turns to Shelby. "You need to practice your riding. Get a helmet. I wouldn't want to see you in the hospital."

Dorian's brow is furrowed. He's got a *What's wrong with this picture?* expression on his face. He knows his grandmother can't stand Shelby, but there they are sitting side by side, both with drinks in their hands. "There's nothing to worry about," Shelby tells him, just as she insisted when she rescued the monster that turned out to be Pablo. Dorian understands that she's taken care of the problem. He leans over to kiss her cheek before he and Teddy go inside. Jasmine has plopped herself down on the painted wooden porch floor. The night is inky, but through the dark the forsythia in the yard glows with a deep, yellow light. Up and down the street the neighbors are watching TV, putting their children to bed, saying good night. Maravelle runs her hand over her beautiful daughter's head, then goes inside for the rum.

"Tell the truth," Jasmine asks her grandmother once her mother has gone. "How come you're out here with Shelby?"

"Oh, Shelby's not so bad," Mrs. Diaz says. She looks Shelby over, then nods. "I've changed my mind about her. We're girlfriends now."

CHAPTER

8

Shelby is a volunteer at the Humane Society on Fifty-Ninth Street. She began with dog walking, coaxing frightened creatures large and small out of their cages after their arrival, training suspicious pit bulls and overwrought dachshunds to walk calmly on a leash. She's quickly progressed to being a member of the intake team for abandoned and abused dogs. She's there on Sunday afternoons and Monday nights at the intake desk, ready with blankets and kibble. She is in charge of the initial exam before the new arrival goes to be seen by a vet tech. Are there wounds, worms, fleas? Is the dog friendly, frightened, aggressive? The adoptable puppies and dogs bring Shelby joy. They are bathed and fed and photographed for the newsletter and website. But then there are the old dogs, the ones who refuse to look up because they've been beaten or neglected. Every night it is a challenge not to bring another dog home.

Shelby understands abandonment and loneliness. Her desire to do right for these creatures is what fuels her. She works odd hours, fills in when other people go on vacation, is willing to deal with the vicious, the mistrustful, the beaten, the desperate. At night, she cuddles up with the General and Blinkie. They both snore, but she wouldn't think of tossing them out of bed. She thinks of Ben, and how she didn't value him when she had him. Some nights she dreams of Helene, and when she wakes she's crying. She hasn't gotten a postcard in some time, and what she misses most is someone knowing she's alive.

People like Shelby don't beg for human companionship. They don't sign up at dating services, or write profiles, or wait in a Chinese restaurant with sweaty palms wearing a black dress. They don't even wear dresses, but there she is on a Thursday night ordering a Tsingtao beer as she waits for the stranger she met online to appear. She blames Maravelle for convincing her she should get back into the dating world after the mess with Harper. Likely she's here because loneliness can drive even the most alienated person to attempt to make contact with another soul, even when it's via a soulless medium. Loneliness is something Shelby thought she could overcome. She told herself being alone was what she wanted, but lately she finds herself looking at couples and hating them just because they're happy. She blames herself for her situation. She ditched a true-blue boyfriend for a married man. She never asked the right questions, like *Why are you still living with your wife if you're so crazy about me?* or *What do you do every other night of the week?* Now a year has passed since the breakup with Harper. Would she even re-member how to have sex? Does she still have a heart left to break? She watches movies she would have had contempt for in the past, sappy ro-mantic comedies, and she actually cries when star-crossed lovers find their way back to each other. She's sat through *Bridget Jones's Diary*

fifteen times. Sometimes the only person she speaks to during an entire weekend is one of the delivery guys from Hunan Kitchen. The sad guy has disappeared, and now there's a new person every time. Shelby has the feeling all of the delivery guys refer to her as the crazy girl who can't shut up. They probably draw straws to see who's the unlucky one to bring her General Tso's chicken and steamed rice.

It took two weeks for Shelby to complete her dating profile. She'd written term papers in less time. She couldn't seem to get it right. She had no desire to look inside her soul and analyze her needs. She couldn't write down the truth, which is simply that she needs someone to remind her she's alive.

> *Twenty-five-year-old woman who carries around guilt, sorrow, and strange desires looking for a man between the ages 20 and 35 who knows how to laugh. I would rather run through the park with a bulldog than have a diamond ring. I don't care what you look like and I hope you don't care about that either. I'm so pale some people assume I'm a vampire. I'm not afraid of a fight. I don't drive or wear lipstick.*
>
> *Turn-ons: Chinese food, New York City, fire escapes, lost souls.*
> *Turn-offs: people, the past, men who are liars.*

When she sent her profile in, someone from the dating service named Mandy Cohen phoned to suggest she make certain changes before posting. "This is pretty harsh," Mandy told her. So now her profile is simplified.

> *Unusual woman looking for interesting man.*
> *Loves Chinese food, long walks, New York City.*

Shelby insisted on tagging on a line. She needed a statement of purpose, otherwise she would seem like an empty shell.

> *Hopes to save a small part of the world.*

She can't understand why, but she's had over fifty responses. Totally unexpected. A landslide of possible dating material. As it turns out, she appeals to a hell of a lot more people than she would have ever imagined. Maybe they picture her as a modern-day Joan of Arc, a fighter with a heart of gold who likes to take long walks and is great in bed. Unfortunately, most of the guys who write to her seem like jerks. One who might have been a possibility wrote that he, too, always wanted to save the world and they were clearly kindred spirits. He had been to Africa with the Peace Corps and now worked for a church group. When Shelby called him he was so serious and kindhearted she rescued him by hanging up on him. She wasn't the girl for him. She'd only make him miserable.

There was only one other respondent who appealed to Shelby, and she didn't ruin it by talking to him on the phone. His email had made her laugh, so they'd arranged to have dinner. But now the time has come for reality, and Shelby finds herself hoping he won't show. They use code names at this service. She is Darklady, a totally stupid name chosen on a sleepless night. What was she thinking? Was she supposed to sound sexy? Exotic? Like a sci-fi fan? It's a persona her seventeen-year-old self would have chosen. Her date is *Youonlylivetwice*, moronic but nonthreatening. They'd messaged back and forth—only a line or two at a time. He'd written, *Don't think I'm a James Bond fan. I forgot that was a Bond title when I picked my handle.* That's when she'd started liking him.

Who says handle? she'd written back. *What are you, a teapot?*

Let's not discuss drugs via the internet, he'd quipped. *Tea. Pot. Seems like you have a one-track mind.*

She was smoking weed when she read his response, and for a moment she felt like she'd actually found her soul mate and he could somehow intuit her true essence, as if things like that ever happened. Still, there was something about this one that made her feel he was a possibility. His turn of a phrase. His love of the New York Mets, which meant a penchant for losers. His low expectations. *I just want to be happy,* he told her.

Have you ever cheated on a girlfriend? she wrote when she felt she knew him well enough to ask a personal question.

Never would. Never could.

Everyone has a bottom line, and this is Shelby's. She'd cheated on someone and she'd been cheated on, and she didn't know which was worse.

I don't believe in cheating, he'd written. *It would be like shooting Bambi. Who can shoot Bambi and feel okay with himself?*

Bambi is a story, she'd written back, moved by the reference.

Bambi is a cultural signpost for morality.

What do you believe in?

Live and let die, he'd written. Somehow the code name didn't seem as moronic.

Do we or don't we? she'd typed when the time came for them to meet. A month had passed since their initial contact.

Oh we do, he'd written. *How could I lose you when I haven't even found you?*

So she's up to this part, the sweating hands, the black dress, the *I should have never done this* moment. The meeting place is a Chinese restaurant on Mott Street, a more upscale sort of place than the ones Shelby usually frequents. Tablecloths, cocktails. His choice. And yet he's late.

"I'm waiting for someone," Shelby says when the waiter hovers near, clearly annoyed that she's taking up table space without ordering anything. He has started tapping his pen on his order pad and muttering. "He's late," Shelby tells him. "There's traffic."

The waiter shrugs. "Maybe he's not coming."

Shelby feels flushed. "Fine. I'll have a beer. Tsingtao."

The waiter looks at her with pity.

"And an order of pork dumplings. Steamed, not fried. And brown rice."

"For two or one?"

The waiter's tone makes her want to announce that she doesn't plan on leaving a tip. Shelby glares at him. "For two."

If her date doesn't show the waiter will know she's a ghost and she'll have to eat two orders of dumplings by herself.

A light rain is falling and outside the street is slick. It will be hard to get a cab on a night like this. About as hard as it is to trust anyone in this world. Shelby begins on the dumplings as soon as they're delivered. She eats like a starving person. Her mouth is full when she looks up to see her date in the doorway, dripping rain, wearing a tan trench coat, shoving a hand through his long, bedraggled hair. *Of course,* Shelby thinks as he gazes around the room for his date. *This is the way it happens. This is what I deserve.* The man in the doorway is her old boyfriend Ben Mink.

He searches the room, expectant, though he's clearly soaked to the skin. He looks great, no longer skinny or gawky, just a tall, hopeful, good-looking man. It's horrible to see the disappointment on his face when he sees her. He looks as if he's been slapped.

Shelby feels a pit in her stomach, but she forces herself to wave. There's no way out of this. "Hey," she calls. "Ben! Over here."

He stares at her, confused.

"It's me. Shelby."

When she signals him over, Ben gazes around at the other customers as if making a silent plea for help. No one meets his glance, so he cautiously makes his way over. He's much taller than Shelby remembered. He has a bunch of dripping wet tulips in his hand.

"Hey, Shelby." Ben notices she's begun eating. "Dumplings. Of course."

"Two orders. I'm still a pig." Her hands are sweating even more.

"Well, good to see you." Ben appears desperate to escape. "I'm meeting someone," he explains.

"Yeah, me," Shelby tells him.

"Excuse me?"

"Darklady? That's me."

Ben narrows his eyes. Then he gets it. She can almost see the truth of their current situation hit him. He slinks down into the chair opposite her.

"What are the odds?" she says with forced lightness.

The waiter comes over. "More beer?"

"Sure," Shelby says cheerfully. She feels like slitting her wrists. "Make it two."

"How the hell do you come to be Darklady?" Ben looks like he's been the victim of a Ponzi scheme. "You're just about the palest person I've ever met. Have you ever even been in the sun?"

"Dark emotionally. Don't take things so literally, Ben."

"What happened to that guy?" Ben says.

"Guy?" Shelby feels a pain shoot through her gut. Ben is staring at her.

"The one you used to bring to our apartment. He left a jacket there once. I threw it out. I figured if I ignored the situation, it would go away. Stupid me."

"Ben," Shelby says. She despises herself far more than he ever could.

"Are you living together?" he asks coldly.

"We broke up."

The beers are delivered. The waiter stands over them with his order pad.

"We might as well eat," Shelby says. She must be insane. She is willing to humiliate herself to keep him at the table. "We're here."

"We are." Ben turns to the waiter. "I'll have the moo shu pork, and she'll have the General Tso's chicken."

"I'll have the spicy shrimp," Shelby corrects him.

"Since when?" Ben is puzzled.

In the past she had always ordered the same thing, but she wants to shock him and make herself seem like a changed woman. "Since now. And I'll take the shrimp toast. And shrimp lo mein."

They sit there staring at each other. "Maybe I'll get mine to go," Ben says.

"You know what's interesting? The dating service thought we were perfect for each other. How crazy is that?" Shelby holds her breath hoping for the right response, whatever that is.

"Insane," he agrees.

"Maybe they know something we don't know," she offers.

Ben laughs out loud. "You're kidding, right?"

So there it is. He's moved on. He stares at the door as if he's really expecting someone else, his real date, a woman with long, dark hair who would never betray him by screwing around with some man she met on the street. They both gaze out the window. It's pouring now.

"I'd give anything for a raincoat. A really good one. Burberry."

"You didn't use to like name brands." Ben is surprised. "You used to make fun of people for spending money on stuff with logos."

"Well that was then. People change. I appreciate Burberry now. It's classic. I'm wearing a damn dress, Ben."

"So you are," he agrees.

When the food arrives they stare at it. Shelby ordered too much. "What were you thinking?" Ben says.

"It looks good." Shelby imagines a fairy-tale scenario: if she keeps him there long enough the magic will start to work. The veil will fall from his eyes and he'll see she's the one for him and that she has been all along.

The food is pretty awful, but Shelby doesn't say so. When the waiter brings two fortune cookies, Shelby shakes her head. "We don't want those," she says. She is more afraid than usual to find out what her fortune is. *A man you love will walk away from you and not look back. A woman will stupidly cast away a true love. A sheet of ice will await you. A dog will be your best friend.*

"Everybody wants fortune cookies," the waiter says.

"Well not us," Shelby tells him.

The waiter nods at Ben. "He wants a cookie."

Ben takes a cookie and nods back at the waiter. They are united against Shelby.

"Are you serious?" Shelby says.

Ben cracks open the cookie. *All your dreams will come true.* He puts the cookie on the table and pushes it away with one finger.

"It isn't a good idea to get a random opinion on your life," Shelby says.

"I should have known it was you," Ben says.

"Yeah?" Shelby hates shrimp and now she has a ton of it.

"I was the one who told you, you could save the world."

"I should have known it was you. Bambi. That should have been a total giveaway."

"Yeah." Ben laughs. "You remember?"

"Fourth grade. You cried."

Ben winces and looks like his gawky old self.

"And Jimmy whatever his name was, that tough guy who wound up in prison, hit you with some rubber bands while you were crying." Shelby nibbles on the shrimp toast. "I got a fellowship that paid for my last year of school. I graduated."

"Seriously? That's great. I can't say I'm surprised."

"I'm working at the Humane Society." *Build yourself up,* Maravelle told her when Shelby called her to discuss what she thought was a blind date. *Do not tell him your troubles or bring up your past.* So Shelby doesn't mention that she's applied to vet school in case she doesn't get in. She's keeping things positive, something she never did when they were together.

Ben has finished his plate of food. He takes out his wallet. "I chose the restaurant. I should pay."

Shelby feels an odd panic rising in her chest. He's about to leave her. She probably has the same crestfallen expression the stray dogs in their cages have when Shelby locks up for the night. "Already? You're going to pay?"

Ben leans forward. "The dating service was wrong, Shelby. We both know that." He smiles and gets up to go. He leaves the tulips and too much money for the waiter. When he's gone, Shelby takes five dollars off the tip and slips it into her purse. She'll use Ben's money to take a cab home. She leaves the flowers for the waiter. Maybe his wife will appreciate them. Maybe his wife will take him to bed and tell him she's never loved anyone the way she loves him, not now and not ever, not in this lifetime.

CHAPTER

9

When the temperatures rise into the high nineties, people in Manhattan will do just about anything to walk over green grass and find space under a shade tree, even if it means being in Valley Stream. Shelby sits in Maravelle's backyard with the dogs. She's wearing a T-shirt and a short plaid skirt. They've filled up a plastic kiddie pool bought at the local dollar store with cold water, fast turning tepid, from the garden hose. Shelby has her feet dipped in even though Pablo is taking up most of the pool, lolling around like a big polar bear. Just as she predicted, the grapevine Maravelle thought was so charming when she bought the house is now pulling the shingles off the garage. There are hundreds of bees gathered around the sweet buds, and Maravelle is doing her best to chop the whole thing down. When she gives up, she fetches them a pitcher of iced tea and some rum.

"I thought you quit smoking," she says when Shelby lights up.

"I started after my date with Ben. It was traumatic. I'll quit tomorrow."

"You should quit today," Maravelle says. "I liked Ben."

"You barely knew Ben! He was always working or in school. We led separate lives."

"You made it that way," Maravelle says. "You never included him."

"The world is mine to ruin." Shelby mixes rum into her iced tea and takes a sip. She licks her lips. She gulps more rum and tea. "Surprisingly refreshing."

"Ben would have done anything for you."

"I thought that meant he was an idiot."

"No," Maravelle says. "It means you're an idiot."

They have dinner on the back porch. Maravelle has been distant lately. She dodges conversation, saying only that there's trouble with the kids.

"Is that creep Marcus back?" Shelby asks.

Maravelle shakes her head. "It's not that. But I'm always keeping watch over them. I used to feel bad for you that you didn't have kids, now I think maybe you're lucky. You don't have anyone to worry about."

"I worry," Shelby says. "I'm a major worrier."

"Trust me. It would be worse if you had kids. They start off breakable. They fall off things, they get lost, they get fevers. Then they get older and things get worse. Their hearts get broken, they have terrible friends, they start to lie to you."

It's Jasmine's night to cook, and she's made orange-flavored beef in Shelby's honor. Jaz's summer job is working as a hostess in a Chinese restaurant, and she spends all her free time in the kitchen learning as much as she can. Mrs. Diaz comes out with some rice, stopping to greet Shelby. "I heard you went out with your old boyfriend, but he walked out on you," she says.

"Well, yes." Shelby gives Maravelle a look. "Was that reported in the *New York Post*?"

Jasmine laughs as she brings out dishes and silverware. "It was reported in the Valley Stream Echo," Jasmine says. "Otherwise known as my mother."

"Well, that ex-boyfriend of yours doesn't know what he's missing," Mrs. Diaz says in support of Shelby, but Shelby is fairly certain Ben knows exactly what he's missing and that's why he walked out of their date.

Dorian arrives home from swim practice, smelling of chlorine; he's so tall and handsome Shelby feels her throat tighten. Do people really grow up this fast? He leans down to hug her.

That's when Shelby realizes what's missing. Until recently, the brothers were always together. "Where's Teddy?" she asks.

Everyone else exchanges a look. This is why Maravelle has been so upset. It's something to do with Teddy. Dorian fills his plate and starts in on his dinner. Maravelle does the same. No one answers Shelby.

"I haven't seen him the last three times I've been here. Is he in a witness protection plan?"

It's a joke, but no one laughs. "Look at that Pablo," Maravelle says in an attempt to hijack the conversation. The big dog is still sprawled out in the tiny wading pool. "He knows how to cool off."

"Am I not supposed to mention Teddy?" Shelby asks.

"Well, I don't want to talk about him," Jasmine says.

Dorian glares at her. "Maybe you should blame yourself for bringing Marcus around."

"It's not my fault! I didn't tell him to take Mami's money or steal from us."

"Jasmine," Maravelle warns.

"Am I supposed to pretend I don't hear this?" Shelby asks. "What am I? The cleaning lady? Because if I am, I forgot my broom."

"What's wrong with you people?" Dorian gets up from the table and heads for the house, most of his food untouched. "You all just turn your back on him and pretend nothing is happening."

"Are you sure you want to know?" Maravelle asks Shelby.

Shelby nods, so after dinner she and Maravelle take the dogs for a walk. "There's nothing so terrible you can't tell me," Shelby says. "You know that."

"He's in with a bad crowd. I didn't see what was happening for a long time."

"How bad?"

The neighborhood is quiet. It's the place Maravelle moved to in order to get her kids away from bad influences. "He's doing drugs."

"I did drugs and I turned out fine," Shelby reminds her friend.

"Compared to what?"

They both laugh, but only a little.

"It's more than just using," Maravelle says. "My mom found a shoe box under his bed full of the stuff. He's been taking money from my purse and stealing from Jasmine's savings. Most of my jewelry is gone."

Shelby used to steal from her mother's purse when she came back from the psych ward. She'd paw through the medicine cabinet for whatever prescription looked like it could put her out of her misery. She was a good girl on the day of the accident, and then she turned bad. But she always loved her mother, even when she stole from her. She loved her like crazy.

Maravelle gives her a ride back to the city, and all the way home Shelby feels the sting of her remorse. She wishes she'd been a better daughter and hadn't caused her mother so much worry. It's her biggest regret, but she was so lost she couldn't think of anyone else back then. Now she's gotten into the habit of calling her mom on Sunday nights, and even though it's late she phones.

"Hey, Shelby," her mom says when she picks up. "You should be here." Sue sounds a bit drunk. "I'm out in the backyard on the picnic table. There are so many stars. You used to think you could count them all when you were a little girl."

"Is Dad with you?" Shelby hasn't talked to him since her mother revealed he hasn't always been faithful. She's afraid of what she might say. *How can you hurt the one woman in the world who waits up for you at night till you're safely home? Who puts up with your moods and your disappointments in life? Who remembers you when you were young and handsome and had faith in the world?*

"He's watching television. It's that show you hate. The singing contest."

"That piece of crap?" Shelby says dismissively, but she goes to switch on the TV and watches without the sound. She almost never misses it. She thinks of her mother outside alone, staring at the swirling heavens, living with a ghost who doesn't even come home for dinner anymore. "Is Dad treating you right?"

"Not as good as Ben treated you," her mom says.

"Suddenly everyone loves Ben Mink."

"It's not sudden, honey," Sue says. "We always liked him."

Shelby doesn't answer because the truth is, it was sudden for her.

Sue says she's growing dahlias. She gave them up because you have to unearth the tubers in the fall and keep them in buckets of dirt to winter over because they can't take the cold. But now Sue has time for her garden and for those big, beautiful flowers that remind her of Shelby's face when she was a child. Upturned and glorious. "When you were little you'd help me dig them up," she reminds Shelby. "You thought the tubers looked like giant worms."

"Was I ever a little girl?" Shelby says wistfully.

"Oh, yes," Sue says. "I have the photos to prove it."

Later in the week Shelby gets an envelope addressed in her mother's neat librarian's script. There's a postcard inside. Her angel hasn't forgotten her after all.

Believe something.

The illustration is of a tree with a hundred black leaves. The veins of each leaf make up a spidery word: *sky, cloud, rose, kiss.*

There's something else inside the envelope, an old photo that Shelby's mom stuck in, the color faded, the edges upturned. It takes a moment before Shelby realizes she is the little girl in the picture. Her mother's handwriting is on the back. *Shelby at five.* She's wearing a sun hat and there's a huge smile on her face. She is surrounded by stalks of dahlias, orange and yellow and pale red, with leaves so big you could write your life story on each one. She looks like a flower in the garden, just like her mother said.

When the phone rings at five a.m., Shelby is dreaming that she's following Helene through a field. There are white and black butterflies rising from the tall grass. There are flowers the size of pie plates. Shelby is her current age, but Helene hasn't aged. She's seventeen and beautiful, and she runs so fast her feet don't touch the ground. When Shelby pulls herself out of her dream to grasp the phone, Maravelle is on the other end of the line. Teddy's been arrested. Shelby is awake in an instant, pulling on her clothes before Maravelle is through telling her the story. She still smells the grass in the field. She feels the sunlight on her skin, though it's a gray, rainy dawn.

"Do you have an attorney?" Shelby asks Maravelle. "And not that old real estate lawyer you dated. Maybe we can get Teddy out tonight. They can't just lock someone up without probable cause."

"There's cause. His whole crew has been arrested for home invasion. It was supposed to be a robbery but the couple was in bed, so they were tied up and terrorized. I think the old man had a stroke. Maybe he's dead."

Shelby sits on the edge of the bed, floored by this news. "Jesus, Mimi."

"That damn Marcus was involved. Teddy swears he was just along for the ride and had nothing to do with the home invasion. He wasn't identified in the lineup by the victim's wife. But he was in the car when the police pulled them over."

"I'm sure he had nothing to do with it," Shelby is quick to say.

"Don't defend him! That's what I've been doing and look where it got us! The robbery happened because they're all on drugs, Teddy included. I don't want him getting out unless he's going to rehab. He'd just go back to the same crowd." Shelby can hear that Maravelle is crying.

"It will get better," Shelby tells her. "Look at me. I was in a mental hospital drugged out of my mind. I sat in the basement for two years and did absolutely nothing but get high."

"Tell me he'll be fine, like you are."

"He will be."

That's what Shelby says, but you can never be too sure. All week she researches possible placements to present to the court. She finds a therapeutic high school near Albany with a great reputation for turning kids around. Teddy's attorney likes the looks of it, but the assignment has to be approved by the judge at Teddy's hearing. That means the judge has to see something in Teddy, a soul worth saving; otherwise Teddy will stay in the detention center where he's currently being held. There's a three-week wait for a court date due to a jammed docket, so Teddy stays where he is, with every other underage offender in Nassau County. Nothing good can come of this. It's a step deeper into a criminal life. He tells his mother not to come visit him. He doesn't want anyone to see him caged up and humiliated.

On the day of the hearing Shelby waits in the hallway of the courthouse in Mineola with Jasmine and Dorian. Teddy's attorney says it's best to have only Maravelle and Mrs. Diaz sit in at the hearing. All the same, Shelby and Jasmine and Dorian are dressed for a serious occasion, wearing clothes they wouldn't be caught dead in anywhere else. Shelby has on a black skirt and a white buttoned-up shirt she found at a thrift store on Twenty-Third Street. Jasmine's borrowed one of her mom's sweater sets, a pale, dignified gray, and a pleated navy-blue skirt. With her hair in braids, she looks like the serious schoolgirl she's become. Dorian, the most somber among them, is wearing a suit and tie. Dorian looks so concerned that every time Shelby glances at him her heart breaks. She's brought along the brochure for the school Teddy will be attending if the judge okays it so Dorian can see that it looks more like a college than a jail. A plain community college with brick dormitories, nothing fancy, but nothing horrendous. It's not what anyone would have wished for Teddy, but it's the road he's taken, and it's the road back.

"I was much worse than he is," Shelby tells Jasmine and herself as they sit on the bench. A woman turns to glare at her. Everything you say in the courthouse echoes, even a whisper. "Well I was!" Shelby says.

"Plus you were bald," Jasmine says.

They both laugh, but it's nervous laughter. It could break in a moment. Dorian pays no attention. He stares down the hall, focused on his brother's fate. Behind the closed doors of the courtroom, Maravelle and Mrs. Diaz sit in the row behind Teddy and his lawyer. They too are wearing black, as though attending a funeral. In a sense they are. Teddy was always the star, the boy who could have done anything, more confident than his twin, a success at everything he tried. It was always going to be Teddy who was going to attend an Ivy League college and win every award. Maybe things came easily for him, but at some point he just quit. Dorian has admitted he's been doing homework for the both of them for the last couple of months.

But Teddy's fate is unknown, and no one can foretell the future. Shelby has borrowed another thousand dollars from her mom to help pay for the lawyer, Isaac Worth, who looks a little like Teddy, only grown up and set right. If the attorney manages to cut a deal, Teddy will be taken directly to the school upstate, where he will remain a student until graduation or upon the occasion of his eighteenth birthday, whichever comes first. It's the best they can hope for—no jail time, no record, and a chance to get him away from the crowd he's mixed up with. When the judge agrees to the placement, they can hear Mrs. Diaz offering thanks to God all the way down the hall.

The court allows Teddy to say good-bye to his family, but he's accompanied by a guard and his lawyer is present. The meeting takes place right there in the hallway. No privacy and not much time. Shelby hardly recognizes Teddy as he approaches. A month in detention and he seems like a stranger: his slouched posture, the regulation T-shirt and khakis, and, more disturbing, the fact that his head has been shaved. Shelby can tell Jasmine is equally shocked to see Teddy is nearly bald. It's a way to make him look like everyone else, to take away his pride. He's always cared deeply about his appearance, making sure his hair was perfect before he went out. Still, when he raises his eyes and smiles, it's the same Teddy, the one all the girls fell for because he knew exactly how handsome he was.

"I look like shit," he says. "Right?"

Dorian goes to his brother and throws his arms around him. Everything seems fine, until Dorian starts to sob. The sound echoes like a shot. People turn to stare. The guard studies the floor.

"Hey," Teddy says with a nervous laugh, shoving his brother away. "What's wrong with you? I just look like crap. It's not the end of the world."

Dorian backs off, wiping at his eyes. "This is bad," he says. "This wasn't supposed to happen to you."

"I've got an idea," Teddy says. "You can take my place." He laughs. "No one would ever know."

Dorian stares at his brother. "Is that what you want me to do?" Would he or wouldn't he? Shelby thinks he would. He would walk into the line of fire, take his brother's place, ruin his own future. That is why she loves him, of course. He's loyal beyond measure.

"Of course not, stupid. I'm playing with you. I got myself into this.

And if one of us would make it through this shithole they're going to send me to, it would be me."

Isaac Worth is discussing the court's terms with Maravelle. "After six weeks you can visit. Other family members can go up later if he's fitting in. It is not a lockdown. It's a boarding school. It was a military-style school, but now they focus on academics and behavior. I managed to get some scholarship money, and New York State will pay for the rest."

Shelby sees the way Maravelle is looking at her attorney. She's shell-shocked, but she clearly trusts this man so he damn well better be worthy, otherwise he'll have Shelby and Mrs. Diaz to deal with. Shelby goes to give Teddy a quick hug. "You can come back from this," she tells him. "Look at me. I just about killed someone."

Teddy shakes his head. "No you didn't."

The kids don't know about Helene. Shelby wanted to tell them, but Maravelle told her it was unnecessary information. "Seriously?" Shelby had said. "It's what defines me."

"Only to you," Maravelle had insisted. "It doesn't matter to anyone who loves you."

"Anyway, you're a thousand times smarter than I was," Shelby tells Teddy now. "You'll figure it out. If you don't think you're worth something, no one else will either."

"What are you? A philosopher?" Teddy says.

"Nope. Just a friend, baby. One who's been where you are now."

Later they drive back to Valley Stream, minus one. No one says much, not even when Dorian starts to cry again, his large hands covering his face. They just let him cry and Maravelle switches on the radio. People say that twins can feel each other's emotions. That if you stick one with a pin the other will gasp as if wounded. Maybe the one who feels the stab of pain is the lucky one, since he's the one who understands human needs and desires.

Shelby begins a letter to Teddy that night. She thinks about the first postcard that came to her in the hospital, how she thought the nurse had made a mistake when she shouted out Shelby's name at mail call, how it mattered that someone, somewhere, knew how she felt deep inside. She writes to Teddy all through the rest of the week. It's a much longer letter than she'd ever expected it to be. She writes during dinner, in between bites of reheated chicken and rice with plum sauce. She writes while the singing competition show she hates and always watches is on. The letter turns out to be ten pages long by the time she mails it on Friday. She's written about things she's never told anyone, not even Ben Mink, how she hated herself so much she held her hand over the flame on the stove in the hope she'd ignite. How she wished she had died on the road. How, on the night of the accident, she bit and kicked whoever tried to save her. She sends along a photo she took of Teddy and Dorian with Pablo, snapped during the week she took care of them, when she still disliked children. The brothers' arms are thrown around one another's shoulders and Pablo is bigger than the both of them put together. *Remember who you are,* she tells him. She thinks about the photograph her mother sent her, when she was little and her eyes were so bright with faith and love. *What's deep inside never changes.*

The next week she writes a list of all the terrible things she's done in her life. She wants him to know he's not the only one with regrets. *Drugs. Horrible, hurtful sex that she now realizes she thought was punishment for all she'd done wrong. She thought that was what she deserved. Betraying Ben Mink. Never letting him know that she loved him. Adultery with Harper when his wife was pregnant and nicer than he was. Stealing two dogs and one cat. Robbery at the junkyard in Queens. Being a bad daughter. Being a bad person. Stealing Helene's life.*

A few weeks later Shelby receives a postcard in the mail. It's stuck into the metal mailbox in the building's cluttered lobby, where people leave umbrellas and newspapers. There are circulars for food delivery and for a tattoo parlor on Broadway. At first she assumes the postcard is from her anonymous correspondent, then she remembers he doesn't know where she lives and can only leave cards at her mom's address. This postcard turns out to be from Teddy. She knows that's a good sign. An SOS from somewhere near Albany. She stands in the hallway because she can't wait to get upstairs to read it. There's a photograph of the school on the front of the postcard, with a bright blue sky and green lawn enhanced by computer magic. On the back he's scrawled: *I still don't believe you were that bad. Thanks for writing.* He's tagged on a smiley face after his signature, as if he were still the little boy Shelby used to babysit for, the one who never gave her any trouble and walked to school without complaint, who worried for his brother, who saw monsters on the corner while he raced by without a second look.

CHAPTER

10

Shelby knows a bad sign when she sees one. Blood in the egg drop soup she had delivered from the Hunan Kitchen. Nothing good could ever come of that. There are two fortune cookies in the bottom of the bag. Shelby throws them into her container of cookies. She has the feeling they would portend doom.

"That is not blood," the owner, Shin Mae, insists when Shelby calls the restaurant to complain. "It's soy sauce."

But the day after the egg drop soup, she gets a call from her father. Her dad rarely uses the telephone and he rarely calls Shelby. His conversational skills are nonexistent. Shelby has a shivery feeling. For some time she has wondered if her mom has been avoiding her. Whenever Shelby wants to visit, Sue is busy, and their plans are always disrupted. I'll see you soon, her mother always says, and then she cancels again. It's been going on for nearly two months.

"You'd better come home," Shelby's father tells her. When Shelby asks why, her father's response is cagey. "Your mom needs you" is all he'll say.

"Is it an emergency?" Shelby has been waiting for tragedy to strike. She's been a bit too happy lately. Something's got to slam her.

"I would say so," her father says.

That's how Shelby knows it hadn't been soy sauce in the soup. It was blood and bad luck. She's glad she dumped the soup down the sink. Her mother hasn't wanted to see her because something has gone terribly wrong. Shelby wishes she could call Ben to discuss her fears, but she knows it's over for good. She knew the minute he walked into the restaurant and looked at her with true panic.

She quickly folds some clothes into a backpack and carries the two small dogs in a tote bag. She slips on sunglasses and grabs the cane she'd bought at the Chelsea flea market so she can say Pablo is a service dog if anyone gives her a hard time on the train. Luckily, the conductor doesn't even look at her when he punches her ticket. She takes a cab from the station to her parents' house. Her father is waiting for her on the porch. They don't have much to do with one another, and he never waits for her like this, so she realizes the situation is even worse than she'd imagined. Her father doesn't even complain about the dogs. Maybe he's not loyal, but this is his wife and it's hard for him to get the words out, and then finally he does. Shelby's mother has stage four lung cancer. Her parents decided to keep the news from Shelby to protect her, even though she's a grown woman and a college graduate. They did so because they thought she was "delicate," meaning her nervous breakdown back in the dark ages. Shelby sits down on the stoop and cries, her hands over her eyes. Her father lights a cigarette even though he quit five years ago.

"That will give you cancer," Shelby says. They both laugh, and then Shelby starts crying again.

"Come on. Snap out of it," Dan Richmond says. "She's right in the bedroom. You don't want her to hear you crying."

Shelby blows her nose on her sleeve.

"Geez," her father says. "Have you heard of tissues?"

"Does she know?" Shelby asks as they go inside.

"Doesn't she always know everything?" Shelby's father has suddenly noticed Pablo's presence. "I thought you had two dogs." He seems nervous about Pablo. In the past, Shelby left the big dog with her neighbor when she came out to Long Island. Her dad has never been a dog person. "What the hell is this thing? A Saint Bernard?"

"A Great Pyrenees," Shelby says. She has begun to think of a plan of action. "I can quit my job and stay while she has chemo."

"She's already had it. They started, but they had to stop. It didn't work. It just made her sicker."

"Is that why she's been avoiding me?"

"She didn't want you to worry. Just so you're not shocked, Shelby—she's bald."

"That's a bad joke." When Shelby came back from the psych ward and shaved her head, her mother had wept. *How could you do this to yourself?* she'd cried.

"No joke. She won't leave the house. That's one of the reasons I decided to tell you. I want you to take her to get a wig."

"Otherwise you wouldn't have told me?"

"That was her choice, not mine. You think I'm the bad guy, I know."

"Cancer," Shelby reminds him. "The wig."

"There's a place on Main Street that sells them, but she won't go with me. I think she'd feel a whole lot better if people didn't stare at her. She'd look like her old self."

Blinkie and the General follow Shelby into her parents' bedroom.

"Hey, Mom." Shelby has decided not to cry. She's already done that.

Her mother is in bed, under the covers. Shelby perches beside her. She tries to peek beneath the quilt.

"Don't look at me," Shelby's mother says.

"Do you think I never saw a bald woman? I *was* a bald woman."

Sue Richmond laughs. When she's convinced to sit up, she leans against the quilted headboard. She's bald and pale and her eyes are red.

"Good Lord, Mom. You look like me."

The General leaps up, and Sue pets him. "Which one is this?"

"General Tso."

"Is he the smart one?"

"Smarter than Ben Mink."

Sometimes Shelby calls Ben, then hangs up when he answers. Their date was such an embarrassment, yet she still has the urge to talk to him. She had her number blocked so he wouldn't know she was the one calling, but he knew anyway. The last time she phoned he'd said, "Shelby?" She hasn't called since.

"I liked Ben," Sue says.

"He was a drug dealer," Shelby reminds her.

"Still. He was nice. And he became very responsible. I always liked him."

"Me too," Shelby admits.

"You didn't act like it," her mom says.

"If he had known me, he would have known how much I cared about him."

"People don't have ESP," Sue says.

"They should," Shelby says moodily. "Everyone should know exactly what everyone else is thinking and then people wouldn't hurt each other so much."

Sue takes her hand. "How did this happen to me, Shelby?"

It's a big question. Shelby asked the very same thing of the psychiatrist who saw her right after the accident. It was in the ER, before she stopped talking, before she realized she would never be the same. The shrink didn't have an answer then and Shelby doesn't have one now. Her mother didn't even smoke. It doesn't run in the family.

Shelby throws herself across the bed. She used to come into her parents' room when she was a little girl and couldn't sleep. "I must have brought you bad luck."

"Don't talk like that," Sue says. "Your dad wants me to get a wig. He thinks I'm depressed, but the real reason is that it depresses him to see me this way."

"You seem depressed. Which would be totally normal, you know."

"I'm not depressed," Sue says. "I'm devastated."

They both laugh again. Hysterical laughter. The kind that hurts your stomach.

"Maybe I should get a blond wig," Sue muses. "Maybe your dad and I will get back together if I look more attractive."

"You are together," Shelby says.

"I mean in love."

Her mom looks so wistful, something twists up inside Shelby. She hates shopping, but she says, "Sure. Let's go. We'll leave Dad in charge of the dogs."

Shelby sits with her dad in the kitchen drinking coffee while her mother gets ready. "Can you be nicer to her?" Shelby asks him.

"I am nice. It just changes when you've been together for close to thirty years."

"Well, pretend it doesn't," Shelby says coldly. "Pretend you're her knight in shining armor."

Shelby's mom comes out of the bedroom wearing slacks and a sweater, a scarf around her head.

"You look great," Dan tells his wife. He glances over at Shelby for approval, and for a second she feels bad for him even if he is a creep and selfish. She grabs Blinkie and plops him on her father's lap. "Oh, great, the blind one. Jesus, Shelby. What am I supposed to do with him?"

"Take good care of him." She stares at her father. "Try to do something right."

They go out to the driveway, but when Shelby starts for the passenger side of the car her mother stops her. "I can't drive," Sue says. "They did a surgery that affected my arm."

"Well I can't either." Her mom knows she hasn't driven since the accident.

"Damn it, Shelby! You can drive me where I want to go this one fucking time."

Shelby is so shocked by her mother's language she immediately gets behind the wheel. She should be able to do this. Any idiot can drive a car. She starts it up. She's got that tremor in her hand again.

"Make a left and turn onto Sycamore," her mother tells her. "Go to Lewiston."

"That's not the way to Main Street. I thought we were looking at wigs."

"I want to go see Helene," Sue says. "I'm not going to argue with you about it."

At the beginning there were often hundreds of pilgrims milling around the Boyds' house, patiently waiting their turn in the driveway, each one hoping for their own healing encounter with Helene. TV stations sent reporters when prayer vigils were held on the front lawn. But there are new miracles and new healers and people have forgotten about Helene. Eight years have passed since the accident, and nowadays only the faithful and the desperate still appear. There is one old woman who drives out from Queens every day to say prayers on the lawn, even in the depth of winter or during rainstorms. She began visiting the family the week after the accident. Now she says she is waiting for Helene to rise from her bed, to give hope to the world. This devotee of Helene's carries all of her earthly belongings in a paper bag. The Boyds will no longer let her into the house. Sometimes this woman calls out to Helene and begs for her to rid her of her demons, and then the police are phoned and they gently escort her to the tiny apartment where she lives with her daughter, who has never been able to speak or walk.

When Shelby parks across the street from the Boyds' house, she's shaking from the stress of driving. She hasn't been behind the wheel since she was seventeen. She hasn't seen Helene since then. "I'm not going in there with you," she tells her mother.

"I didn't expect you to." Sue flips down the visor and checks to see if she needs to straighten her scarf.

"She can't really heal people, Mom. If she could wouldn't she have healed herself?"

"Don't go anywhere," Sue tells Shelby. "Wait right here."

Shelby watches her mom cross the street and go up the path. There's a shrine on the lawn, with pamphlets that describe the miracles Helene is said to have performed. The old lady is there kneeling on the lawn. She brings a blanket with her so she won't get grass stains on her skirt. She is here because of the stories of drug addicts who visit Helene once and never touch the stuff again, of women who can't get pregnant who have babies nine months after a visit, of men who can't be faithful who renew their vows, of a blind woman who could see while she was in Helene's bedroom and described it perfectly, down to the pink bedspread, the same one she had on her bed when she was a girl.

Shelby sinks down in the driver's seat and lights up a joint even though Sue doesn't allow smoking in her car. Shelby inhales once or twice, then realizes her hands are shaking even worse, so she stubs it out. From what Shelby knows, there's no cure for what her mother has.

Shelby can't see through the windows of Helene's room. She thinks of crouching beside the house with Ben. That was the night she realized he loved her. She could cry if she let herself. She's ruined everything she's ever touched. The windshield has steamed up, and after a while the whole world outside is foggy. Shelby laughs to think her mother told her not to go anywhere. Where the hell would she go? After an hour, Sue comes back out and gets into the car.

"That took a long time. What was it like?" Shelby asks.

Sue is fussing with cleaning off the foggy windshield with her scarf, so it takes a moment before Shelby realizes her mother is crying.

"I told you she couldn't help," Shelby says. "This kind of thing just gives people false hope. It just exploits her, Mom, don't you see that?"

"You're wrong. She did help me. She made me realize how lucky I've been." Sue wipes her eyes with her sleeve. "I went there wanting to know what my life has been worth, and now I know, I've had you all this time, Shelby. I've realized more than ever what a precious gift that is."

"I wish it had been me instead of Helene," Shelby says. "I should have died."

Sue turns and slaps her. The slap is so hard Shelby hits her head against the window. "Mom!" she says, stunned.

"Don't you dare say that!" Sue cries. "Don't even think it! Do you hear me? You're the best thing that ever happened to me, Shelby, don't take that away from me. You're my gift."

"Okay," Shelby says, sobered. Her mom is sobbing now. Shelby doesn't feel stoned anymore. She's heard that people on chemo can have their brains affected. Maybe that's what's happened to her mother.

"And don't look at me like I'm crazy," Sue tells her.

"Okay."

"And don't keep saying *okay*. It doesn't sound like you, Shelby. Say *fuck you* or *kiss my ass*."

"Okay, kiss my ass." They both laugh. "So do you want to go to that wig shop?"

"Kiss my ass," Sue says. They laugh harder. They laugh until Sue says, "Did you know your dad has a new girlfriend? This time it's serious."

"You're crazy," Shelby says. "You always think the worst. He was probably never dating that woman at Macy's."

"That one didn't last long. This one is different. She's a nurse. He told me he wanted the chance to be in love again. He has no idea that being in love is bullshit. It's knowing someone down to their soul that matters. That's what love is. It's difficult and it's real and it doesn't change." Sue sniffs the air. "Did you smoke pot in here?"

"A little," Shelby admits.

Sue rolls down the window. "His girlfriend works at the hospital where I was being treated. We became friends. She invited us for Thanksgiving dinner."

"Fuck him," Shelby says. "I hate him. Fuck her, too."

Her mom takes Shelby's hand. "Actually, I'm glad he'll have some happiness."

Shelby looks at her mom, eyes shining. "You can't be this good."

"Oh, don't get me wrong," Sue says. "I hate him, too."

"How can he do this to you?" Shelby says of her father.

"I don't care, I have you," Sue says.

Shelby says nothing. The fact that she's the high point of someone's life is pathetic. She's probably never loved her mother more than she does at this moment. Maybe she didn't even know what love was before today. "Where should we go?" she asks.

"Take me someplace new. Someplace I've never been before."

"You trust my driving?"

"At this point, does it matter?" Sue says wryly.

They drive around aimlessly for a while, up past the high school, then around by the mall. Shelby and Helene used to come here all the time. Shelby notices another branch of the pet store she managed. She heads for it.

"This is where you're taking me?" Sue says when Shelby parks. "I've been to the mall, Shelby honey."

"But have you been to the pet store?"

It's a Saturday and the mall is crowded. As soon as they go into the pet store, however, Shelby feels at home.

"It smells like hamsters," Shelby's mom says. Sue has a good nose, that's for sure. They head toward the fish department, which is less offensive.

"Remember when I had a Siamese fighting fish?" Shelby says. She was ten years old at the time.

Her mom remembers. "Jackie Kennedy."

"That was a crazy name."

They're in front of a huge tank of angelfish.

"They've never cut Helene's hair," Sue says. "Did you know that? Not since she was seventeen. It reaches all the way to the floor. It's still a beautiful color."

There's a big black and white angelfish over on the side by itself. Shelby can tell something's wrong with it by the way it's tilting. If this were her store, she'd separate it from the others.

"I asked her mom why they haven't cut it short so it will be more manageable and she said Helene always liked it long. She brushes it for Helene twice a day."

"Helene always said her mother didn't listen to her. She wanted to get a tattoo of a horse on her arm. She probably would have cut her hair short and dyed it blue if she'd been the one who lived and I was in a coma."

"It wasn't supposed to be you," her mom says. "You were supposed to live."

"Because I'm living such a brilliant fucking life?"

Shelby's voice cracks, so she moves on, to the goldfish. She hates goldfish.

Shelby's mother follows her. "Because you're such a good person, Shelby."

"I'm nothing, Mom! Don't you understand that? You gave birth to a nothing!"

Sue moves toward her. At first Shelby thinks she's going to slap her again, but instead Sue throws her arms around her. "Love of my life," she says.

A group of kids head down the aisle, so Shelby and Sue move away from each other.

"Stop making me cry." Shelby wipes her eyes.

They stroll arm in arm through the pet food section.

"I wish I'd gone to Italy," Sue says. "I always wanted to do that.

And I wanted to live in California. Maybe not forever. Just to try it. A cottage on a beach."

"Really?" Shelby is surprised. She cannot imagine her mother in California.

"And I wish I'd had more sex before I married your father."

"Mom!"

"I'm telling you these things so you won't make the same mistakes I did."

"I already have," Shelby informs her. "And more."

"But you have time. You can still do everything, Shelby."

They are in Shelby's least favorite section. Puppies.

"Let's stop." Sue leans on the railing. There are two pugs and a little poodle and a dopey-looking golden retriever. "I always wanted a dog, but your dad was against it."

"Why did you always do what he said?"

"What makes you think I did?"

They both laugh. Shelby's dad is kind of clueless. He's probably sitting in the same spot where they left him with Blinkie on his lap. Maybe he's talking to his girlfriend on the phone.

"I was in love once," Sue says. "My college roommate's brother. I was at Wellesley. But he was too much for me. I didn't know if I could measure up in their family. They were all somebodies."

"So you picked a nobody?"

"I already knew your father from high school. He was working in his father's store. I'd see him when I came home during vacations. We weren't a match, but I thought he was loyal and decent. Maybe I was afraid to go for real love. Don't do what I did," Sue says.

"Okay," Shelby says.

"I mean it. Don't feel bad about Ben. I let my life happen. I don't want that for you." Sue is becoming distraught. "Don't take the easy way."

"Okay." Shelby crosses her heart with her hand. "I'll do it the hard way."

"This isn't a joke!" Sue says.

"Mom, I promise."

A salesgirl spies them watching the puppies and comes over. "Want to see one?"

"The fuzzy one," Sue says.

Shelby doesn't have the heart to say no. Her mom sounds like a little girl.

The salesgirl gets the poodle out of its cage. It's wriggly and excited.

"He is so cute," the salesgirl says.

She dumps the poodle into Sue's arms, and the dog leaps up to lick Sue's face.

"This isn't sanitary," Shelby declares. "They say dogs don't have germs in their mouths, but they do. They lick their own asses."

"Oh, Shelby, stop looking at all the negatives. He is adorable. Hey, buddy," Sue croons. The poodle is white with a tiny black nose. "Little bitty buddy."

Shelby knows a sucker when she sees one. Her mother is falling for the poodle.

"He can fit in a tote bag so you can take him everywhere," the salesgirl blathers. "You can take him to the supermarket."

"We're not interested," Shelby tells her.

The salesgirl ignores Shelby. She knows she's got a potential buyer in Sue. "He really seems to like you."

Shelby glares at the salesgirl, who is apparently completely oblivious to the negative vibes Shelby is sending out. The salesgirl leads Sue over to a play area, where customers can get down on the floor with a puppy. Shelby stands on the other side of the half door watching her mother tossing a stuffed animal for the poodle to fetch.

"We're supposed to be getting a wig, Mom."

Sue Richmond gazes up, bright-eyed. "I love him." She sees Shelby's panicked expression. "I know I can't get him. It wouldn't be fair. I can't get him, then leave him all alone after I die."

The poodle clambers onto Sue's lap.

"You're not dying," Shelby says. She sounds unconvincing even to herself.

Sue snuggles the puppy and whispers something to him.

"Fine. He's cute," Shelby admits. "He's like a cotton ball."

"I want him more than I've ever wanted anything," Sue says.

Shelby heads over to the salesgirl, who is letting some teenagers play with the golden retriever.

"We've got a problem with the puppy." Shelby reaches into her backpack and brings out her old ID, from when she was still the manager of a sister store.

"I didn't know you were a manager." The salesgirl is nervous.

"I'm taking that puppy to a veterinary hospital. I think it may have some medical issues. Ever hear of kennel cough?"

"I didn't hear him cough," the girl says, flustered.

"Get your hearing checked," Shelby suggests.

Shelby briskly returns to the play area, where she's left her mother. She picks up the poodle. "Let's go."

Sue follows her through the pet food aisle. "We still have the poodle," she says, confused.

Shelby grabs two cans of puppy food and stuffs them into her backpack.

"Shelby! Are you crazy?"

"We're taking this dog. We're liberating him."

"That salesgirl is going to get fired, Shelby. I won't have it!"

They've come to the checkout, so Shelby stops and shows her ID to an older man working the register. "I'm taking this puppy to be seen by a vet. The girl in the back had no choice but to let me take him."

The older man glances at her ID card. "Okay, Miss Richmond."

They walk quickly, and when they get to the parking lot, they run. They get into the car, laughing like wild women.

"He called you Miss Richmond," Sue says. "That's a first."

Shelby hands the poodle to her mother. "Happy?" she says.

"Oh, Shelby, he is the cutest thing. Your father's going to have a fit, not that I give a damn." Sue pets the dog curled up in her arms, his nose hidden in her sweater. "Hi, Buddy," she says.

"Tell me you're not calling him Buddy."

"Yes I am. And when I die and you come to get him, I want you to go on calling him Buddy."

They drive along Main Street. They're not stopping at the wig store. Instead they go to the park and let Buddy play in the grass. He pees first thing while Sue and Shelby sit on the bench near a picnic table. Shelby takes out the rest of the joint she began in the car.

"Are you going to get arrested for stealing the puppy?" Sue asks.

"The cops have bigger criminals to go after." Shelby lights up and inhales.

Sue studies her. "I hear it helps people with nausea and pain."

"So they say."

Sue takes the joint, inhales, then starts to cough.

"Keep the smoke in," Shelby advises.

"Kennel cough," Sue says, and they both laugh. Sue inhales a few more times. "It doesn't do a thing," she insists.

Shelby retrieves the puppy and has it sit in Sue's lap again. She thinks of all the dreams her mother had. "Want to go to California?" Shelby asks. "I'm at your service. I'll do whatever you want."

"I don't care about California. I love you more than anything in the world, Shelby. More than my own life. More than Buddy."

"You've only known Buddy for an hour," Shelby jokes.

"Love has nothing to do with time or space." Sue takes another puff. "This is so weird."

"What?" Shelby smiles. Her mother sounds like a little girl again.

"I really want ice cream. I haven't been hungry for weeks."

"Let's go to Baskin-Robbins."

They walk back to the car, Buddy in Sue's arms.

"Your favorite was always cherry vanilla," Sue says. "I like pistachio."

"Dad always brought you chocolate."

"That's how much he knew me," Sue says, as if their relationship was already in the past.

The puppy has fallen asleep, wrapped in Sue's sweater. He looks perfectly comfortable. A white cotton ball.

"This is my perfect day," Sue says once they're settled in the car again. She reaches into her purse and brings out a card. "I've been carrying this around to give to you."

Shelby feels a rush of some raw emotion she can't place.

"From your angel," Sue says.

"Is it Helene?" Shelby asks.

"No. Helene can't get out of bed, honey. You know that. Your angel is a big man. Like a wrestler. Maybe a sumo wrestler."

Shelby laughs.

"He left his car running," Sue says, "so he could make his getaway if anyone saw him. I was watching through the living room window the whole time. He waved to me."

Shelby grins. Her mother really is stoned. "And did he have wings?"

Sue laughs. "Of course not! Let's get serious here. Let's go get our ice cream. I'm starving."

Sue hands over the postcard, and Shelby studies the photo. It's her in her fourth-grade class photograph. There she is, in the front row. She looks so cute, with her long brown hair and her frilly dress. She has a big smile, as if she's sure of a bright future. Shelby turns the card over. She feels a tightness in her chest. *Love something.*

Her mother is stroking the little dog. "You're my baby," she says.

The afternoon has turned gray. Rain will soon fall. Shelby had planned to take the train back to the city after supper, but she decides to stay and sleep on the couch. She used to read piles of fairy tales. Her favorites were always tales of transformation: brothers who became swans, beasts who hid their kind hearts. She always put her faith in animals rather than in human beings. After they went to Chincoteague, Shelby begged her mother for a horse. Sue said their neighborhood wasn't zoned for horses, so instead they went out to a farm in Blue Point, where they fed someone's ponies handfuls of hay. It has taken her this long to realize how cold it was that day, and how her mother was shivering, but still stood with Shelby in the barn for over an hour.

Shelby wants to spend tomorrow with her mother. She feels her love inside her as if it were as tangible as blood and bones. They'll go out for ice cream every afternoon and try every flavor there is. She'll start house-training Buddy. She'll learn how to make onion soup, her mom's favorite. Things will get worse, but there's no reason to think about that now. Tonight Shelby will look out the window to see if her angel returns, and if he does she'll ask him how he knows so much about love. She wishes he would come to her tonight, climb in through the window to lie down beside her and explain how it's possible to love someone so much and still manage to carry on when you have to let them go.

CHAPTER
11

Shelby sits on the picnic table in the backyard. It's cold and there's a light snow falling and her mother has just been buried. The past months are a blur. October and November were swallowed up by illness and hospitals. Toward the end Shelby left her dogs with Maravelle and set up residence in her parents' living room. Her mother's hospital bed was right next to the couch, and sometimes they held hands as they slept. Shelby found all of her old books in a box in the basement. She read the color-coded series of Andrew Lang's fairy tales to her mother. They became lost in an enchanted cottage with vines growing over the window. It was dark and it was quiet and they could hear each other softly breathing. Every story had the same message: what was deep inside could only be deciphered by someone who understood how easily a heart could be broken.

"Wake up," Shelby would say whenever her mother drifted off as she was reading. "The best part is just about to happen." But as time went on, Sue was asleep nearly all the time, with Buddy beside her in bed. Shelby had to pick up the poodle and carry him outside so he would pee. He always ran right back inside. *My baby,* Sue would say, *how can I leave you?* Shelby was never certain if her mom was talking to her or to Buddy. Now it's over and they've left her in the cold ground. Shelby can't bring herself to go inside the house. Her fingers are freezing and her toes are turning to ice inside her new fleece-lined boots, but she doesn't care. She has the grill out, and she's burning the old Misty books. She doused them with lighter fluid and they flared with fire and all the pages turned orange, then blue, then black. It's over. All of it. It's smoke.

Dozens of neighbors are in the living room, partaking of the casseroles they brought over. There's macaroni and cheese and meat loaf and chicken and dumplings. Comfort food. The same recipes Shelby's mom used to make when Shelby had her nervous breakdown. Back then, Shelby had wanted to waste away; for weeks she only consumed what was pure: water, green apples, celery. Now, she opens her mouth and lets snowflakes fall onto her tongue. She's empty and she feels like she'll stay that way.

Maravelle and Mrs. Diaz attended the funeral, but afterward Shelby assured them there was no need for them to come back to the house. She'd rather they take care of her dogs, left at the house in Valley Stream. The truth is she didn't want them to see her in her parents' basement. She is never going to sleep on the couch again, and her mother's hospital bed has already been picked up by the furniture rental company. She thinks she spied Ben Mink and his mother among the mourners, but she's not sure, since she couldn't bring herself to look at anyone and see their pity. She hasn't seen Ben since their mortifying date, when he walked out on her and she knew he was right to do so. If Ben had even tried to convey his sympathies, Shelby would have fallen apart.

"Maybe you should spend the night with us," Mrs. Diaz had suggested before they dropped her off. "You can sleep in Jasmine's room."

"Mami's right," Maravelle had said. "You shouldn't be here alone."

But she is alone, no matter where she is, no matter whom she's with. She was being driven home from the cemetery by the Diazes because she didn't want to get in the limo with her father. His girlfriend had attended the funeral. Her name is Patti something. She introduced herself to people as a friend of Sue's. Shelby didn't catch her last name, or maybe she didn't want to. *It's the funeral,* she wanted to scream at her father. *Couldn't you wait one more fucking day?* Shelby loves Maravelle; she wishes she could spend the night in Valley Stream, but being with Maravelle and her mother would only make her sadder. She doesn't have a mother anymore. There's no one to whom she's the most important person in the world.

Shelby's father is in the kitchen with Patti and some friends. Shelby doesn't care that people say widowers with good marriages always marry again quickly. She knows how lonely her mom was in her marriage, how much she wished for something more. All Shelby cares about is that her mother is in the ground, miles away, all alone on a dark evening when the snow is falling. Shelby may have screwed up her own life, but she has high standards for everyone else, including her father. She expects people to act like human beings.

Shelby certainly doesn't want to sit in the living room and hear how sorry people are and what a wonderful person her mother was and that it's all for the best that Sue Richmond isn't in pain any longer. Instead she is burning her childhood books in the grill in the backyard. She wants to be alone, only she isn't. Her mother's little poodle, Buddy, has gotten out through the pet door. Shelby's mom had the door put in when she couldn't get out of bed anymore. She was afraid that people would forget about the dog, and they have. He looks bedraggled. "Hey," Shelby says to the poodle.

Buddy doesn't look at her.

"Hey, stupid, can't you hear me?" Shelby says, then she feels horrible. Her mother loved Buddy, and now he's sitting on the steps with a broken heart and Shelby's calling him stupid. She promised her mother she would take him, and she wonders if anyone has thought to feed Buddy during the past few days. She gets off the table and goes over to him. Buddy looks down, as if he expects Shelby to hit him. She picks him up and feels him shaking; it's all too sad, his chicken-thin bones, his fuzzy baby fur. He slept next to Shelby's mother every night. Now he's cold. Shelby tucks him inside her coat. She can feel him shivering against her chest. She'll be damned if she leaves him here with these people who've come to honor her mother and didn't even notice whether or not her dog is alive.

Shelby watches the books burn. She wonders if words are pouring down on other people's houses, sad words, like *beast* and *mourn* and *sorrow* and *mother*. She pokes at the cinders as the paper turns black and flaky. A few sparks fly up. There goes her childhood, nothing but ashes. Shelby slips out of the backyard with Buddy curled up near her breastbone inside her coat, then walks along the path that sparkles with snowflakes. She's reminded of the time when she would get lost on purpose and her mother would look for her, shouting her name as though calling for a lost dog. Now she burns with regret when she thinks that she hid from her own mother. She should have leapt up and waved her arms. She should have gotten into her mom's car and said, *Thank you for rescuing me.*

On a whim she stops at the mailbox before she heads off. It is a Sunday evening, there's been no delivery, but she opens the box. Inside is a postcard. It's blue and it looks like a piece of ice. Shelby reaches for it. The front of the card is an illustration of heaven in blues and black and silver. There are constellations she recognizes: the archer, the crab, the fish, the lion. There is a shooting star in the sky and a tiny photograph of her mother from a yearbook back when she was the school librarian. Shelby's eyes smart with tears. It is so cold they feel frozen. She flips the postcard over. *Remember someone.*

She folds the postcard into her coat pocket and heads off. She has a trembling feeling. She wants to believe in faith and trust, but she doesn't think she can. The snow is starting to collect, and it crunches under her boots. She heads over to the 7-Eleven. When she steps inside, the heat of the store is overwhelming. There's loud music playing. Elvis's "Blue Christmas." It's almost Christmas, not that Shelby cares. She hasn't even noticed that decorations are going up or that most of the houses on her block are strung with colored lights. At the counter there is an electronic Santa who cries out *Ho Ho Ho* every time someone passes by. He does it when Shelby asks for a pack of Marlboro and a Bic lighter. She hasn't smoked for some time, but what's the difference now? At the last minute she buys a pair of striped gloves displayed beside the counter. They're purple and black and look like they'd fit a toddler, but the fabric stretches and shapes to each individual's hand. There's a No Dogs sign, but the guy at the register doesn't notice the bump under Shelby's coat. Or maybe he thinks she has a tumor and is too polite to ask.

Shelby lights up in the parking lot. The smoke and the cold air hurt her lungs. Her father won't notice her gone. He never came to search for her when she was missing as a teenager, calling her name like a dog's. Shelby perches on the concrete stoop outside the store. If Helene were here she'd do something silly to cheer Shelby—she'd throw her arms out and spin in a circle, she'd tell a joke, or just sit beside Shelby and sing "The Itsy Bitsy Spider" or some other nursery song. Shelby opens her coat so Buddy can see out. He doesn't seem to want to go anywhere. He's probably the kind of dog who doesn't like to get his feet wet. Shelby leans up against the brick wall and blows the smoke away from Buddy's head. When she was in high school the wild kids hung out here.

Shelby never came here. She was a good girl with a 3.8 average who planned to go to NYU and study history. Now the past is the last thing she wants to remember.

There's one lone teenager in the parking lot tonight. He has a gold ring in his nose and his hair is long and messy. He's stomping his feet against the cold. He wears a light jacket, no gloves, no hat.

"Hey," he says to Shelby.

"Hey." She nods dismissively.

"Cold out," the kid says.

Great, Shelby thinks darkly. *A conversationalist.*

"What you got there?" He nods to Buddy.

"A dinosaur," Shelby says. "Tyrannosaurus."

"Hah. Looks like a dog to me."

"A poodle."

Shelby hopes this bit of information will be enough to satisfy this lurking kid. He's just about the last person on earth she wants to talk to.

"My friends are late," he tells her. "They were supposed to pick me up."

As if Shelby cares.

"Are you twenty-one?" he asks.

So that's the reason for all this friendly conversation. He wants something.

"Do you really think I'm going to buy you beer and put myself in criminal jeopardy because you're too young and stupid to get yourself a fake ID?"

"I'll take that as a no," the kid says.

Shelby laughs. She hadn't expected a sense of humor.

"Well, I had to try," the kid tells her.

"Leave me alone," Shelby says. "My mother's dead."

She's started to cry, so she turns her head away. The snow is really coming down now. Everything is white. Buddy has settled and his breathing is more even; maybe he fell asleep. He's a teacup poodle, which means he weighs less than six pounds.

"I believe in reincarnation," the kid informs her. He just doesn't get that Shelby wants him to leave her alone. Clearly, he's not going anywhere till his friends come for him.

"Good for you," Shelby says. "What are you, a Buddhist?"

"Nah, it's common sense. We're too fucking complex to just disappear. We get recycled. We do it all over again, only different. Better."

The thing about crying is, once you start it's not easy to stop. Shelby sits there crying, while the kid goes into the 7-Eleven. He comes out with two steaming cups and gives one to Shelby.

"So we don't freeze to death. The coffee looked like crap, so I got us green tea."

The tea in the foam cup warms Shelby's hands through her gloves. She takes a sip. It tastes fresh, like grass or new leaves.

"Want me to walk you home?" the kid asks.

"Yeah, right. I want a stranger to walk me home. Maybe you're a psycho mass murderer. And by the way, I'm twenty-six, practically old enough to be your mother. So I hope you're not hitting on me."

"My mother's dead, too. Lung cancer. I was three."

"Sorry." Just what she needs, to feel bad for him.

The kid sits down with his back against the wall. He lights a cigarette. Camel. No filter.

"Do you get the irony in your smoking?" Shelby says.

The kid doesn't answer. He just smokes.

"Do you think your mother came back?" Shelby asks him.

"Definitely. She's a cardinal who lives in my backyard."

Shelby snorts and sips her tea.

"I don't care if you don't believe me," the kid says.

"How do you know it's her?"

"How do you know it's snowing? Some things are what they are."

A car pulls up; the headlights are blinding. Snow falls in the streams of light. The flakes are big and wet, and they're sticking when they hit the cement.

"Are these your friends?" Shelby asks.

"Nah. My friends don't drive Volvos."

It is indeed a Volvo.

Ben Mink, Shelby's ex-boyfriend, gets out. It's the kind of car he always said he would buy, the safest model on the road. "Shelby?" he says.

Shelby's eyes are still aglow from the bright headlights even though they've been turned off. Maybe she's going blind. Is it really Ben Mink? They haven't seen each other since their nonexistent blind date. Shelby never contacted the dating service again, but she should have. She should have asked for her money back.

"What are you doing here, Shelby?" Ben asks.

"I couldn't stand all the good intentions of the neighbors who came to honor my mother," she tells him.

"So instead you're sitting here in the cold with Aaron Feinberg?"

Shelby looks at the kid.

"Hey, Ben," the kid says. "How about buying me a six-pack?"

"Yeah. Right," Ben remarks. "In your dreams. I'm not getting arrested for you, Feinberg."

Shelby is confused. "You know each other?"

"He lives on Western Avenue," Ben says. It's around the corner from Ben's parents' house. "My sister used to babysit him."

"Could you please not mention that?" Aaron huffs. "It's humiliating."

"I came to the funeral," Ben tells Shelby. "You left so fast I didn't get to talk to you. I thought I'd see you at the house, but by the time my mom had finished the pot roast to bring over, you'd split. I've been driving around looking for you for close to an hour." Ben puts his hand out to help Shelby up. Inside her coat, Buddy starts moving around. The dog sticks his head out. "What the hell is that?" Ben asks.

"A poodle," Aaron tells him.

"My mother's," Shelby says.

"Let's get out of here, Shelby," Ben says.

They head for the Volvo with Aaron following them. "Could you give me a ride home? My friends didn't show up and I'm freezing my ass off."

"I don't think so," Ben says.

"It's not out of our way," Shelby murmurs.

Ben gives her a look.

Shelby shrugs. "He's a kid."

"Get in the back, Feinberg."

Aaron hops in the back. Shelby slides into the passenger seat. She takes Buddy out of her coat and deposits him on the floor near her feet. He just sits there, like he's afraid to move.

Aaron Feinberg leans forward, one arm on the back of Shelby's seat, the other around Ben's seat. "You wouldn't happen to have any weed, would you?"

"What the hell are you doing with this guy?" Ben asks Shelby. "He's bad news."

"The hell I am," Aaron says.

"I saw you at the funeral," Shelby admits to Ben. "I just couldn't talk to anyone."

"Except for this idiot?" Ben says of Aaron. "Here we are, Feinberg," he tells the kid as they turn onto Western Avenue. "Now get the hell out."

It's a pretty nice house, big, brick, with a double lot.

"Thanks, Ben Mink the big Stink," Aaron says as he opens the door.

Shelby laughs despite herself, but covers her mouth with her gloved hand when Ben throws her a look.

"Get going," he growls at Aaron.

"Look for cardinals," Aaron reminds Shelby as he gets out of the car. "She'll be there."

"What's that supposed to mean?" Ben asks as they watch Aaron lope toward his house.

"He thinks that when his mother died she came back as a cardinal," Shelby informs Ben.

"His mother's not dead. She's a psychologist. Marian Feinberg. My parents made me go to her a couple of times when I was a teenager and they found drugs in my room."

"Are you kidding me?"

"I told you he was bad news."

Shelby laughs. She nearly doubles over.

"You think it's funny? He's a liar and a bullshit artist looking for sympathy," Ben says.

"I think he just wanted me to feel better."

"Did you?"

"I kinda did."

"Sucker. How about I sell you the Verrazano Bridge or the Eiffel Tower?"

Ben is the kind of person who can put aside the way Shelby betrayed him in a time of sorrow. By now, Shelby knows she was an idiot to dump him. Ben could say *I told you so*, but he doesn't. They can almost act as if they were friends. Maybe he's been her angel all along.

"Are you leaving me postcards?" she asks.

"Postcards?"

"With advice. Suggestions for life."

"Nope. You never listened to my advice," Ben says. "I hope whoever it is doing it is faring better than I did."

There are very few cars on the road and it's slippery, but Ben doesn't mind driving. Shelby has yet to drive in the snow. She's afraid of flashbacks. The sound of Helene hitting the windshield. The broken charm bracelet. How Shelby howled and couldn't get up off the ice. She's afraid of ruining someone else's life. She wonders if there's some sort of poisonous antibody in her blood that hurts anyone she's close to. Maybe she should live on an island, like lepers were made to do. Ben says he doesn't mind going back to the cemetery so that

Buddy can say good-bye. Shelby thinks that's the dog's problem, the reason he's so quiet and depressed. He wasn't at the funeral, so he doesn't know where his beloved owner is. Maybe he thinks she's coming back.

They park on a side road. Ben climbs over the fence first. Shelby hands Buddy to him, then scrambles over.

"How are we supposed to find it?" Ben asks.

"There was an angel nearby."

Ben laughs. "This place is filled with angels. Maybe one of them is sending you messages."

"I'm not crazy," Shelby says.

"I know that." Ben looks at her, hard. "I'm the one who told you that."

They walk on, Shelby carrying Buddy. They actually have to trudge.

"There are more dead people in the world than there are alive people," Ben says. "I never realized that before."

"Is that supposed to be comforting?" Shelby asks.

Shelby's mom had told her months ago that Ben had a great job; he makes over a hundred thousand a year. Still, it's a surprise when he informs Shelby that he's bought a house out here, in Dix Hills.

"You're moving back?" When they were young they couldn't wait to get out of town; it was all they talked about.

The snow is shin-deep, and Shelby has to blink in order to see.

"Yeah, well, I'm getting married," Ben says. "That's what the new house is all about. She's a pharmacist, too."

"Aha," Shelby says. Her heart has dropped. She just keeps breathing.

They walk on. Ben is obviously waiting for more of a response. He doesn't get it.

"Is that all you have to say?"

"Congratulations?" Shelby tries.

What is she supposed to do? Tell him she ruined their relationship like she ruined everything else and she doesn't wish him luck for a single second even though he's walking with her through a cemetery in a snowstorm?

"What's she like?" Shelby says, hoping her jealousy doesn't rise through her skin in green puffs.

"Her name is Ana. Her family is from Cuba, but she grew up in Northport. We met at a conference and it turned out we had mutual friends."

Shelby didn't know Ben had friends. She doesn't. Only Maravelle. She can't imagine who else would put up with her.

Now that Ben has started talking about his intended he can't seem to stop. He has a dreamy expression. "She has long black hair. She calls me Benny."

"Great," Shelby says. "Perfect. Don't tell me any more. Okay?"

"Sorry," Ben says. "I didn't think you'd care."

Shelby walks faster. She's afraid she's crossing over graves because it's impossible to tell where the paths end under all the snow. Finally there is the angel near her mother's grave site; Shelby is sure of it. Her wings are feathered stone. It's hard to tell where the fresh graves are because of the new cover of snow, but Shelby finds the spot.

"You've got a natural sense of direction," Ben says.

"Is that supposed to make me feel better? And did you have to tell me how beautiful Ana was?"

"I wanted to tell you I was getting married before someone else did. And I didn't say she was beautiful."

But Shelby can tell from Ben's tone that she is. He just doesn't want to wound Shelby any more than he already has with another woman's beauty. The dog starts to whimper, so Shelby puts him down in the snow.

"Here you are," Shelby tells Buddy. "So now you know, she's not coming back. Not if you wait for a hundred years. She's left you and you're all alone, so get used to it."

Buddy stands there shivering.

Shelby doesn't even know she's crying until Ben puts his arms around her. "I'm sorry," he says. "Shelby."

She sobs until she can't breathe. When she pulls herself together, she backs away from him. She takes off one of the gloves she bought at the 7-Eleven and blows her nose in it.

"Lovely," Ben jokes.

Shelby laughs. Then she looks down. She doesn't see the dog.

"Oh, no," she says. Everything is white. Blindingly white. "Damn it, Ben, the dog is missing!"

Shelby is in a panic. She starts clapping her hands together and calling for the dog. She wanders blindly through the snow. "Buddy," she calls. Her mother will never forgive her. It was the one thing she asked of Shelby, and she can't even do that right.

Ben comes up behind Shelby and takes her arm. "Over there," he says.

Shelby turns. There is the poodle sitting beside the angel. Shelby's sobbing must have scared him. He's too afraid to move. Shelby runs and picks him up. He's soaked with snow.

"Buddy," she says. She feels about ten years old and so lost no one will ever find her.

Ben Mink is there. "It's okay," he tells her.

"Is it?" Shelby says. How could she ever have thrown him away?

"It will be," Ben says.

They walk back following the tracks they left. Soon those tracks will be gone. A foot of snow will fall by midnight. Shelby climbs the fence first. Ben hands the dog over, and follows. Once they get into the car, they turn up the heat and Shelby towels the dog dry with a blanket Ben keeps in the backseat.

Ben gets out and goes around to the trunk. When he gets in again and sits behind the wheel, he's got a large, fancy box. "I bought you something. I knew I'd see you. I just didn't think it would be at a 7-Eleven."

"It's not my birthday or anything," Shelby says.

"It's just a present, Shelby."

"Because my mother's dead?" Her voice breaks and then she's embarrassed.

"Because I wanted to give this to you. I've wanted to for a long time."

Shelby opens the box. It's a Burberry raincoat. The last time she saw him she'd gone on and on about wanting a Burberry raincoat and he must have believed her.

"Ben," she says.

"I was an ass the last time I saw you. I didn't want you to know how much you used to mean to me. When we were together I could never afford to get you anything nice. This is for old times' sake."

Shelby decides she doesn't want to go back to her parents' house. She has a timetable for the Long Island Rail Road in her pocket, so Ben drives her to the station. This is as over as a relationship can get. She used to mean something to him. Ben gets out of the Volvo to wait for the train with her. Shelby has Buddy tucked into her coat. The raincoat is draped over her arm.

"Well, that was fun," Shelby says. "Remind me to invite you to the next funeral."

"Maybe she will be a cardinal," Ben says.

Shelby laughs. "You said that kid was a liar and bad news."

"That doesn't mean he's not right."

When the train arrives Ben hugs Shelby as best he can without crushing Buddy.

"It's okay if your girlfriend is beautiful," Shelby says. "I want you to be happy."

Ben grins. "Really? You never did before."

They laugh and embrace, then Shelby gets on the train. At this hour, it's almost empty and she has a double seat all to herself. There is so much snow it's like taking a train through the clouds. Buddy's even breathing means he's fallen asleep again. She'll keep her promise to her mother and take him home. As they near Penn Station, Shelby considers leaving the raincoat behind for some needy person to find. It's not really her style. Then she realizes she's the needy person. She didn't thank Ben, and she probably should have, but maybe he knows that she's grateful. Maybe he understands that saying thank you can be just as hard as saying good-bye.

CHAPTER

12

Ever since her mother's death Shelby has had trouble sleeping. She's filled with regret, it's in her blood and bones, it lies down beside her with its head on her pillow and whispers a list of all she's done wrong. She wishes she hadn't burned her childhood books and could read them every night; perhaps then she would find some peace. She wishes she had spent more time with her mother, and that she could call her on the phone. She dials her home number late at night, but either no one picks up or her father answers, his voice full of worry and sleep. Her father has sent her all the sympathy cards from her mother's friends and from the co-worker she had when she was a librarian. *We loved her so. She was one of a kind. We will miss and mourn her.* In between the Hall-marks, there's a postcard. It's plain white, no illustration this time. *Trust someone,* the message reads in black ink. It is so simple and so pure that Shelby fears it's the writer's last message.

As the weather improves, Shelby takes to roaming the streets whenever sleep eludes her. *Walking is man's best medicine,* Hippocrates stated and maybe it's true. In the evenings she heads along Broadway, merging with the late-night crowd. Occasionally she stops for a drink at Balthazar on Spring Street, where her usual waiter knows she wants the cheapest white wine. On other occasions she stands outside a tattoo parlor called Scorpio in the East Village, although she never goes in. Would she be transformed once she stepped over the threshold, with her sins and sorrows revealed to all in ink? On one occasion, while she was considering if she should finally get the tattoo she's always had in mind for herself, someone inside opens the shop door for her. "Just looking," she calls as she hurries away.

Shelby often thinks about the tattooed girl in Union Square and how they might have exchanged lives on the day Shelby took the dogs. In fairy tales, such things happened, you stole from someone, then were handed their fate as a punishment. She has always wondered what the difference was between herself and the girl in the park, why she had been saved from her own desire to destroy herself. Shelby was the one who had to be tied down to her hospital bed, who would cut herself with anything she could get her hands on, including plastic forks and spoons. But that girl is like a little sister inside of her now. She doesn't know why she didn't turn out like the girl in Union Square, screaming at passersby, caught in the web of her own pain, but on nights when she's reading her veterinary journals, and the dogs are sleeping, she wonders if it's possible that when she rescued them, they rescued her as well.

The winter has been a hard one, and in April it's still chilly. Shelby sleeps in sweaters, and sometimes in the Burberry raincoat Ben gave her. When she thinks of him she wants to cry, but she doesn't. She wonders if it's possible that she's lost the ability to produce tears. When her apartment feels too small, she sits on the fire escape, the way she used to with Ben. In the spring chill the Hudson turns a silvery color, as if the moon has fallen straight down to the river bottom, a cold, white stone. On clear nights it's possible to see stars in the black sky above Tenth Avenue, a rarity in the city. A few brave leaves have shown themselves on the flowering pear trees, but they tremble in the wind that comes off the river, and some of them freeze solid on thin, wavering branches.

Shelby has had a terrible cold, which turns out to be pneumonia. At night she feels like she's drowning. She coughs so loudly her downstairs neighbors, who fight so furiously she can hear shoes hitting the wall, complain about her hacking. She orders egg drop soup from the Hunan Kitchen, and throws most of it away along with the fortune cookies. *The lost are in need of a compass,* she thinks her fortune will read. *What becomes of someone who is unbecoming?* Her dreams are all of water. Sometimes she spies a girl swimming. She knows it's not Helene. Helene never went into the ocean; she was terrified of sharks and crabs. Then Shelby realizes she's seeing herself out in the sea, the girl she used to be before all of this happened, when she still had hope and a future she wasn't afraid to know.

Her illness worsens; she cannot stop coughing. She finally goes to the ER at Bellevue one night when she can't breathe. She's given antibiotics and an inhaler and is told to keep hydrated. *She who drinks water will never thirst for knowledge.* As she's leaving Shelby stops to lace her boots. An orderly looks her up and down. She stares back at him, annoyed.

"Interested?" the orderly says with a thick Russian accent. "I'm single."

Only now does Shelby realize he is the one who took her to see the old man who collapsed on the pavement years earlier, on the day she met Harper Levy. She can hardly remember Harper's face, he's become a ghost in her memory, but she will never forget this orderly. Now Shelby has long hair that reaches past her shoulders and is likely her best feature. Maybe that's why the Russian doesn't recognize her. All the same, she feels as if she's stumbled upon an old friend. She goes up to him, surprising him with a kiss on the cheek. "You did me a favor once," Shelby tells him.

"Good for me," he says, amused.

On her way home from the ER, Shelby wonders if there was ever a year in which spring never came. She sits out on the fire escape to have her dinner, hot and sour soup and shrimp toast. *A girl who is cold has only herself to blame. If you have burned a book, don't complain that there is nothing to read.* Shelby has on two sweaters, her raincoat, and a scarf looped around her throat. The weather is cloudy and miserable, but birds have built a nest on the fire escape. Shelby enjoys watching the nesting birds as she recovers. But one pale morning she wakes to find the nest has been abandoned. Some larger bird, perhaps a hawk that is said to circle the neighborhood, has torn it apart. A single blue egg has been left behind. She looks it up in her copy of *Birds of America*. Her birds would have been robins, another rarity in Manhattan.

This is the weekend when Ben Mink is getting married. Shelby was invited to La Scala restaurant in Huntington for the wedding dinner. Ben is nothing if not gracious, unless you cheat on him behind his back, then he calls you every name in the book and slams out the door so he can cry in the hallway and hold his broken heart in his hands, so damaged and ripped apart it's clear he's never coming back. Although Shelby never bothered to RSVP, she's kept the invitation taped to her refrigerator. She's torturing herself with it every time she gets something to eat. There is a photograph of Ben and his impossibly beautiful bride-to-be, Ana. Shelby has spent the past week obsessed by wicked thoughts. She is vindictive, even when she's the guilty party. Perhaps it's always true that when you wreck your own life you blame everyone else for your misfortune. She wants Ben's wedding day to be ruined and has imagined dozens of possible scenarios, from lightning strikes to floods. Now her wish has come true. It's April and it's snowing. She feels a stab of joy when she wakes to see six inches of powdery white has fallen onto Tenth Avenue. No wonder the robins abandoned their nest. Perhaps Ben should do the same with his marriage. Now the wedding guests will have trouble on the Long Island Expressway. Their cars will skid and swerve, and those who do manage to arrive at the service on time will drag in wearing boots, the hems of their dresses soaking wet.

If she were to go to Ben's wedding she would cut in during the first dance. She'd have on a long black skirt and hiking boots; she'd be so awkward and bitter no one present would imagine she was Ben's old girlfriend, the one who dumped him and then regretted it ever after, the way she's regretted everything in her life. It's a good day to be alone. She's horrible company, worse than usual. Even the dogs leave her be. Shelby tries not to think about centerpieces of roses and orchids and a red velvet wedding cake. Ben actually talked about those things to her on drunken evenings when he thought they'd be the couple to be marrying. He wanted to go to Mexico on a honeymoon. He had it all planned.

In the afternoon Shelby walks through the snow to East Third Street. On Ben Mink's wedding day she finally goes inside the tattoo parlor to mark herself for her sins. She stomps fluffy snow off her boots. Three men are in mid-conversation, which stops dead when they see Shelby. Because of the weather they're clearly surprised to have a customer, particularly someone like Shelby. She used to resemble a homeless person, someone who could snap, who might have a knife in her pocket. People often crossed the street when they saw her, bald head, torn red sweatshirt, but now, in her Burberry raincoat and new pair of boots, she may look too upscale for her surroundings. All the walls are covered with tattoo patterns, some intricate and tribal, others colorful and traditional. There's low jazz playing on the radio. The men all have elaborate tattoos. One guy says something to his cohorts, then approaches Shelby. He's dark and brooding, a large man with a demeanor that can be taken as threatening. He appraises Shelby in a way that makes her feel uncomfortable.

"Just looking?" he says with a scrim of sarcasm.

"I'd like a tattoo." For some reason Shelby feels judged. Her hackles are up. "Isn't that what you do?"

"I've seen you lurking around before, but you always disappeared."

Shelby furrows her brow. "I don't lurk." Then she thinks of the time the door opened and she managed to avoid a shadowy figure. "Well, maybe sometimes," she admits.

The artist has dark, liquid eyes, with an intense gaze that goes right through her. "Where do you want it?" he asks. When he sees that she's puzzled, he grins. In his amused expression she sees the glimmer of another side of him. "The tattoo?"

Shelby has considered her choice for a very long time. "Over my heart."

"Are you sure?" He's not handsome, but something about him draws her in. Can it be that stepping through the door of this shop has brought her into a world where another fate is possible?

"I'm sure," Shelby tells him. She hopes that if you reveal something on the outside, it won't cause as much pain on the inside. It will float to the surface and leave you alone.

The tattoo artist holds up his hands, as if giving in to someone who is clearly making a mistake. "You're the customer."

They go into the back room. The tattooist says his name is James. He informs her that he learned his craft at the School of Visual Arts on Twenty-Third Street and in prison. If that's supposed to scare her, it doesn't. She's always felt she should be in prison for what she did to Helene. She used to fall asleep in her parents' basement waiting for the police to knock on the door.

"Drugs," the tattooist tells her. "When you're young and desperate for something you act before you think."

"I don't believe you were ever young," Shelby blurts. Then, embarrassed, she apologizes. "Sorry. I don't know why I said that."

"Because it's true. Old soul."

There are several tattoo chairs separated by black curtains and one faux leather table that reminds Shelby of something a masseuse might use. The room smells like sweat and incense. For a minute Shelby's afraid she might have to get naked. She already feels overly exposed. "I'm not undressing," she says.

"Did I ask you to?"

Again, she feels embarrassed. They exchange a look that makes her even more ill at ease.

"Just the clothes that cover the area," he tells her.

Shelby slips off her raincoat and sweater, then sits on the table.

"Do you want me to tell you about the process?" James pulls up a stool. "Some people feel more comfortable if they know what I'm doing. Like when a doctor explains the steps of a surgery before he starts cutting."

"Don't tell me anything," Shelby says.

She tugs her T-shirt over her head. She's wearing a bra, which she assumes she can keep on. It's nothing special, she doesn't believe in name brands like Victoria's Secret, despite her Burberry raincoat from Ben. Her bra is simple, black, a little too small for her, something she didn't realize until this moment.

"We haven't discussed the art," James says, his eyes all over her.

"It's a name."

"Of course." He sounds contemptuous. "You want a heart with that? And a *forever*?"

Shelby glares at him, unsettled. "Do you make fun of all your clients?"

"Names are usually a bad idea." He sits beside her on the table, close enough so that their legs touch. Shelby feels burned. She moves her leg away. She's here for only one thing. She doesn't want to talk to anyone, she wants to get this over with, but the artist won't shut up. "I think of life as a book of stories," he goes on. "You move through the stories and the characters change. But once you have a name on your skin you are stuck with one story, even if it's a bad one."

Shelby is surprised by the way he expresses himself. It's not what she would have expected given his tough appearance. But she disagrees with him and isn't afraid to say so. "Well, I think of life as a novel. You can't just hop out of the mess you're in and into another story. You carry it all with you."

"You're wrong," he says.

Maybe she is. She tells him about *The Illustrated Man,* how it's a book of stories, but those stories are threaded together, tattoo by tattoo, until they become a novel. Bradbury's book is a hybrid and that's why she loves it so. That's what life is, Shelby claims.

"I'll have to read it. Sounds great."

"You read?" Shelby says.

It's supposed to be a joke, but it falls flat. James smiles wearily. He's used to this kind of judgment. Everything he's wearing is black, including heavy black boots, not unlike the ones Shelby used to wear. Now her pretty leather boots have high heels. Frankly, they're not very good for trekking through snow. James takes off his sweatshirt, and she sees his arms are colored sleeves filled with dragons and roses, skulls and blue-black geometric patterns. She wonders if James's tattoos come alive in burning color when he sleeps. If she spent the night with him would she know everything there was to know about him?

When he sees her staring, James rolls his shirt up his forearm. Inside a circle of thorny, blue vines there is a name. *Lee.* "Sometimes what feels right turns out to be wrong. It turns love into a burden."

Shelby actually feels a surge of jealousy when she sees the name inked onto his arm. She wonders whom he might have loved so deeply that his love became a burden. Still she shrugs. She has been planning this tattoo since the accident. "I want a name, and I don't much care what you think."

Her eyes are burning. There is a wave of grief rising to the surface. She didn't think she could cry anymore, but now it is happening in this highly inappropriate place. Shelby covers her face with her hands, mortified. Maybe it's because it's Ben Mink's wedding day and she's here alone and she still hasn't punished herself enough for her crime. "I don't cry," she manages to say.

Before she can leap off the table and pull on her shirt, James embraces her. He doesn't say anything; he just lets her cry. He doesn't tell her *It's okay* or *You'll be fine* or any of that other crap people try to tell you when you're breaking apart. For a guy who talks so much, he knows when to shut up.

"I'm an idiot," Shelby says when her tears subside. "I'm ready. Let's get this over with."

"Is it Ben's name you want?"

Shelby looks at him, more confused than ever. "You know Ben Mink?"

"I'm Jimmy," the tattoo artist explains. "From fourth grade? Out in Huntington? James Howard."

This is worse than she could have imagined. He's someone she knows, or at least she did, once upon a time. In their fourth-grade class photo session he leapt up and down so much the photographer finally tied him to a chair with a jump rope. "You're the one who shot Ben with rubber bands when he cried over Bambi."

"I didn't hurt him." James squints at her. "Did I?"

"You did. I think he has a scar. He's probably still embarrassed over that incident."

"Should I call him and make amends? I did that in AA, but I had so many other people on my list I didn't even think of Ben." James gives her a sidelong glance. "Are you two still together?"

"He's getting married today. You really don't have to worry about Ben. He's fine without amends. How did you know we were together in the first place?"

"Who do you think he bought his drugs from back home? He never mentioned the Bambi incident, so I thought he was over it. But he was always whining about you when he picked up his weed."

"Really?" Shelby is flattered.

"He was madly in love with you."

"Well, not anymore. Now he's marrying a beautiful Cuban wo-man."

"I doubt that he loves her," James says.

"He happens to love her a thousand times more than he ever loved me." Shelby's heart is racing. She doesn't want to talk about love with James Howard. "Can we get on with it?" she says briskly even though her heart is fluttering. Perhaps she has arrhythmia, a syndrome she's been reading about in a veterinary text that affects elderly dogs.

James brings out a book of lettering so Shelby can choose the style she prefers. "This isn't invisible ink," he warns. "What you write on your skin is there forever."

Shelby notices the word *Trust* written across one of his wrists when he gives her the book. She loves the thin, Gothic lines. It's just the sort of print she wants. Without thinking, she reaches for James's other arm to see what's written there as well. He pulls back; it's a gut reaction, but a strong one. Shelby nearly topples off the table, until James puts an arm out to stop her fall. They're both breathing too hard. Now she can see the ink. *Someone* is written across his other wrist. It's the most recent postcard message she received. She looks at him and he looks back at her and she can feel something between them, but she's not sure what it is. "You've been writing to me? Why would you do that? We hardly knew each other."

"I was there that night. I was high and drunk," he tells her, "and the road was a mess. I probably would have crashed if I kept driving, but you spun out coming the other direction. I stopped because your car was blocking the road. I was the one who pulled you out of the car."

Shelby is half-naked and freezing. What she remembers most about that night is how cold it was. But she remembers there was someone who told her not to close her eyes. He told her not to fall asleep. He said *Stay here* and she did.

"What about Helene?" Shelby asks.

James shakes his head. "She was crushed. I couldn't get her out. But you were breathing. What they say about saving a life is true," he adds. "You're responsible for that person forever. That's why I wrote to you. Even though you didn't really know me."

"My mom saw you leave the cards. She thought you were an angel."

"I'm not." James laughs. "Far from it."

It's a good thing James gets up to put the book of lettering away. Shelby's not sure what she might have done if the spell hadn't been broken. She wants to stop her attraction to him before she does something she'll regret.

"I had a brother who died when I was ten," he tells her when he comes back. "Meningitis. The doctor said it was just a cold and he would be fine but he wasn't. He died in the middle of the night, in the room we shared. I was there with him, in the next bed. We'd both gone swimming. We'd snuck away and biked all the way to Northport. Then he died and I didn't. I shouldn't have been saved. So I knew what you were going to feel. That's why I stayed with you until the cops came. As it turned out, I happened to have some drugs in my possession, so I didn't get to visit you in the hospital. The best I could do were the postcards."

"They were good postcards," Shelby says.

"Yeah?"

"Sometimes I thought you were the only one who knew I was alive."

James reaches for his wallet. Inside there is a small black butterfly. The charm from her bracelet, broken that night. "I've been keeping this for you."

Shelby takes it in her hands. Perhaps her luck has been returned to her at last. James leans in to rub on some alcohol. He runs one finger along her skin, and she shivers involuntarily. "I assume the name you want is Ben," he says.

She shakes her head. "Helene."

James stops, rattled. "You expect me to be a party to that kind of remorse and self-hatred?"

"You still feel bad about hitting Ben with rubber bands. I might as well have murdered Helene. At the very least I need to remember."

"Do you think you're the only one who's ever done something terrible? I assaulted people and robbed them. I did these things on purpose. It wasn't an accident like what happened to you with Helene. Anyone could have crashed that night. In AA it took me three weeks to get through the list of people I had to make amends to. But I couldn't call my brother. I couldn't make amends to him."

One of the other guys in the shop moves the curtain aside and starts to come into the room.

"Get out," James growls at him.

The guy slinks away.

"I'm not sure whose idea it was to go swimming on that day," James says, "but I'm pretty sure it was mine."

It's then Shelby realizes the printed *Lee* marking his forearm isn't the name of a girlfriend or a lost love. It's his brother. She vaguely recalls him. He was a year older, wild, always in trouble. "I remember. He shot off fireworks in the gym."

"It doesn't help to carry them around, Shelby. That's something I know for sure. It helps to let them go."

But Shelby is the customer and she sticks with her choice. Before James begins to work, he tells her to breathe evenly and deeply. He'll do his best not to hurt her. "The first one's the worst," he says. Shelby turns her face away, but she tears up at the first stab of pain. She can't believe she's crying in front of him again. This time she can't stop. "It's okay if you cry. Just don't move," he tells her. On the night of the accident she did exactly as he said. She stayed alive on the road. Her skin burns, the way it did then, and by the time James is done Shelby has stopped crying. He deftly drapes the fresh ink with surgery cloth dipped in lidocaine, which he tapes to her skin. Then he gives her some tablets of Vicodin from his own stash. "To use sparingly," he warns. She's to leave the bandage on for several hours and not shower.

"I hope you're happy with it," he says. When Shelby takes out her wallet at the counter, he won't let her pay. "No. Not this time. It's on the house."

"I'm glad you shot those rubber bands at Ben," Shelby confides when he walks her to the door. "He deserved it. You don't have to feel bad about it anymore."

"Just to be totally truthful, when I found you that night, you tried to get away from me. But then I told you, you could trust me."

Shelby has no memory of this. "Really? And did I?"

James laughs at her, and there's the glimmer of who he was before his life came to grief. "I don't know, Shelby. You tell me."

The snow is melting and Ben's wedding most likely wasn't ruined after all. When Shelby reaches her apartment she hears voices inside. Maravelle has a key for emergencies, and there she is with Jasmine, making themselves at home.

"Where have you been? We've been calling and calling. Don't you ever answer your phone?" Maravelle hugs Shelby before she can take off her raincoat.

Shelby grimaces and pulls away. The tattoo is killing her. There's an itch under her skin, and she can tell it's only going to get worse.

"What did you do to yourself?" Maravelle asks.

Shelby slips off her coat and pulls down her shirt to expose the bandage.

"You idiot!" Maravelle says. "How is that going to look when you're eighty?"

"I'm trying to be in the here and now," Shelby responds.

Jasmine chimes in. "I want a tattoo!"

"Not on your life." Maravelle throws Shelby a warning look. "You see how you influence her?"

"Hardly," Shelby says.

Jasmine has turned out to be everything Shelby was not: the prom queen, the valedictorian, the good daughter. Now Jaz has a big announcement, one she wanted to tell Shelby in person. She's been accepted to Yale. She found out at the start of the week. Shelby throws her arms around Jaz. "I can't believe you waited a whole week to tell me!"

"It was so hard not to tell you, but Mami and I thought you would need some positivity today, considering Ben and the wedding."

Maravelle announces they intend to spend the night to cheer Shelby up. They've brought pillows, bags of candy, flannel pajamas. Maravelle will sleep on the couch, Jasmine on a quilt on the floor. They've also brought the ingredients for chocolate chip cookies, and Maravelle begins the search for mixing bowls and a cookie sheet.

"I don't own a cookie sheet," Shelby informs her. "I don't cook. I order. I think you've mistaken me for a normal person."

"Fine. We'll use aluminum foil instead. My mami used to do it that way."

Shelby has a sink full of unwashed dishes and no clean sheets and her tattoo is killing her. It's not the pain, it's the itch, like something is trying to get out of her skin. "You should leave," she tells them.

"We're not letting you be alone tonight," Jasmine informs her. "Not on Ben's wedding day."

"Seriously. I'm fine," Shelby insists. "I'm happy for him."

"Get real," Maravelle says. "Nobody's happy for their ex-boyfriend."

"Now that my mom finally has a boyfriend she's an expert," Jasmine quips.

"He's not my boyfriend." When Shelby gives Maravelle a look, Maravelle grins and says, "In the first place, he's not a boy."

It's all very proper, but Maravelle has begun to see Teddy's attorney, Isaac Worth. He's taken her to dinner several times, and he was recently allowed to come to Sunday night supper with the family. He brought potato salad, his mother's recipe, which Shelby hears was delicious. Mrs. Diaz put Maravelle's new beau through his paces, questioning him, and he rated a *not bad,* which is *excellent* in anyone else's book. Last Saturday, Isaac drove Maravelle upstate to visit Teddy. When they sat down to lunch together, Teddy narrowed his eyes and asked, "Do I get free legal services from now on?"

Maravelle reports that Isaac Worth quickly said, "No. Because you're not going to need an attorney again."

Ever since, Maravelle has been on cloud nine, though she's downplaying the situation. "I hardly know him," she claims.

"Should we refer to him as your beau?" Shelby teases.

"How about your steady?" Jasmine suggests.

"Just a friend," Maravelle insists. "Thank you very much."

While the cookies are baking, Jasmine and Shelby take the dogs out for a walk. It is freezing on Tenth Avenue, with a wind rising off the cold, half-frozen river. They head across the West Side Highway. Shelby carries Blinkie while the other dogs enjoy what's left of the snow. The black butterfly charm is in her pocket. Soon it will be spring, maybe tomorrow. As evening falls, the wet street glows as if sprinkled with diamonds. Shelby remembers the angel crouching down on the pavement on the night of the accident. She didn't know who or what he was, but she let him cover her with his coat.

"Ben's a great person," Jasmine says as they trek along the riverside. "He just wasn't right for you." Jaz is much smarter than Shelby ever was at her age. "You have a different path."

"Yeah." Shelby laughs. "Alone."

Jasmine laughs. "You're not alone."

Shelby hugs Jasmine, and then they take off running, the dogs leaping beside them, Blinkie in Shelby's arms. Shelby never wanted to get involved with Maravelle and her kids. She wasn't looking for friends. Tonight they will sit up till all hours and watch movies; they'll finish the chocolate chip cookies and order Chinese food. If there's a fortune, Shelby won't read it. She can see the future without it: Jasmine will grow up. Maravelle will fall in love. As for herself, she's still not sure she wants to know.

When Jaz and Maravelle have fallen asleep, Shelby locks herself into the tiny bathroom. She tugs off her T-shirt, then eases the tape away from the bandage, even though James told her not to fuss with it until the following day. When she sees what he's done she feels tears stinging her eyes. Instead of Helene's name, he's inked a black butterfly. It's the exact image of the charm from her bracelet, the one he held on to ever since that night. He's telling her what happened isn't something she has to pay for, for the rest of her life. And then she knows she trusted him on that night, and that maybe, possibly, she'll trust him again.

Shelby is waiting outside when he gets off work on a Friday night. It's late, nearly midnight. James is wearing a black coat and a knitted cap and is almost invisible in the dark. "You," he says when he sees Shelby standing there.

"I didn't get the tattoo I asked for."

"Did you come to get your money back?" James grins since the tattoo was free. He starts to walk toward Broadway. Shelby keeps pace alongside him.

"You can buy me dinner if you want to apologize," she tells him.

"Apologize?" He glances at her and frowns. "Helene's name isn't your story."

"You know my story?"

James shrugs. "I know what it isn't."

They're passing by a Chinese restaurant that doesn't look half-bad. Shelby pauses to gaze at the menu posted in the window, then she realizes James has walked on. She has to dash to catch up with him. "What was wrong with that place?"

"I don't eat Chinese food." James keeps going.

"Seriously? Never?"

"Nope. I lived behind a Chinese restaurant in Queens for a couple of years. I ate there every day. How about this place?"

It's a bar that serves hamburgers. They go inside the dark tavern and get a booth. Shelby orders a cheeseburger and a glass of white wine. James asks for a Diet Coke and a salad.

"I'm a sober vegetarian," he explains. "It sounds terrible, I know. Like I'm in a cult. But if you eat the crap they call meat in jail long enough you never want to see the stuff again. And if I drink, I let the monster out of the cage."

"If I feel, I let my monster out," Shelby says.

James leans forward. "I'd like to see that."

While they're waiting for their food they discuss the best death scenes in their favorite movies. Shelby thinks it's the bloody death in *Alien*. She could watch that moment over and over again. James insists it's Marlon Brando in *Apocalypse Now*.

Then Shelby realizes there's an even better one. "Actually, the best death scene is Bambi's mother."

James laughs. "Did you have to bring up Bambi?" He gulps some Diet Coke. "Did Ben get married that day?"

"I assume so. Why? Do you care?"

"Do you?"

She's no longer sure. By the time their meals arrive Shelby has realized there is something seriously wrong with her. She can't eat and she's ordered another glass of wine, which will make her more tipsy than she wants to be. "Don't tell me you still want to make amends to Ben?" she says.

"No. I just want to thank him for being stupid," James says. He has this way of looking at her that gives her chills. Shelby can't even drink after that.

They leave together and wind up walking down East Seventh Street. This is where he lives. "Can you wait here?" James sounds unsure. Maybe he expects her to take off running. Maybe she should. He's warned her that he has a monster inside him, but she has one too. She nods and waits on the stoop. She has a shivery feeling, as if she's stepped into a dream from which she can't wake. When James comes back outside he's got a white German shepherd with him. It's the sort of dog you would find in a dream.

"You didn't say you had a dog." Shelby sinks down to pet the shepherd, who is aloof but tolerant, just like the General. Her favorite type. She had always found dogs that dance around desperate for approval annoying. This is a real dog. Dignified, but willing to accept Shelby's praise when she tells him what a good and gorgeous boy he is.

"His name is Coop," James tells Shelby as they meander down the deserted street. "I found him near Cooper Union. He was dumped out of a car, half-dead, and there I was, so I figured it was fate."

The trees look black and the sky is dotted with blue-black clouds. Shelby feels strangely happy walking along in the dim night. There are bats in the tower of a church overlooking a small park. There's a sprinkling of gold-tinged stars in the sky. They've entered a moody, tattooed world, but they laugh as they talk about their worst days at school. For Shelby that day was when she forgot her homework and humiliated herself by crying in front of her entire fourth-grade class. She locked herself in a stall in the girls' room and wouldn't come out until the principal asked her mother to talk to her. For James, there are so many horrible incidents he has to list them. The day he was suspended for shooting rubber bands at Ben, of course, and the day his brother set off a cherry bomb in the gym and he took the blame, the day of their fourth-grade photo when the photographer tied him to the chair. *There you go, you little shit,* the photographer had told him. *I was in the navy. See if you can get out of these knots.*

"Believe me, I tried," James tells her. "That bastard knew his knots."

When the dog has finished with his business, they go up to James's apartment. It's bigger than Shelby's place, but not by much. It's certainly emptier: a bed, an old couch, and a long trestle table littered with drawing paper and bottles of colored ink. There are intricate tattoo patterns taped to the wall, all blue and black. A heron in flight, a rose that never blooms, a constellation of stars. Alongside are original illustrations for a graphic novel, *Nevermore,* just published by a small press in Queens. Several copies are stacked on the table, fresh from the publisher. The images are vivid: a young man called the Misfit, who dons a black coat like the one James wears. A raven is perched on his shoulder and a monster looms before him. All in shades of black and blue, grim and heartbreaking and glorious.

"Did you write this?" Shelby asks.

"It's a comic. The story is mostly what you see."

As Shelby flips through the pages, it becomes clear that the raven is the soul of the main character's deceased brother. The Misfit has lost the power of speech, and his brother, the Raven, speaks for them both. Together they fight demons in New York City, of which there is an endless supply. Each time another one is defeated, the Misfit comes closer to forgiveness, a state of grace he never can quite reach.

"It's a beautiful story," Shelby says. "Or is it a novel?" she jokes, bringing up their original argument.

"It's a novel made up of stories. Like *The Illustrated Man.*" He holds up a battered copy of Bradbury's book he picked up at the Strand bookstore. "You were right about this."

He's sitting on the couch, and Shelby goes to sit beside him. "The best book ever," she says. Instead of speaking, James pulls her onto his lap and kisses her and she kisses him back. Shelby wants to see what it's like to kiss an angel. As it turns out, it's a little too good. It's the best kiss she has ever had. She can feel the monster of desire inside him, and she feels it inside herself. They are desperate for each other, or maybe they're just desperate. Shelby could go on kissing him, but she forces herself to stop. James lets out a groan. "Shelby," he says, but she wrenches away. She knows what will happen if they keep on this way. They'll wind up having sex, then she'll take him home and he'll be nice to her dogs and they'll love him, and she'll never get away. If they could go back in time to before the terrible things happened, back to when she could feel something, there might have been something between them, but it's too late now. Shelby is moving to California. She hasn't told anyone, she can barely believe it herself, but her letter of acceptance from the University of California at Davis School of Veterinary Medicine has arrived. She sleeps with it under her pillow, to ensure it won't vanish.

James gets the message that she's wary. He backs off, a gentleman, even though Shelby isn't a hundred percent certain she wants him to be.

"That's why I never came forward and sent the postcards instead," he says. "I thought I'd scare you."

Shelby gives him a look. "I'm not scared."

"You seem like you are. You look like Bambi."

"I do not! And if anyone should be scared, it's you."

James laughs. "I'm terrified." He kisses her again, then stops, leaving her breathless. "Tell me right now if this is what you want. I want to hear you say it."

For so long Shelby has prided herself on feeling nothing. Every time she held her hand over a flame, every time she ruined a relationship, every time she shaved her head, it was proof of who she was. A girl no one could hurt. Why would she open herself to him now when she'll soon be leaving?

James takes her silence to mean she doesn't want to end up in bed with him. "Right." He scoops her off his lap and grabs his jacket. "Let's go. I'll walk you home." He gives her a copy of *Nevermore* on the way out. "For your once-upon-a-time files," he suggests.

"Thank you," Shelby says formally.

"You can write me a thank-you note if you want to," he says with some bitterness.

"Maybe I will."

They take Coop and walk toward Chelsea. When Shelby slips her hand into his he doesn't respond. "Don't tell me you're afraid of the dark," he says. He's getting sarcastic again. He's pulling away. Not that she can blame him. She's Miss Conflicted. Miss Weak-in-the-Knees. Why would she let him go, when she's been waiting for him all this time?

"I have four dogs," Shelby tells him.

"Okay." James looks more confused than ever.

"One's a Great Pyrenees. One's blind. One's a poodle."

Most men hate poodles, but James doesn't flinch. "What's the fourth one? A Great Dane?"

"A French bulldog. I stole him from a homeless person. I grabbed him and the blind one. Actually, I stole the Great Pyrenees, too."

"You're a dognapper. Do you dress in black and wear a mask?"

"I stole a kitten, too, but I gave her away."

"Good move," James says. "You're not a cat person."

Shelby goes to kiss him. "This is what I want," she tells him.

She brings him into the apartment. She's got the jewelry box on her night table, and for some reason James goes right for it.

"Hey," Shelby says, embarrassed.

But it's too late. James has found the postcards. He turns to her with a grin.

"Okay, I saved them," Shelby says.

"So I see."

"You knew I would."

James shrugs. He greets her dogs, and as Shelby suspected, although they're suspicious of Coop, they seem to love James. James leans up against Ben's great-aunt Ida's dining room table and rubs Pablo's head. He happens to have dog treats in his pockets, which makes him all the more attractive, except to the General, who has a sour expression. The General is making growling sounds low down in his throat.

"I don't like the way he's looking at me," James says of the bulldog. "Like I'm a rival." James grabs Shelby and pulls her into the bathroom, so they can be alone. "How do you turn around in here?" he asks.

She shows him by sitting on the sink and wrapping her legs around him. "We're hiding from our dogs," she whispers.

They can hear Buddy whining in the hallway. A little paw stretches under the door.

"I'm not hiding anymore," James says. "No more postcards."

This time she doesn't stop him from doing anything. Maybe he was a monster once, and maybe she was too. Maybe the only thing they have in common is that they're survivors. But this is not the past, this is not the icy road. This is what she wants in the here and now.

Shelby has come home from the clinic at the Humane Society to find Teddy and Dorian hunkered down on the steps outside her building. At first it seems like a hallucination. But it's not her imagination. That is definitely Mrs. Diaz's Subaru parked on Tenth Avenue, and those are the twins making themselves comfortable on the stoop. One is supposed to be in Valley Stream, and the other is in a boarding school he is not allowed to leave.

"You're kidding, right?" Shelby says. It's the end of a bright spring day, and the air is clear and sweet after a brief shower. "Tell me you're not here."

"Hey, Shelby." Teddy stands to embrace her. "You don't know how good it is to see you."

Still too handsome for his own good, and still a charmer.

"We decided to visit you," Dorian tells Shelby. At least he has the decency to look guilty.

"You drove up and got him?" Shelby asks Dorian. "With your grandmother's car and a learner's permit?"

They've been wandering around the city all afternoon and are clearly exhausted and depending on her. The boys explain that Teddy signed in to the clinic at his school complaining of a stomach virus, then, as preplanned, he climbed out the window, ran through the field, dove under the bushes, and squeezed through a hole in the fence to where Dorian was parked and waiting.

"Like a jailbreak," Shelby says.

"More like a day off," Teddy corrects her. "The nurse doesn't come back till eleven at night. My buddy delivers the dinner trays, and he's going to cover for me."

"And you came here because you'd like me to be arrested for harboring a juvenile who has defied a court order?"

The twins exchange a look. Maravelle always says that, as toddlers, they slept in the same bed. They hated to be separated, and it's been hard on both of them.

"We came to you because I can't drive without someone over twenty-one in the car," Dorian tells her.

Shelby laughs. "You're kidding, right?"

"Really, Shelby. Legally, I can't. If I get caught I'll never get my license."

It's all clear to Shelby now. They came to her because they've realized how much trouble they could get into, and they want a driver. "If you think I'm driving you back to Albany, you're mistaken. I don't drive."

"You have to," Dorian pleads.

"Actually, I don't." Shelby unlocks the front door. Why then does she feel the heat of Dorian's eyes on her back, pleading even when he doesn't speak? The twins follow her upstairs, where the dogs are overjoyed to see them. She asks Dorian to call the Hunan Kitchen and order them some supper. While he's on the phone she turns to Teddy. "Are you happy that you've involved your brother in an illegal act?"

"I wasn't thinking of it that way."

"You have to start thinking," Shelby advises him.

She has a copy of *Nevermore* out on the table, and Teddy scoops it up. "You read this stuff? Comics?" He seems surprised.

He settles onto the couch to read while Dorian clips on the dogs' leashes to take them for a walk and pick up their takeout. He looks the way he did when Shelby first met him, back when she hated children, or thought she did until she took care of him and Dorian and Jasmine.

After dinner Shelby says, "Let's go now. Before I change my mind."

They pile into the car and get onto the West Side Highway headed for the Thruway. Shelby's heart is pounding. She's rarely driven since the night of the accident, and now she's responsible for Maravelle's sons. Her hands are sweating as she grips the wheel tightly. Dorian's in the passenger seat, directing her. He seems to think he's an expert. "Stay in the middle lane, then no one can merge into you."

Teddy's sprawled in the backseat, engrossed in *Nevermore*. In James's book the Misfit cries ice instead of tears. He can freeze a lawn, a street, an alleyway, a heart. And yet he's nothing without his brother. Teddy has reached the end of the story. "So there's the good brother who is a raven who has to pay for the bad brother's sins. This is one fucked-up story your friend is telling. He's just ripping off Cain and Abel, you know. It's nothing new."

"That's not what he's doing." Shelby glances at Teddy in the rearview mirror. James never got to be sixteen, the age Dorian and Teddy are now. He went from being ten to being a hundred. "He's writing about guilt and sorrow."

"Aren't you supposed to be looking at the road?" Dorian says to her.

"The author's brother died," Shelby tells Teddy. "He didn't have a second chance."

"Am I supposed to feel sorry for him because he feels responsible for his brother? Should the bad brother jump off the roof or something?

Save the world from his despicable self? And what makes you think this is a second chance for me? Maybe it's what puts me over the edge into true evil."

"Give me the book." Shelby reaches behind her.

"Not while you're driving," Dorian tells her.

"I got all the bad genes," Teddy says. "Everyone knows that."

"Bullshit," Dorian says.

Teddy's referring to their father, a man with a criminal past who spent time at Rikers and hasn't seen the boys since they were four years old. Occasionally the children's father will send Maravelle a check, which she tears into tiny, confetti-like pieces. She says if she takes nothing, she owes him nothing.

"You know it's not true," Shelby tells Teddy. "Don't waste your life trying to prove that it is."

They stop at a service station. The boys pump gas, then head to the store for snacks and drinks. By now, Shelby is drenched in sweat. Driving has taken all her concentration, and her muscles are tense. She wonders if she could go to jail for this escapade.

"Sorry," Teddy says when the boys get back into the car. Dorian has obviously had a talk with him. "I know you're helping me."

"The story is about how much he loves his brother," Shelby says. "That's all it is."

"He gets it," Dorian says.

It's pitch-dark when they reach the school. Shelby squints as the head-lights pierce through the black night. Dorian directs her to pull over beside a field; he tells her to cut her lights.

They all get out and stand in the drifting darkness. The world beyond the field feels dangerous and broken. There is the scent of the woods nearby, swamp cabbage and loamy earth. The brothers kid around, punching each other and saying good-bye, then embrace in a bear hug. "Wait till I'm out of here," Teddy says. "We'll be back like we were."

When Shelby goes to hug Teddy, he's so tall she has to stand on tiptoes so she can whisper, "You can do this."

Teddy grins at her. "I still don't believe you were ever that bad."

"I was a monster," Shelby says.

"No," Teddy says. "Not you."

The journey home seems to take forever. Dorian switches on the radio to make sure Shelby stays awake. There's a Bob Dylan station, and his nasal, heartbreaking voice suits the long, dark drive. When "Don't Think Twice, It's All Right" plays, Shelby starts to cry. This is why she never wanted to have a heart. She wishes Teddy could have met James, that he could have seen how good a man a monster can become.

"It's probably better not to cry and drive," Dorian says.

"Right." Shelby blows her nose on her sleeve, and they both laugh. "I did this in fourth grade and was embarrassed for the rest of the year."

"I can see why."

They laugh again, but they're both exhausted. Shelby pulls off the highway in search of a diner. They order French fries and coffee, and then get back on the road again. They have to circle around Manhattan, which looks as if it's made from silver and gold. On the Throgs Neck Bridge, Shelby should be panicking, but she stays in the middle lane, as Dorian suggested, and she does fine.

When they're almost in Valley Stream, Dorian says, "I'll tell my mother about today. You don't have to."

She's so proud of him, and he's not even her kid. "I don't care what they say about twins. You're you even when you're without him," she tells Dorian. "I'll bet when you were little you let him do all the talking for you."

Dorian shrugs. "He was better at it."

"No. You're better at it," Shelby says. "You're better at a lot of things, and you're going to have to accept that."

Dorian gazes out the window at the familiar streets. "You're a pretty good driver." He grins at Shelby. "You're just going to have to accept that," he tells her.

CHAPTER

13

Shelby is drawn to the places she went to when she first moved to the city. She goes to Union Square on Greenmarket days, when farms truck in fresh vegetables and fruit and there are jars of honey and jams, along with brilliant flowers, the dew still on their leaves. Everything smells like mint. She does her shopping, a box of strawberries and some soft green lettuce, then gets a hot tea from the deli and finds herself a bit of space on a bench.

Today Shelby's got Blinkie with her. He's getting old and she hates to leave him alone for too long. He's so small he fits in her tote bag. She thinks he may be shrinking, vanishing bit by bit. She wonders if Blinkie knows where he is, the park where she stole him on a hot summer day. She still looks for the tattooed girl whenever she's in the area. It's been so long since she's spied her, Shelby assumes she's vanished, but suddenly she sees her crossing the park, walking briskly. Shelby decides to follow her. She tosses her tea in a trash can and trails along behind the tattooed girl toward Broadway. She's surprised to discover their destination is the Strand Book Store, open since 1927, home of over two million books, perhaps the best bookstore in the world. It's one of James's favorite places and has become one of Shelby's as well.

The tattooed girl goes in and waves to someone, then heads downstairs, two steps at a time. Shelby follows as if she were in a dream. She's always thought that if she didn't end up as herself, she would have been the tattooed girl. She wants to see what her alternative fate might have been.

The basement of the Strand is filled with boxes of books delivered from the loading dock. "Geez, Shawna, how about being on time?" a young, handsome clerk with a ponytail calls to the tattooed girl.

"Screw you, Henry," she shoots back. "Like you're punctual."

The girl grins and this Henry grins back. Up close the girl's tribal tattoos are quite beautiful, yet Shelby can't help but think of what Maravelle said to her when she looks at the blue swirls across the girl's face. *How is that going to look when you're eighty years old?*

The girl and Henry begin unpacking new shipments of books. It's dusty and dark, but they're talking the whole time until Blinkie barks. Then they both turn to look at Shelby.

"Did you say something?" Henry asks. He's young, maybe twenty.

"I'm looking for the graphic novels," Shelby blurts. She's got *Nevermore* on the brain. Every time she reads it she discovers more about the way James thinks about the world and his place in it. She's fallen in love not only with him but with his story.

"Did you just bark?" Shawna asks.

"Do you work here?" Shelby asks.

"No, I'm unpacking these boxes for free," Shawna says. "I like to do crappy work for nothing."

"Second floor," Henry the clerk tells Shelby. He turns back to his co-worker. "Are you coming to Leah's tonight?"

"Probably," Shawna says. "I just hate going to Queens. It's like going to Neverland when you're the Red Queen."

"Which one of us is the Queen?" the handsome clerk jokes.

He and Shawna both laugh. "Off with your head," Shawna says. Shelby is motionless as she listens in. "Anything else?" Shawna asks coldly when she realizes Shelby's still standing there. Really, the tattooed girl is a woman, likely in her early twenties, only a few years younger than Shelby, an employee of the Strand Book Store who's got better things to do than talk to a stranger.

"You'd better show her," Henry says. "She seems like she needs help."

Shawna nods, and Shelby follows her to the elevator.

"Do you like working here?" Shelby asks.

"What are you, the CIA?"

Shelby shrugs. "I was just curious."

"I love it. Not that it's any of your business. I love books, so what's not to like?"

"I didn't know that about you," Shelby says.

Shawna narrows her eyes. She still looks fierce with her tattoos swirled across her face. "Why *would* you know that?"

"I wouldn't," Shelby says. "I guess I mean from looking at you I wouldn't have thought you were a reader."

"Yeah, well, don't judge a book by its cover," Shawna says. "I've probably read more books than you have. That's the great thing about working here, you find treasures you never heard of before."

There's a rumbling sound and a little yip coming from the tote bag. Shawna peers into the bag. "There's the barker," she says.

She clearly doesn't recognize Blinkie. That's good. Shelby's heart is pounding. There's no way on earth she would ever give Blinkie back.

"I'm too irresponsible to have a dog," Shawna says. "I'm sticking with books. They never let you down and they don't judge you." The elevator door opens and Shawna nods. "Your floor."

"See you," Shelby says.

"I doubt it," Shawna says.

They look at each other. They're nothing alike.

"Right," Shelby says.

As long as she's up here, Shelby takes a look around. She finds *Nevermore* displayed on a wooden table along with the new releases. Shelby grabs a copy and sits between some stacks of books. Ben Mink used to do this at the Book Revue in Huntington, where he read for hours when he was young and broke. Shelby loves the cover of *Nevermore*. When she looks at it she imagines she is seeing a part of James's soul.

There's a kid reading a graphic novel across from her. He glances over. "That one's great," he says, nodding to *Nevermore*. "You've got good taste. You like monsters?"

"Sure," Shelby says. "It takes one to know one."

The kid laughs. "That's why the best heroes used to be villains and vice versa."

Shelby leaves the comfort of the Strand. She hopes she finds a bookstore that's half as good in California. On the walk home, Blinkie's breathing changes. Shelby sits on a bench and peers into the tote bag. Blinkie's eyes are closed and he's struggling for air. She says his name but he doesn't respond. Shelby feels a wave of panic. She hasn't allowed herself to see how bad off he is. She hails a cab and gets in. "Ninth Avenue and Thirty-Second Street," she says. "Fast."

She calls James as they speed uptown and lets him know where she is. She tells him Blinkie will be fine, but she doesn't believe it. By the time she gets to the veterinary hospital, he's barely moving. She goes to the desk even though other people are waiting with their pets. "I have to see Harper," she says. "It's an emergency."

"He's with a patient," the girl at the desk remarks without looking up. She has long black hair. Maybe she's the one who was with Harper the morning Shelby found out he was a cheater who cheated. Shelby doesn't care about that betrayal anymore. She only cares about Blinkie.

"Tell him it's Shelby," she insists.

"He has another patient right after this one."

Shelby turns and pushes through the doors. She races along the corridor leading to the examining rooms.

The girl from the desk chases after her. "You can't do this!"

Leandro, the janitor, has come out to see what the ruckus is all about. He waves when he sees Shelby. "Are you okay?" he asks. "We never saw you again."

"My dog is dying," Shelby tells him.

Leandro nods and brings her into an examining room. "I'll get the doctor," he says. "Don't worry."

Shelby stands weeping over Blinkie in the tote bag. She doesn't hear Harper come in until he is beside her. "I heard you were here," he says. "There's my man Blinkie." Harper gently takes the dog out of the tote bag. "When did this start?" he asks.

"I don't know. This morning I think. He couldn't walk."

"Has he been drinking? Peeing?"

Shelby is furious with herself. She, who is about to start veterinary school, has been in denial. She looks at Harper through her tears. "Renal failure," she says.

Harper places a hand on her shoulder. His touch is familiar and comforting, despite what happened between them. One thing about Harper, he sucked when it came to people, but he loved dogs. That's why Shelby is here. "He's old, Shelby. Maybe fourteen. Maybe more. You don't want him to suffer."

They both know once this sort of failure begins, there is no cure, only horrible pain if the situation continues.

"I don't want anyone to suffer."

"Maybe you shouldn't be in here when I do it," Harper suggests. "You're upset."

Shelby shakes her head. "I'm not leaving him."

"I didn't think you would," Harper says. "You're loyal."

Shelby stands beside Harper and the two technicians he calls in—not the girl with the long black hair, fortunately. She pets Blinkie and cries. "Hey, baby," she says. "You're my baby."

Blinkie's one eye is closed, and he doesn't move when he's given a shot of morphine to settle him before the IV is inserted. Harper is calm and he speaks soothingly. "That's right," he says to Blinkie. "You're a good boy." It takes only a few moments for Blinkie to die. "That's because he was ready," Harper says. "He probably lived ten extra years because of you, Shelb."

Harper hands her a paper towel, and Shelby blows her nose. Blinkie looks so tiny and empty.

"Why did you bring him here?" Harper says. "Don't get me wrong, I'm glad that you did. I just wouldn't have expected it."

"Because you're good at this," Shelby says, "and I wanted the best."

"Thank you. I wish I had been better at other things."

"You're not," Shelby says.

"I'm sorry about what happened." It sounds like he really is.

"Did she have a girl?"

"Elizabeth Jasmine Levy. We call her Jazz."

Shelby smiles in spite of herself. "That makes me hate you less."

Harper laughs. He hugs her, then lets go. She can pick up Blinkie's ashes at the end of the week. Shelby leaves without paying. Harper can cover it.

She goes to a deli around the corner and texts James the address. When he arrives he sits down across from her, out of breath, wearing his black coat. Due to a traffic jam, he got out of the cab he was in and ran the last ten blocks.

"I should have been with you," he says.

"It happened too fast." She shakes her head. Her nose is completely red. She's been sobbing with long, shuddering sighs, and the deli guys have been muttering to each other and eyeing her nervously, waiting for her to snap. Now they're keeping an eye on James. When he notices them staring he snarls, "Is there a problem?"

One of the guys calls back, "It's fine. There's no problem."

James orders two café con leches with covers. They're not staying. "Blinkie wasn't okay, Shelby." The counter guy brings over their coffees, averting his eyes as James pays him. "He could barely stand," James tells her. "I had to hold him on the stoop when I took him out last night to make sure he wouldn't tilt over."

"I didn't even notice. How can I be a vet?"

"Baby," James says. "He was old. You just didn't want to see it."

They hold hands. "Blinkie's dead," Shelby says.

"You saved him."

"It was the reverse. Like us."

"I assume I'm Blinkie in this equation."

Shelby doesn't care if the deli guys are watching. She goes to sit on James's lap. Nobody says anything. Nobody disapproves or thinks they're crazy or asks them to leave. They know love when they see it.

12

CHAPTER

14

Shelby's most frequent visitors have been deliverymen from Hunan Kitchen, but that's over now. The Hunan Kitchen has closed down. The owner sold out to a tapas restaurant, which doesn't deliver, and is so packed on Friday nights the crowd spills out onto the street. The neighborhood is changing; it's much more upscale, filled with art galleries and women in fashionable clothes and high heels. Shelby's upstairs neighbor, the waiter she used to depend upon to walk her dogs in times of emergency, has moved to a cheaper apartment in Brooklyn and three NYU students have taken his place. There's a lot more noise with the young women tenants, with music playing late into the night and their rowdy friends traipsing up and down the stairs. Shelby occasionally has pizza with them (Kyla, Jackie, and Erin, all from Scarsdale) out on their fire escape, which is more spacious than Shelby's. Individually they tell her their secrets. Kyla wants to drop out and move to a sustainable farm,

Jackie is in love with her cousin's husband, and Erin thinks she's fat and hasn't looked in a mirror for over a year. She peers into a frying pan whenever she's putting on makeup and needs to get a glimpse of her reflection. Needless to say, Erin is Shelby's favorite of the three.

Because Shelby doesn't expect visitors, especially at ten on a Saturday morning, when her buzzer sounds, she ignores it and goes back to sleep. James has a key, and whenever Shelby doesn't answer he comes up and gets into bed with her. He's currently at work, so Shelby figures whoever it is will go away. Yesterday she worked a double shift at the shelter, and she could easily sleep all day today. But the buzzer keeps on vibrating, and eventually she gets out of bed and pushes on the intercom, recently fixed by the landlord, who has made a suspicious series of improvements to the building, as if getting ready to sell. "Hello?" Shelby says.

"Shelby, is that you?" the voice asks.

It's her father. She hasn't seen him since the funeral. Whenever he's called she's made excuses and gotten off the line as quickly as possible, but there's not much she can do now that he's right downstairs. Shelby pushes on the buzzer that allows him into the building while quickly pulling on a pair of black pants and a T-shirt, then tosses the dirty dishes into the sink. The dogs start barking as soon as there's a knock.

"Four flights up?" Dan Richmond says when Shelby opens the door. He's winded, leaning on the banister. He's carrying a box that looks fairly heavy. "I heard you were living like this. Your mother told me about it."

"Yeah, it's small," Shelby says. As in tiny. As in she's poor. Or hadn't he noticed?

Shelby's dad steps inside and places the box on Ida Mink's dining room table, then plops himself on the couch next to Pablo. "I see you still have the dogs."

He hasn't noticed that Blinkie is gone. The only dog he knows is Buddy, Sue's poodle, who is staring at him.

"Hey," Shelby's father says to Buddy. "I know you. Come over here."
Buddy doesn't move.

"He always hated me," Shelby's father says. "The feeling is mutual, buster," he tells the poodle. "Do you have some water?" he asks Shelby.

Though she's in shock to have him in her apartment, Shelby goes to get him a drink. She lets the water run for a minute, otherwise it's a hazy brown color, then fills a tumbler. Shelby's father drinks it in one gulp. Shelby perches on a dining room chair.

"Nice table," her dad says.

"It was Ben's great-aunt Ida's."

"Patti and I got married," her dad tells her.

Shelby doesn't move. She feels a little like Buddy. Wary as hell.

"Last weekend," her dad adds.

"Well, I guess congratulations are in order." Shelby gets up and fetches herself a glass of water, mostly so her father won't see that the tremor in her hand has returned due to his visit. It only happens when she's especially anxious. She thinks back to last weekend. She and James watched all four Alien movies in bed, stopping only to order takeout from the salad place on the corner since Hunan is no longer an option. They were probably in bed together watching Sigourney Weaver fight for her life while Shelby's father was getting married.

"We're moving to Florida, so we figured we might as well go all the way." It's an unfortunate turn of phrase, and Shelby's dad must realize that from the look on her face. "You know what I mean. Make it legal. And the house is sold."

"Is there anything else? Like Martians have invaded or I'm really adopted?"

"Shelby," her dad says. He shakes his head, like he's the put-upon party.

"No, seriously, what else are you going to spring on me?"

"You just can't be happy for me," Shelby's dad says.

"Bingo," Shelby says. "You've got that right. So she's Mrs. Richmond now?"

"Shelby, it hasn't been easy."

"Especially for Mom," Shelby reminds him. "She's dead."

Her dad ignores the dig. "I packed up some of your things. I added some of your mom's belongings that I thought you would like. She had that teacup collection. You liked to play with it when you were little."

"Does it look like I use teacups now?" Shelby lashes out. "You clearly don't know the first thing about me."

"I don't know anything about you because you don't tell me!"

"Did you ask?"

"You never want to talk to me."

He's got her there. Maybe it's not all his fault. She hasn't included him in anything since the accident. "I'm distracted. I got into vet school."

Shelby's dad's face brightens. "Wow," he says.

"Yeah. A really good one. In California."

"We're moving to Boca," her father says. "We bought a condo."

"I want to see the house before I leave," Shelby says. "I want to say good-bye." She feels about eight years old. "It was my house."

"It was," her dad says. He takes out an envelope and hands it to Shelby. She opens it, suspicious.

"This is too much," Shelby says when she sees the check.

"You think I don't love you," her father says.

"Because you don't." Shelby lowers her head so he won't see her tears.

"Shelby, I do. I loved your mother, too, I just wasn't good at it." Her father finds a tissue for her in his pocket. She blows her nose and hands it back to him and they both laugh. "I thought you might turn the money down," he says.

"I'm not stupid," she sniffs.

"You definitely are not," her father agrees.

"Should I say thank you?"

"You should." Her dad gets up to go. "But we both know you're not going to."

All the same, Shelby hugs him good-bye. "Good luck in Boca," she says.

"Your mom always wanted to go to California. She'd be happy for you."

Shelby's dad pats her head as if she were a little girl, a flower in a garden, and then before she has time to change her mind and say thank you, he's gone.

⌣

A few weeks later Shelby's father's new wife sends a change of address card, along with a nice note. *Come and visit Florida sometime! We have a beautiful guest room!* It's June, and Shelby figures it's likely hot as hell in Boca. *Thanks,* Shelby writes back, *but I'll soon be headed to the other coast.* It happens to be perfect weather in New York on the day of Jasmine's graduation party. It's a sunny Saturday and the roses are blooming. Even Long Island looks great. Mrs. Diaz and her friends from the hospital have made all the food. Jasmine has dozens of friends, and they all appear to be guests, as hungry as they are excited. The school upstate has allowed Teddy to come home for the weekend festivities; he's excelling in his classes, plus he never got caught making his great escape. Anyway, that's all behind him now. He's starting to realize that he's in charge of his own future. His somber expression makes him seem older than he is.

Shelby gets teary when Maravelle makes a toast to the best daughter in the world. It makes her miss her mother even more than usual. Shelby's graduation present for Jasmine is the watch her mother gave her when she got her high school diploma. It never really suited Shelby, and once she's in school, she'll be handling blood and vital organs. A plastic watch will suit her just fine.

"Seriously?" Jasmine says when she unwraps the gift. "Isn't this too nice for me?"

They are standing beside the grapevine, which has come back despite Maravelle's continuing attempts to kill it. Jasmine is wearing a white gossamer dress. She's barefoot, and her hair, once upswept, has fallen down her back.

"Nothing is too nice for you," Shelby tells her.

Later, when Shelby and Maravelle are setting out plates for cake, they stop to watch the kids dancing. Jasmine is the Queen of Valley Stream, exactly what Shelby told her would happen when she ran away and had to be convinced the move would be a positive change.

"You made it through," Shelby tells Maravelle.

"So did you." Maravelle hands Shelby a graduation present. Shelby graduated this week, too. James was in the audience cheering her on. When he took her home he ran the bath, which he had scrubbed clean—not an easy task—and they got into the tub together and drank strawberry milk shakes. It was the perfect way to celebrate.

"Your mom would have been proud of you," Maravelle says now. "I know I am." Her gift to Shelby is a photo of Jasmine, Teddy, and Dorian in a gold frame.

"Why were you ever friends with me in the first place?" Shelby asks. She was a bald, nasty loner who wore a red sweatshirt and combat boots, just in case the world crashed down on her and she had to kick her way out.

"I saw who you were," Maravelle says.

"Who was I?"

"My best friend, stupid."

"Yeah, well, I'm going to a state where there's no winter," Shelby says. "So who's stupid now?"

They're going to miss each other like crazy. Maravelle throws her arms around Shelby. "You're always welcome here," she tells her. "No matter what. No matter how far you go."

Shelby hates good-byes, so she slips out mid-party and heads for the train station. Once there, she changes her mind. Instead of heading back to the city, she buys a ticket to Huntington. James has gone to see his mother, as he does most Saturdays, and Shelby can surprise him. But that's not the real reason for her decision. She wants to see her house. She phones her new upstairs neighbors and asks Kyla, the one who wants to be a farmer and likes animals, to take her dogs for a walk.

Being on the train is like being in a dream, the hazy green landscape flying by, the low whistle. It's nearly dinnertime when Shelby arrives. There's no one on the streets, only the hum of lawn mowers in backyards and an occasional dog walker. When she gets to her house she stands in the driveway. The old paint is being scraped off, but the workmen have finished and left for the day. Clearly, the new people intend to remodel the place. Shelby goes up to the front door. There's no answer when she knocks. She peers under the mailbox, and sure enough there's the extra key taped there. Her mother always wanted to make sure that Shelby could get into the house, even if no one was home. It can't be breaking and entering if you have a key, so Shelby unlocks the door and slips inside. The place is so empty that her footsteps echo. The house should look bigger without furniture, but it seems tiny to Shelby. The appliances are all missing, no refrigerator, no stove. New ones will be installed and there'll be a complete kitchen remodel, something Shelby's mom had always wanted.

Shelby meanders through the rooms, which feel sad and unfamiliar. Then she goes down to the basement. What had been her lair is filled with boxes that belong to the new people. She sits on the stairs, where she often thought she spied Helene. This was her safe place, where no one could find her and nothing could hurt her, but nothing familiar remains. Even the washing machine is gone. Shelby says *Mom* out loud just to test what will happen. Maybe time will shift and she'll be seventeen again and everything will be different. She won't go over to Helene's that night, she'll have a cold and stay home in bed, and in the morning Helene will call her and everything will be all right. But the word *Mom* rises up and disappears. It sounds like a sob. It's dusty in the basement, and Shelby realizes that even when she was a recluse her mother must have cleaned up when she was asleep. She was always watching over Shelby.

Shelby leaves through the back door, as she used to do when she roamed the neighborhood after dark, meeting Ben Mink. The picnic table is gone. The new people must have had it hauled away with everything else. The grass is patchy, but a few plants in the borders are growing; they refuse to give up. There is a stray stem of a dahlia. One that managed to get through the winter. Shelby starts walking to James's house. His car is in the driveway. His father died the year after his brother passed away, so on the weekends it's James who drives his mother to the market and to her doctors' appointments and to the cemetery. On his way back to the city he often stops at the beach where he and his brother went swimming. He never goes in the water, not even on the hottest days. He likes to watch the birds. Sometimes he brings along a pad and a pen and some ink so he can work on illustrations for the sequel to *Nevermore*.

But this Saturday is different. James has come to tell his mother he's leaving. He's going to California with Shelby. When he quit working at Scorpio, the guys threw him an after-hours party to which Shelby was not invited. "Don't tell me what went on," she advised when James finally came to her place at four in the morning. "I didn't drink, but I almost tattooed your name on my back," he told her as he got into bed. Shelby laughed and drew him close. "Very funny."

It's their private joke: never write someone's name on your skin if you know what's good for you. "Our love will never be a burden," James promised her that night. He was sober and very serious. "Never is a long time," Shelby told him. "Not at all," he said, his hands all over her. "Not for us."

The Howards' house is identical to the house where Shelby grew up, only the Richmonds' house was painted gray and this one is dark green. There's a picnic table in the yard, like theirs, only in better condition. James mentioned he painted it last summer. There are some roses growing here, red with centers so dark they're almost black. Birds perch in a sycamore tree, peering down at her. Shelby thinks they're robins. She raps on the back door for some time and hears Cooper barking like mad before James finally swings it open, eyes narrowed with suspicion until he sees her. Shelby can't tell if he's horrified or delighted. He's certainly puzzled. Coop runs to greet her warmly, rubbing his head against her.

"I thought you were going to a party and I was picking you up at Maravelle's."

"I went. But I wanted to see my house."

"How was it?"

"Not mine anymore."

James glances at the house where he grew up. "Well, this is mine. When I told my mother I was leaving New York, she didn't say anything. She just froze me out. As usual."

"You don't live here," Shelby says. "You just pay your penance here."

James eases himself onto the picnic table and lies on his back in order to look at the sky. Shelby lies down beside him, the way she and her mother used to do. The sun looks like it's falling to earth. Everything is red. They go inside, down to the basement, which served as James's bedroom when he was younger. Coop hops onto the bed and curls up. Shelby and James lie down beside the dog, entwined. James tells her he used to lie in his bed thinking about her. He says that every time he was with a woman, no matter where he was, he was with Shelby inside his mind.

"Mind-fucked," Shelby says.

"I'm serious," James says. "It was always you, Shelby."

She goes to wait in the car while he finishes packing up. She's not the kind of girl who has to befriend someone's mother, and she's sure his leave-taking will be difficult. He's come here every week to run errands and help his mother, despite the fact that he says they've never been close. It's growing cooler, and Shelby wishes she had her Burberry raincoat. She hugs herself to keep warm. She's so wrapped up in her thoughts about leaving for California she doesn't notice Mrs. Howard has come out of the house and is approaching. When there's a tapping on the window, Shelby nearly jumps out of her skin. She buzzes down her window. She says the first thing that comes into her head. "I'm sorry for your loss, Mrs. Howard."

"When you lose a son, people being sorry doesn't do much good," Mrs. Howard responds coldly.

"But you have James," Shelby says.

"James is it? I thought that was the son you were talking about since you never knew Lee. Now I'm about to lose Jimmy, too, thanks to you." Liz Howard stares Shelby down. "I don't think you're sorry at all, Shelby Richmond."

Shelby's heart is beating too fast. "I am."

Mrs. Howard isn't wearing a sweater. She must be cold standing out on the curb. "He was in jail, you know," she says.

Shelby understands. Mrs. Howard is trying to drive her away. "He told me," she says gently.

Mrs. Howard appraises her coolly. "Young girls can be stupid."

"I'm not that young." Shelby sees that James's mother has a little tremor just like she does when she's anxious. Right now, for instance, Shelby is shaking. "And I'm not stupid."

James is headed down the path, a duffel bag slung over his shoulder, his dog following. He's wearing the same coat he wore on the night of the accident, the one he covered her with until the ambulance came. He slinked off, and Shelby's mother came to lie beside her on the asphalt until she was lifted into the ambulance. He stops to reassure his mother. "All the bills for next month have been paid. Mr. Boyd is going to look over the lawn until you hire someone."

"Do you think I care?" his mother says.

"Probably not."

He opens the car door, and after Coop leaps in the back, James gets behind the wheel. "That went well," he says darkly. Shelby is watching Mrs. Howard. Her face has fallen, her complexion is chalky, and her tremor has worsened. She understands that Mrs. Howard can't afford to show her love for James. She can't lose another son.

"She cares desperately," Shelby says.

James gives Shelby a look. "You think you understand my mother?"

"Trust me," Shelby says. "You're her everything."

James gets out of the car in order to speak with his mother. They stand there for quite a while, and at the end of their conversation James hugs her. When he gets back into the car he looks at Shelby with admiration. "Anything else I need to know?"

"Yes," she says.

They stop in Northport and drive to a strip of land called Asharoken. As far as Shelby is concerned the only thing he needs to know is whether or not he really wants to leave this place. She wants him to be sure. They park and walk along the rocky shore as the sky hangs down in bands of gray and blue twilight. Coop runs off to chase seagulls. James tells her that when he dreams, it's always of this beach. If his brother ever were to return, it would be here.

"There are beaches in California," Shelby says.

"What if he comes back and I'm not here?"

James picks up a rock and throws it as far as he can. Shelby feels a chill. She may have lost him to the burden he carries. He has been trapped here since he was ten years old. Under this pale sky there is a soul as free as a bird and a man who has never taken off his mourning clothes. Shelby folds her arms around James and presses her face to his.

She can hear his heart beating against hers. He's in there somewhere, just as she was when she couldn't say anything or believe in anything or want anything or see anything or be anything. She was hiding inside, waiting for an angel.

"Do something," she says.

It is a late Sunday afternoon like any other, except for one major problem. Ben Mink is at the door. Not at the lobby door downstairs that a visitor has to be buzzed through, but right here on the fourth floor.

"Ben," Shelby says when she opens the door to see him, stating the obvious and doing her best not to let on that she's having an instant panic attack. They've been packing and there are boxes everywhere.

"It's me," Ben says.

One of the girls from NYU unlocked the door in the lobby for him. He probably looked harmless, like the nice guy whose heart you break. He's holding a bunch of tulips, yellow and deplorably cheerful.

Shelby is wearing sweatpants and an old T-shirt that may be Ben's. Her hair is in braids and she looks about fifteen years old. She's been reading a text on skin diseases in canines. Other than that, the most she's done so far this morning is brushed her teeth and had coffee and an energy bar. James took the dogs for a long walk before he went out to his publisher's in Queens. He has begun a sequel called *Evermore,* in which the Misfit must travel through an enchanted woods alone, without his brother, but with a series of loyal companions: a dog, a white horse, a woman who will never betray him.

"God, this place looks terrible," Ben says when he comes inside. The dogs mill around him. "Who's this?" he says when Cooper warily comes to sniff him.

"He's Coop," Shelby says. James will soon be home, and Shelby would very much like to get Ben out of here before then.

"Another dog?" Ben looks around. "Where's Blinkie?"

Shelby leans against the arm of the couch. "Not here, Ben."

"What does that mean? Does that mean he's dead?" When Shelby nods, Ben is distraught. "Are you kidding me? Blinkie is dead and you didn't tell me?"

Ben is wearing a suit and tie, and he looks completely out of place in the mess of the apartment. He tosses the tulips on his great-aunt Ida's table.

"I didn't want to bother you," Shelby says.

"Well, thank you for not bothering me," Ben says with biting sarcasm. "Blinkie was my dog, too, wasn't he? I paid for his dog food and he slept in our bed, but what the hell, don't bother me and tell me he's dead." Ben sits on one of Ida's chairs. It's the only clean space in the room. "You still have the table," he says.

"Are you here for the table?"

Ben notices the half-packed boxes scattered across the floor. "What is all this?"

Shelby tells him she's moving to California. "I got into Davis."

"But don't feel like you have to tell me that either!" Ben's face furrows with anguish. "It was my idea, after all, but what the hell."

"Oh, Ben. How are you?" Shelby asks, worried. She can still chart his moods.

"Miserable."

"You look it."

"I don't want to be married," Ben tells her.

"Ben." Shelby doesn't think they should be having this conversation.

"At least not to her." He is looking right at Shelby with a fevered expression. "Ana and I are all wrong for each other." That is why he's here. He's come back for her.

"Marriage is difficult," Shelby says. When Ben laughs, she adds, "So I hear."

"It wouldn't be with you," he tells her.

"Yes, it would be. Come on, Ben. It would be ten times worse."

"It was always you," Ben says. "Everything I've done since has been a mistake."

"That's not true." Shelby feels her heart opening to him, but they're each other's pasts now. "I was a horrible girlfriend. You were always so nice, and I was the worst. You were smart to dump me. And you're right. I should have called you about Blinkie."

"Did you bury him? Did you have a funeral and everything?"

Shelby goes to the bookcase and brings out a little metal box. Blinkie's name is printed on it. She paid extra for that. "He's in here. I'm taking him to California."

Shelby hears footsteps on the stairs. In her shock over Ben's admission of unhappiness, she'd forgotten about James. He's arrived with an order from China Sea in hand, the next best thing now that Hunan Kitchen has closed down. James stops in the doorway when he sees Ben, dropping his hand to pet Cooper when the dog races to him.

Ben looks at James, then glances at the overjoyed German shepherd. He's beginning to see the light. "It's his dog?"

"Ben?" James says, surprised. "Ben Mink?"

"He stopped by for his great-aunt's table and chairs," Shelby tells James. "He just got here."

"I don't want them. And that's not why I'm here. I'm here to see you." Ben is still staring at James. "Jimmy Howard?"

James comes in and deposits the takeout on the table. "Don't worry," he assures Ben. He just can't help himself. "I don't have any rubber bands."

"Is he serious?" Ben says to Shelby. He turns to James. "You have the fucking nerve to mention the rubber bands? That was a trauma for me. I didn't live it down for years."

"To tell you the truth, I'm glad for this opportunity to make amends to you," James says. "I get the whole Bambi thing now. I actually think it's the most disturbing thing in film."

"Do you?" Ben says. "Because I think the most disturbing thing in real life is that you're fucking Shelby and living in my apartment."

"It's not your apartment," Shelby says.

"I have my own place," James tells Ben.

"Congratulations," Ben sneers. He grabs the bag of food and takes out one of the white cardboard containers and some chopsticks. He opens the General Tso's chicken. "Same order, different delivery boy. You don't mind if I eat at my aunt Ida's table, do you?" he asks James.

"Go right ahead. I hate Chinese food," James tells him.

"He hates Chinese food," Ben says pointedly to Shelby. "So how did this happen? An online dating site? I was the first choice for a match for her, you know," he tells James. "He's been in prison," Ben informs Shelby. "He was the guy I bought drugs from."

"We fell in love," James says.

"Really? Well, fuck you." Ben has begun to eat the General Tso's chicken, which he always hated. "You know nothing about Shelby. Were you there for her when she really needed someone?"

James throws Shelby a look. He was there, but neither of them can say anything that will hurt Ben anymore.

Ben has noticed a copy of *Nevermore* on the table. "What's this supposed to be?"

"James wrote and illustrated it," Shelby says.

"He's a writer?" Ben says mournfully. "I'm the one who loves books. I made you read Ray Bradbury."

"*The Illustrated Man,* right?" James says. "Brilliant."

Shelby has to get Ben out of here. She slips on her boots and grabs her raincoat.

"It's Burberry," Ben says to James. "Who do you think gave it to her?"

"Let's go for a walk," Shelby says to him.

"I don't want to go for a walk." Ben takes a threatening step toward James. "I doubt very much that you understand Bambi," he says.

"I just wanted you to know I'm sorry for what I did back then," James says. "I acted like an asshole and I got what I deserved."

"Really? Because it seems like you got Shelby."

"Come with me." Shelby grabs Ben's arm, and they go downstairs. "I don't know where I would have been without you."

"You'd be right here with that guy." Once out the door Ben sits on the stoop, and Shelby sits beside him.

"No. I wouldn't. I'd be lost."

"So you're saying you're in love with him? The guy that made me cry in fourth grade?"

"It was a bad year for everyone. And yes. I am. I really am, Ben. I don't think I knew how to love anybody before."

"Perfect," Ben says. "You had to learn now."

Shelby takes his hand and laces her fingers through his. "Do you think Ana wants the table?"

"It's too old-fashioned for her. She hates anything with history."

"She's right," Shelby says. "It's a piece of shit. I'll leave it for the next tenant."

They both laugh. "Good thing Ida is dead," Ben says. He glances at Shelby. "Do you miss Blinkie?"

"I miss everything," she says. "I miss you."

"But it's him, huh? Fucking Jimmy."

"He was there the night it happened. He's been writing to me all along. That's how I fell in love with him." Shelby is sitting on Tenth Avenue in the clothes she slept in, so she's especially grateful for the raincoat Ben gave her. She wears it all the time, and she suspects she'll put it to good use in California. "What happened with Ana?"

"She wants bigger, better, more. She wants to move to a fancier house than the one we already have." He shakes his head, as if trying to shake off his confusion. "We're having a kid," he says.

Shelby feels a twinge of jealousy, but only a little pinprick. "Ben, you will be a great father. I wish you were my father."

"That's perverted," Ben says.

"I mean it. Everyone should have a father like you."

"You don't want to go back in time?"

Shelby laughs. "To when we were miserable?"

"Jimmy," Ben says sadly. He gives her a sidelong look. "It was never going to be me, right?"

"Are you kidding? I wouldn't be here without you." Shelby hugs him so tightly that Ben laughs and backs off.

"I'm glad it all happened," he says. "Even the bad parts."

"There were bad parts?" Shelby says, and they laugh together. She hugs him one last time so she can listen to his heartbeat. She doesn't want to see him walk away, so she turns and goes inside. Upstairs, James is at the table, eating spicy tofu.

"You hate Chinese food," Shelby says.

"I might as well get used to it. How's Ben?"

"He'll be fine." Shelby notices the fortune cookies on the table.

"How about you?" James asks.

Shelby strips off the cellophane. The crinkly sound reminds her of a wind chime. She cracks the cookie in half. She has never read a single fortune. She thought she knew what her future would be like, but as it turns out life is far more mysterious than she would have ever imagined.

What is behind you is gone, what is in front of you awaits.

"Shelby," James says. "It's a fortune cookie. You hate them."

"Not this one," Shelby says. "This is the one I was waiting for."

CHAPTER

15

People in town don't know each other the way they used to when Shelby was a girl. Everyone knew who she was back then, the girl who had an accident on Route 110. Now she's just another stranger in town. No one says *Shelby Richmond, you're the one who almost killed your best friend, who spent years in your parents' basement doing penance. You're the girl who disappeared.*

It's August, the month when the orange lilies along the road are fading. Shelby recently bought her first car, a used Toyota 4Runner. She used part of the money her father gave her, her inheritance. This morning she headed out to Huntington on the Long Island Expressway. James went out the evening before so he could take his mother to dinner and present her with the cash he got when he sold his car. Shelby was nervous driving again, and her hands shook, but here she is. She wonders if she didn't drive for all those years simply because she didn't want to return to the scene of her crime. Certainly after she lost her mother, there'd been little reason to come back. Yet it's the place she dreams about. In her dreams it's always snowing, the road is always slick with ice.

Now that she's here Shelby feels a tight knot of terror in the back of her throat, as if she were one of those women in horror movies who just keep unlocking the door even though they're pretty damn certain there's a monster on the other side. Shelby has decided to see Helene before they leave for California. It's been more than ten years. People say if you face your worst fear the rest is easy, but those are people who are afraid of rattlesnakes or enclosed spaces, not of themselves and the horrible things they've done.

All of Shelby's belongings have been packed up and sent on to the apartment they found on the university's housing list. There's a yard and a bedroom that's bigger than her entire New York apartment. Shelby Richmond, who struggled to finish high school and spent three months in a psychiatric hospital, who assumed she would work in a pet store for the rest of her life, if she managed not to get fired, is going to veterinary school. She and James will spend the next few weeks traveling cross-country with the dogs, camping out in state parks along the way.

Last night Shelby stayed at Maravelle's. Shelby and Maravelle became friends by accident, and by accident they've become family. Leaving Maravelle was hard, even though she promised to visit in the spring. Leaving Jasmine was equally difficult, especially when she started to cry. But it was Dorian who got to her, the way he hugged her. And it was Teddy, who wasn't there, who sent her the message she needed most on a postcard.

Be happy, he'd written. *You deserve it.*

Shelby is driving along Route 110. This is where it happened, on the left side of the road. The asphalt used to dip into a hollow, but there's a guardrail now. A bunch of plastic flowers has been tied to the metal with string. Shelby used to be so empty inside she could hold her hand over the flame of a burner on the stove and not feel a thing. She tried her best to destroy herself, but she's still here. Her heart is beating, she can feel it sometimes, when she lies beside James, when she thinks about her life, the force inside her that wouldn't let go.

In Shelby's old neighborhood the trees are so big they meet in the middle of the street to form a bower. The new people are in her house and they've repainted; it's yellow, a color Shelby's mom never would have chosen. Sue Richmond preferred the basics: gray with a white trim. Shrubs have been planted, and the driveway has been re-tarred. When Shelby climbed out her window to wander through town, she always avoided Helene's street, except for the cold night when she and Ben sat under Helene's window, and then again the day her mother insisted she drive her here. The first time she came to Helene's house she was in second grade. They were best friends from the moment they met. Shelby noticed Helene's house was smaller than hers, even though Helene had two older brothers. Helene's father had made the basement into a bedroom for the boys, and Helene had an upstairs bedroom all to herself. *I'm the favorite,* she told Shelby, who marveled at her confidence, even back then. Shelby was an only child and she didn't feel like the favorite, not until her mother was dying. *I never want to stop watching over you,* Shelby's mother had told her, and then she wondered why it had taken her so long to know she was loved.

Shelby parks across the street from the Boyds'. People still make pilgrimages to see Helene, but she certainly didn't cure Shelby's mother, although Sue said she felt healed after her visit. She said she could feel Helene's spirit. Helene's brothers have families of their own; it's just her mom and dad who take care of her along with a series of volunteer caregivers who are still dedicated to Helene. Shelby has done the research on Helene's injuries in the medical library at school. She knows that Helene's vertebrae were broken, that her windpipe was crushed, and part of her skull was smashed. There was no oxygen to her brain for at least seven minutes. Helene will never come back. Shelby knows it's true in theory, but she needs to make sure that a miracle is out of the question.

Bill Boyd is on his front lawn pulling weeds from the border of lilies. As soon as she spies him Shelby feels like turning the car around. He sent her candy on her birthday one year. He sent a card that said she could come visit anytime, but she never responded. It's too late to leave. She's already pulled over to the curb and the window is open and the dogs start barking when they see Mr. Boyd. He turns and stares at the 4Runner. Shelby can tell he's squinting to see if he recognizes the driver. Clearly he doesn't. How could he? Shelby's a grown woman with a car filled with dogs, not the girl who used to sleep on a rollaway cot in Helene's bedroom.

"Hey, Mr. Boyd." Shelby waves. Helene's father walks to the edge of the lawn, still staring. Zero recognition, so she calls out, "It's me. Shelby."

She half expects Mr. Boyd to cross the street and spit on the ground. As he approaches, she gets out of the car and steels herself for whatever happens next.

"Shelby? Is that you?" Mr. Boyd looks old. Shelby must have been in his house a thousand times, and yet she barely recognizes him. "You look exactly the same," he remarks.

Shelby almost smiles. "No, I don't."

"You do!" Mr. Boyd gazes past her into the 4Runner. "Geez. You've got a lot of dogs, kiddo."

"Only three." Shelby laughs. It's an insincere, nervous laugh. "I had four, but I lost one."

"Maybe they need to pee," Mr. Boyd says.

"They probably do."

"Come on. You can let them out in the backyard."

"Are you sure? They'll pee on your grass."

"That's the point, Shelby. They look like they could use a run."

Shelby clips leashes on Pablo and Buddy and lets them jump out. Then she lifts the General up. The General doesn't need a leash. He's a leader, not a follower.

"Any more in there?" Bill Boyd jokes. The General goes right over, as though Mr. Boyd were an old friend. "Hey there, pal," Bill says.

Shelby follows Mr. Boyd and the General across the street, then up the driveway to the back gate. She feels dizzy. She's not sure what constitutes a miracle. Will Helene rise from her bed? Will the roses on the wallpaper bloom and bees stream in through the windows? Shelby's heart is beating so fast she stops in her tracks.

"It's okay," Mr. Boyd says when he sees her hesitation.

Pablo takes the opportunity to urinate on the wishing-well decoration at the side of the driveway. It's where pilgrims drop little slips of paper with their wishes written down.

"Geez," Mr. Boyd says. "He pees like a horse."

"He's a Great Pyrenees." Shelby's eyes are burning. "Mr. Boyd," she says, and then she just clams up.

"It's okay, Shelby. I know you're sorry. I never held you accountable. Well, maybe that first night, but I think I went crazy then. Come on in the backyard."

Shelby follows Mr. Boyd through the gate. She lets the dogs off their leads. They've been in the car all morning and are happy to explore. She still misses Blinkie, and sometimes, in the middle of the night, she thinks she feels him beside her.

"I always wanted a dog," Mr. Boyd says.

"So did my mother. She got Buddy four months before she died. He's the poodle. She made me promise I'd take him after she was gone."

"Oh, I know Buddy," Mr. Boyd says. "Your mom used to bring him with her to visit Helene."

"I didn't know that," Shelby says.

"I'm sorry about your mom, Shelby. You couldn't find a nicer lady."

They are quiet for a moment, thinking about Shelby's mother and Helene and how unfair the world can be.

"So what happened to you?" Mr. Boyd says. "Afterward."

"I had a nervous breakdown. Then I moved to the City and worked in a pet store. Then I went to college. Now I'm moving to California to go to vet school."

"Seriously? No kidding! That's a surprise."

"I know. To me, too."

"I don't mean it that way, it's just that you were always so squeamish. I once had to take a splinter out of your foot after you girls walked around town barefoot. You screamed your head off. I thought one of the neighbors was going to call the police. Now you're going to be doing surgeries. That is quite a switch."

Shelby remembers the splinter incident. Mrs. Boyd gave her an ice-cream sandwich afterward, but she was crying so hard she couldn't eat it. Now Diana Boyd is at the back door watching them.

Mr. Boyd waves to his wife. "She probably thinks the circus came to town and dropped off a dog act."

"Let me get them back into the car," Shelby says.

"I don't mind them. They add some life. After the accident everything just stopped here. Helene's in her bedroom, so her mom thinks she's still here."

"Maybe she is."

"If you're going to be in medicine, then you know what her situation is." When Shelby makes a funny little sobbing sound, Mr. Boyd pats her on the back. "Don't go choking on me now."

"Do you think Mrs. Boyd would mind if I went in to see Helene?"

Mr. Boyd calls to his wife. "It's Shelby Richmond. She's here to visit Helene."

"Shelby. Come on in." Diana Boyd motions to her. "But not with those dogs."

"I'll throw a tennis ball around for them," Bill Boyd says. Shelby looks at him, mutely. She feels a sort of terror inside her. Mr. Boyd misinterprets her hesitancy. "I'll take good care of them."

When Shelby goes inside, Diana Boyd hugs her. "I'm so sorry about your mother. I recognize Buddy out there." They both gaze out the window to watch the poodle chase a tennis ball. "I used to visit her when she was getting her treatments and I'd take Buddy for walks when I could. At least a couple of times a week."

Shelby is surprised by how little she knows about her mom's day-to-day life.

Mrs. Boyd smiles wanly. "Your father had already taken up with that nurse."

"He married her. They moved to Florida."

"I know, dear. Mr. Boyd and I went to the wedding."

"There was a wedding?"

"It was just a little gathering at the house before they moved. Patti made all the refreshments. They probably didn't want to upset you by inviting you. You know, your mother came here to see Helene once a week. For a while she brought Buddy over every day."

"She did?"

"She said Helene was like another daughter. Helene had spent so much time at your house growing up, and she always loved when your mom came by. Her whole face would light up. Sue was such a kind person. Kindness like that radiates, and Helene could feel it."

"I know I should have come to see Helene before this," Shelby says. "I've thought about her every day since it happened."

"We've had plenty of visitors. So I'm sure Helene hasn't minded."

As they head down the hall, Shelby can hear the pumping of the oxygen machine. Her heart is beating too fast and she tries to slow it to an even rhythm. There is the same wallpaper Helene chose when she was thirteen, with rosebuds that have never bloomed. Another volunteer is sitting beside Helene's bed knitting, an elderly lady in a gray suit.

"Mrs. Campbell, this is Helene's old friend, Shelby," Diana says to the volunteer. "Sue Richmond's daughter."

"Well, isn't this a good day with an old friend here to visit," Mrs. Campbell says to Helene. "Don't be afraid to talk to her," she tells Shelby. "She loves when you do."

Shelby can hear the thud of her own pulse. Helene is in bed beneath the white sheets. She was such a skinny, coltish girl, but now she's heavier. Her hair is still beautiful, masses of thick auburn. Helene is facing the wall, staring at it. There are patterns of sunlight coming through the window. A shadow that looks like a rabbit, one that's a square, another that looks like a garland of leaves. Shelby stands at the foot of the bed. For the first time in years she is not stuck in that moment inside the snow globe. She is right here.

"Helene," she says. "It's Shelby."

Helene blinks.

"She knows you're here," Diana Boyd assures Shelby. "She definitely does."

Shelby can hear the dogs barking in the backyard. Helene shudders.

"She never did like dogs," Diana remarks. "Even as a little girl."

But she did, Shelby thinks. She wanted a little Westie and cut out pictures from a magazine. "I think about you every day," Shelby tells Helene.

"She appreciates that," Diana says.

"I wish it had happened to me," Shelby says. A broken sob escapes. Helene shudders again.

"She doesn't like it when people are upset," the volunteer warns Shelby. The volunteer who never even knew the real Helene.

"You know what's best? If you just brush her hair. That calms her down." Shelby looks at Mrs. Boyd. She's afraid to touch Helene. Mrs. Boyd urges her on. "It's fine, Shelby, really."

Shelby goes closer. She can smell the faint oily odor of shit from the bag attached to Helene and the scent of lavender powder. Shelby takes the hairbrush and gently begins to brush Helene's hair. Diana is right. The motion seems to settle her. Is this when a miracle can happen? The room is darker than before, the roses on the wallpaper are more deeply red than Shelby had remembered them.

"It's me," Shelby whispers. All she can hear is the rhythm of the oxygen machine. She thought she would be more upset than she is. It's peaceful in this room. And yet, Shelby doesn't feel as if she's with Helene. She's with someone, but the Helene Shelby thinks about every day isn't in this bed. Mr. Boyd is right about that. And it's equally true that the girl Shelby once was isn't here either. If she were, Shelby would want to put her arms around herself and tell the Shelby she used to be that she has a good heart and that the person who will punish her most in this world is herself.

"You're good at this," Diana tells Shelby as she brushes Helene's hair. "You're a natural caregiver."

Good enough for Shelby to be left alone with Helene while Mrs. Boyd and Mrs. Campbell go to the kitchen to fix lunch. Shelby pulls a chair closer to the bed.

"Helene," she says.

What Shelby wants is the most difficult miracle of all. She wants to be forgiven. She takes Helene's hand in hers, and though it is impossible for Helene's brain to dictate what she should do, her hand responds, perhaps involuntarily, perhaps not. She holds Shelby's hand, and then lets go. It is the exact moment Shelby has waited for. She couldn't leave without it.

Out in the yard, Mr. Boyd is still throwing the tennis ball for the dogs, but only the General is interested. The other dogs lie in the grass,

exhausted. Shelby has said her good-byes to Mrs. Boyd and now comes
to stand beside him.

"It's a good thing you tired them out," she tells Mr. Boyd. "They
have a long ride ahead of them."

"I was right, wasn't I? It's not Helene."

"Not the same Helene. No."

James has arrived with Coop, walking from his mom's house, and
he's packing his belongings into the 4Runner. He honks the horn and
waves at Mr. Boyd.

"Jimmyboy," Mr. Boyd calls.

James comes into the yard with his dog. "Hey, Bill," he says warmly.
The men shake hands. When Shelby gives James a look, he shrugs.
"Small town."

"I've known Jimmy since before he was born," Bill Boyd says. "I'm
going to help his mom out with her yard work after you leave, unless I
hitch a ride to California."

"You wouldn't trust my driving," Shelby says.

"No one could have done any different, Shelby. It could have happened to anyone." He gives her a brief, heartfelt hug. "I'm glad you
made it, kiddo."

James loops an arm around her. "She was always going to make it."

Neither of the men asks where she's going when Shelby crosses the
lawn. She stands at Helene's window. She looks inside, and then she lets
herself move forward into whatever fortune awaits.

They stop at the beach in Northport one last time. The rocks here are
mossy and green. It's low tide, and the scent of salt is bitter. James gets
out and walks along the shore. He leaves his black coat on the rocks.
Later, when the tide comes in, it will float out to sea, like a dark flower,
but they'll be gone by then. Shelby knows they won't get through New

Jersey until the evening, but she doesn't mind. She thinks of the way angels arrive, when you least expect them, when the road is dark, when you're bleeding and alone and hopeless, when you're sleeping in a basement, convinced that no one knows you're there.

As they drive, Shelby thinks of her mother's last day on earth. Shelby crawled into her hospital bed, and curled up beside her so she could thank her for everything. The nights they looked at stars, the trip to Chincoteague, the way she spoke to the nurse in the locked ward, the times she searched for Shelby when she was missing. Shelby told her that if she had a hundred lifetimes she would want Sue to be her mother in every one, just as for a hundred lifetimes she would want James to be the one who stopped on the road that night. She would want him to say *Stay here*. She would want him to know her when no one else did.

It's late when they reach Pennsylvania. After checking in and paying a camping fee, they park in a field. The campground is nearly empty. Neither one of them owns a tent. They're used to New York City; they didn't even think of what they might need to camp out. They've got pillows and blankets, so they set up a bed in the back of the 4Runner with three of the dogs curled up beside them and Pablo sprawled out in the backseat. The countryside is quiet, but in the middle of the night something wakes Shelby. She leaves James sleeping and takes the dogs out to a field where the tall grass is already turning yellow. They scatter, then race to gather around her when she whistles.

James notices she's gone. He's a light sleeper. He gets out of the car and calls for Shelby to look up at the sky. There are so many stars above them she could never count them all. She lies down in the tall grass and listens to the last of the season's crickets. The landscape is so like the one in her dreams Shelby half expects to see Helene, but all she sees is the moon, which will follow them until they reach California. It's the farthest Shelby's ever been from home. She's looking forward to seeing an ocean she's never seen before. She trusts she'll find her way.

ACKNOWLEDGMENTS

Many thanks to Marysue Rucci, Jonathan Karp, and Carolyn Reidy for their remarkable kindness and support.

Gratitude and love to my beloved agents Amanda Urban and Ron Bernstein.

Thank you to everyone who has made being at Simon & Schuster such a delight, especially Dana Trocker, Anne Pearce, Zachary Knoll, Susan Brown, and Jackie Seow.

Thank you to Miriam Feuerle and everyone at Lyceum Agency.

Many thanks to Madison Wolters for tech, word, and research savvy.

To Andrew and Lisa Hoffman, gratitude always.

Endless gratitude to Kate Painter for invaluable help on all fronts, literary and human.

To Pamela Painter, my deepest gratitude for her invaluable friendship and literary expertise.

Thank you to my friends and family who have offered so much love and support, especially to Mindy Givon, Jill Karp, Gail Roberts, Tal Givon, Sue Standing, Susan Laskowski, Alexandra Marshall, Allyssa McCabe, Eric Karlberg, Gregory Schmidt, Lucy Fisher, Charlie Cuneo, Megan Marshall, Jessamyn Cuneo, Janet Prenksy,

Nina Rosenberg, Deb Newmyer, Dr. Marilyn Antokoletz-Hoffman, Laura Zigman, Ann Leary, Sue Miller, Jodi Picoult, Nancy Freed, Shellie Klurfeld, Karina Van Berkum, Luanne Rice, Barbara Kohler, Jacquie Duva-Pearson, Lisa Menschel, Elaine Markson, Gary Johnson, Erica DelVecchio, and Ashley and Harriet Hoffman.

To Jacob and Tessa Martin, love and gratitude for all you do.

And a huge thank-you to Ross Hoffman and Dorothy Crawford for giving me a home where I could finish this book.

Thank you to all of my old friends from Long Island.

Thank you to the editors of the literary magazines where some sections of *Faithful* were originally published.

Thank you, Leonard Cohen.

And thank you to the many bookstores that have given so much to me both as a reader and a writer, with special gratitude to the bookstores in *Faithful*: Book Revue in Huntington, New York, and Strand Book Store in New York City.

To my own Shelby, xo always.

ABOUT THE AUTHOR

Alice Hoffman is the author of more than thirty works of fiction, including *Practical Magic*, *The Dovekeepers*, *The Museum of Extraordinary Things* and *The Marriage of Opposites*. She lives near Boston.

Visit her website: www.alicehoffman.com